W·CLARK
PUBLISHING
A STATEMENT IN LITERATURE

LICKIN' LICENSE

From Lust to Love to Deception and Death

An Urban Erotic Romance

by

Intelligent Allah

Wahida Clark Presents Publishing, LLC
60 Evergreen Place Suite 904
East Orange, New Jersey 07018
973-678-9982
www.wclarkpublishing.com

ISBN 13-digit 978-0-982841426
ISBN 10-digit 0-9828414-2-6

Library of Congress Catalog Number 2010936251
1. Urban, Erotica, Lesbian, African-American, Brooklyn, NY, Street Lit – Fiction

Cover design and layout by Oddball Design
Book interior design by NuanceArt
Contributing Editors: Jazzy Pen Communications and R. Hamilton

Printed in United States
Green & Company Printing. LLC
www.greenandcompany.biz

Acknowledgements

I'm from Brooklyn, so I know heads in 'hoods all over New York City. I've been locked down since '94, so I'm cool with dudes all over the New York State prison system. I'm an active member of the Nation of Gods and Earths, so I know brothers and sisters with knowledge of self across country. My family is deep and it extends from Florida to Albany, New York. But if you fall in any of these categories and you're not mentioned, don't take it personal. The shout-outs will come later. These are acknowledgements of the people I recognize for directly helping me over the years to become the writer I am. The fiction I write is the result of me writing in virtually every field there is, with inspiration, instruction and insight from a lot of people.

My peeps (formerly The Ill Cipher and Masked Villains) that I ran the streets with and started writing rhymes with back in '92. My physical brother Uneek and my righteous brothers Victorious (East Medina Entertainment), Whyz Ruler (Intelligent Business Investments), I.B. and Be Born. I was just dabbling in poetry until y'all influenced me to start spiting. Two of the nicest emcees I met Up North—the only heads that inspired me to write a 50-bar verse after hearing them on separate occasions: Jah Gunz a.k.a. Dirty Gunz (E.N.Y.) and D.B. a.k.a. Donnie Boy (Harlem). Writing rhymes helped pave the way for nearly every type of writing I've done, from articles and screenplays to copywriting and editorials to essays and fiction.

My comrades that introduced me to writing as a means of fighting for my freedom and challenging unjust prison conditions. The late Power Ruler Nation Allah, R.I.P. Divine G (Author of Baby Doll and Money Grip, among other books.

Larry "Luqman" White, Gene, Arnold, Baba, Pooch, Kasiem, Quick, Q, Abdul Majid and all the other brothers who served on the editorial boards of The Lifers' Call and Ujima with me.

The college instructors who helped me step up my pen game. Professor William G. Martin and Assistant Professor Michael Hames-Garcia from Binghamton University. Professors Tad Richards, Delia Mellis, Rachel Levitsky, Jane Schlubach and Amanda Vladick from Bard College. I had no interest in some of the things I had to write about, but the process of researching and writing helped me a lot. The writing instructors from other writing courses I learned from over the years. Robert Gover (Writer's Digest Novel Writing Workshop), Pattie Eagan (Shawangunk Valley School), Kathleen Reid (Rising Hope, Inc.).

Elise S. Zealand for serving as editor of my articles and essays early on and blessing me with *The Elements of Style*. My professor and instructor of the Harvest Moon Collective poetry group: the late renown poet and author Janine Pomey-Vega who helped me advance my poetic skills and focus on *The Elements of Style*. R.I.P. Arin Arbus for your analytical eye and insight on characterization and screenwriting. Zenola Watkins for always giving me an intelligent woman's view on my work. Gysia a.k.a. Kwame Ersell (*Brooklyn: Lessons on Young Lives in Chaos*), where would I be had you not schooled me on fiction early on? Zach Tate, the Ambassador to the Elite (Author of *Lost & Turned Out* and *No Way Out*), thanks for not being a yes-man and being a grown man. You're home now, so take over this industry! Rashawn Hughes (Author of *Under Pressure*), I owe you a lot as a confidant and fellow writer. Papooch a.k.a. F. Gee Heyward (Author of *Game Like Honey*), the most active go-getter I met in prison. Casio Mike (Author of *2 Sides to a Story*) and The Twinz (Authors of *Crime Pays*), watching each of y'all make it happen from scratch in the pen was an inspiration. DeVine (Author of *Humor From Behind The Walls*), a woman of your intellect and ambition is a rare source of motivation for me. Keep writing. My fellow East New Yorker, Dee from The Pink Houses, I've never seen anybody write as much as you do. I'm waiting on Texas Tom (LOL). Stroke from Harlem, for reading and giving me feedback on everything from my 'hood tales to my romance. Glad you're home, but I wish you could've critiqued *Lickin' License*. Dr. Supreme Understanding Allah (*Author of How to Hustle and Win* and *Rap, Race and Revolution*), for giving me a voice in the book *Knowledge of Self: A Collection of Wisdom on the Science of Everything in Life*. Winthrop Holder, for giving me a voice in the book *Classroom Calypso*. God Kalim, for giving me a voice in *The Five Percenter*. Everyone at theurbanbooksource.com for giving me a platform. Freyda Dinshah, for publishing my work in American Vegan.

The people who gave me feedback on *Lickin' License*. Joan Burke Stanford of Jazzy Pen Communications, from one editor to another, you're the truth! My mother Margaret for your editorial assistance. June from Bushwick, for the Spanish spelling. Everyone else that gave me overall assessments. Nut from Crown Heights, some publishing company needs to put you on their payroll. Kay from Newburgh, good looking on the Balmville info. Sha-Rize from the BX, you went in hard on me. Peace Soldier—Nothing Else matters but freedom!!! Yusef from Albany, thanks for speaking your mind Breezy from the BX, don't be so hard on Vanessa. (LOL) Science from Brownsville, I'll be following you out there, so catch me at a signing. Khalil a.k.a. Bless, my ENY homie, when I thought I was done, you proved me wrong. Big King from L.I., I appreciate you helping me logistically to make this a reality.

Wahida Clark. We go about six years back at least, since you were in the pen. I always told you I respect your hustle. Thanks for keeping me busy on the editorial side and now letting your company be an outlet for me to showcase my talent. As I always tell you, stay focused, stay real and stay up!

Kisha Upshaw and the entire WCP staff, from the readers to the typists. A lot goes into bringing a book from manuscript to store shelf. People just don't know. No business can prosper without a strong team! To all the writers of WCP: Tash Hawthorne (*Karma With A Vengeance*, Parts 1 & 2), Cash (*Trust No Man*, Parts 1 & 2 and *Bonded by Blood*), Missy Jackson (*Cheetah*), Mike Sanders, (*Thirsty*, Parts 1 & 2), Victor L. Martin, (*The Game of Deception*) and Anthony Fields (*The Ultimate Sacrifice*). Every book y'all put out helped fuel me to step it up and move with WCP.

For everyone about to taste *Lickin' License*, I dare you not to touch yourself or your significant other (LOL). After you've tasted *Lickin' License*, post a book review on amazon.com. Thanks to my cousin Bunny in The A, you can go to Facebook and MySpace directly to let your words be heard and learn more about me. You can send me your feedback at Intelligent Allah #95A4315, Box 1000, Woodbourne, N.Y. 12788. I need you to help me get my mind right while I work on *Lickin' License* 2: *More Sex, More Saga*. I write for me, but I'm motivated by you. Peace.

Dedicated

*To every woman who was motivated by lust but
was fortunate enough to find Love*

WAHIDA CLARK PRESENTS

LICKIN'
From Lust to Love to Deception and Death

LICENSE

A NOVEL BY
INTELLIGENT ALLAH

CHAPTER ONE
CANDY

Sex was in the air. The woman's long legs were spread as far apart as possible. Her back sunk into the leather couch of her office. Her slanted eyes rolled to the back of her head. She thrust her pelvis forward as her body jerked uncontrollably as if she was having an exorcism. She felt like she was floating. Her lips quivered. The euphoric sensation of her throbbing clit was all she sensed. Her oak desk, the photos on her walls, the ultra modern lamps, the breeze from the ceiling fan— they all were non-existent. The only important thing was the tongue between her thighs. It made her feel so good that she could not utter a sound, although her mouth was wide open. Candy's manicured fingernails clawed the crushed velvet couch as she climaxed. Finally, she managed to whisper, "Thank you."

She opened her eyes as Vera removed her face from between her legs. Candy watched the firm figure of the nineteen-year-old wiping her cum-soaked lips. Vera's gold and brown dreads hung to her slim waist, just above her large, round butt. Her body was a work of art. It appeared to have been perfectly sculpted from chocolate and it tasted just as sweet.

"Why you lookin' at me like that?" Vera asked.

Candy leaned up until she was sitting in the center of the couch. "Come here," she whispered.

Vera smiled, stepping forward. "What's up, baby?"

Candy gazed at Vera's perky B-cups, and then grabbed a handful of her butt. "You know your body is so beautiful, right?"

Vera giggled.

Candy turned her around and gently kissed on each of her butt cheeks then slid her tongue between them.

"Ahh," Vera whimpered.

In seconds, Candy had Vera slumped over the arm of the couch, jabbing her tongue into Vera's crack. She slid her hand underneath Vera and massaged her clit simultaneously. Clutching Vera's waist with her other hand, Candy tried to stop her from squirming uncontrollably. The more Vera moaned the more wet Candy became. Seconds turned to minutes and time flew as their sweaty bodies overheated with lust.

"I can feel it, Candy." Vera began panting. "I'm cumming."

Candy slurped and rubbed faster until she felt Vera's delicate body go limp and her panting stop. She stood and patted Vera on the butt. "Come on," Candy said as she led Vera into the private bathroom connected to her office. The two women lathered and rinsed each other's bodies, a sensual routine to which they had become accustomed.

Thirty minutes later after the two women were dressed, Candy glanced at her watch. It was 10:10 a.m., ten minutes past the opening time at Candy's Shop—Harlem's hottest hair salon. Candy was sure Leah was waiting out front. The gorgeous Latina was her most reliable employee, always on time. "You ready?" Candy asked Vera.

Vera nodded.

She and Candy walked out of the office and through an area filled with lockers and benches that served as a dressing room. They stepped into the brightly lit, spacious beauty shop that housed five work stations equipped with state-of-the-art hair tools and chairs. The walls were covered with mirrors and photos of women who had their hair done at the shop, plus snapshots of exclusive hairdos from *Essence* magazine. Candy grabbed a remote off a table covered with magazines. She pointed it at the iPod doc beneath one of the two large flat screen televisions. The surround sound system began blaring Jay-Z's *Empire State of Mind* from the speakers discretely situated throughout the shop.

"Hey, Candy," Leah said, stepping into the shop. "Sorry I'm a few minutes late." She smiled at Vera. "Vera."

"Hi, Leah," Vera responded.

Candy turned to Vera. "Call me later."

Vera winked and stepped out of the shop.

Candy looked at the smirk on Leah's face and shook her head, before sitting down. "Don't even say it, girl."

Leah laughed. "You are just too much. You and these young girls."

"She's a grown woman."

"Technically, but barely legal. You got her by what? Eleven years? You really need to stop taking advantage of these young girls."

Candy was silent, noticing the seriousness in Leah's tone and facial expressions.

"She'll be twenty soon, so you can say ten."

"Didn't you say she got some crazy-ass brothers? They'll probably kill you if they find out you turned out their sister."

Candy sucked her teeth. "Yeah, yeah," she mumbled, thinking of how wild she heard Vera's brothers were. But she knew they would never find out about her. Vera feared her family learning about her sexuality. It was the reason that she was comfortable traveling, all the way from Brooklyn where she and her brothers lived, to Harlem to see Candy.

"Just be careful," Leah said as she made her way to her station and began setting up for work.

Meisha stepped through the door. "Newww Yorkkk. Concrete jungle where dreams are made offf," the chunky brown-skinned Harlemite sang along with the music in the shop. "Owe."

A short, dark-skinned Diva donning Fendi heels followed behind Meisha. She strutted over to the chair at her workstation as if she was a model on *Rip the Runway*. She set her Fendi bag down and removed her matching shades, revealing her hazel eyes. "Chanel has just entered the building. Thank you, thank you." She bowed and smiled. "No autographs, please. Thank you."

Leah burst into laughter. "Y'all are crazy. Only in Candy's Shop."

The ladies exchanged hellos and hugs. They began preparing for their customers to enter the shop. Leah, Chanel, Meisha and Candy were the four stylists that made Candy's Shop more than Harlem's go-to spot for hairdos. The shop was where women came to discuss the latest gear by Roberto Cavalli, what brother would be the next official sex symbol to replace Denzel Washington after he retired, who was the last person shot or arrested in Harlem and what handsome thug was coming home from jail with a hard dick in his pants and pussy on his mind.

While Meisha added on to whatever was mentioned, Leah usually brought some mental stimulation to the conversations—the type of mental stimulation she got from Long Island University, where she majored in business management. Despite the professionalism Leah and the other stylists brought to the shop, Candy was searching for another beautician. She had fired the last one because of the woman's laziness. Candy liked a festive environment in the shop, but she took her business seriously. She had opened the shop 10 years earlier in the summer of 2000 with the help of Leah. Leah had always had a business mind, but she didn't have the money Candy had accumulated from hustlers she dated. Candy felt guilty knowing that Leah's insight helped create the shop, but Leah had no ownership in the shop. But Cabndy was all business and the business was all her's. The shop had helped her maintain a luxurious Harlem apartment with two closets full of designer clothes and the customized BMW M3 she steered to the bank each week to deposit $1,000 into her savings account.

Chanel stepped outside and returned with two Sak's Fifth Avenue shopping bags. "All right, all right, y'all. It's that time of the month and I don't mean the red light special," Chanel said. It was customary that each month a different person in the shop gave out gifts to everyone who worked there. Chanel began pulling out clothes from the bag—a Christian Dior blouse for Leah, a Fendi clutch for Meisha. "And last, but not least," Chanel said, stepping over to Candy. "A Michael Kors shirt for the hottest chick in Harlem."

"Thank you," Candy said, hugging Chanel. "This is hot." She held up the silk lavender piece so everyone could see it.

"Girl, that's nothin'. You know how we do," Chanel said.

Candy smiled. It was those displays of camaraderie that Candy loved about the shop. She watched Chanel walk away and then peered into the mirror in front of her.

The five foot ten redbone adjusted her weave. She had the body of an Amazon and the face of a beauty queen. People often told her that she needed to leave the hair business behind and pursue modeling.

"Hey, Candy," Leah called out.

"What's up?" Candy responded.

"You give any thought to that idea I gave you for starting another business?"

"Yeah, jotted down some ideas."

"Ahh, here we go," said Chanel, shaking her head. "Heifer

got a punk-ass beauty salon; now she wanna be Bill Gates out this bitch."

"Wish I was Bill Gates," Leah said. "He lost seven billion last year and he still the richest dude in the country with fifty billion."

"You heard that, Chanel? Billion. Can you spell that?" Candy laughed.

"I hear that hot shit," Chanel mumbled.

"Now, Leah, as I was saying before East New York's finest ho interrupted. I'm thinking about hair care products."

"There's a big market for it, but there's an even bigger industry supplying." Leah pointed at the assortment of products in front of her. "There's about a dozen brands here alone that I'm using."

"I know, I know, I know. That's why I have to find a niche."

"You should go online and do some research. See how big the market is, then see how big the industry is. Then see where you can fit in."

"Yeah, guess I'll hit Google and see what's up."

"Good morning, ladies," Rich announced, as he walked through the front door and removed his aviator shades. The stylish hustler lived in a penthouse on 100th Street, where the Upper West Side ended and Harlem began. He seemed to switch up his women and cars by the week. He had a tall, athletic build and the complexion of Taye Diggs. According to the rumor mill in Harlem, he had a dick like a donkey and the stamina of a cheetah.

Rich stopped in front of Meisha. He pointed at her curly hair, then his cornrows, which Meisha had styled a few days earlier. "You ready?"

"One minute," said Meisha. "Sit down. I gotta make a quick call."

Rich sat and leaned back, rubbing his hands together, as

Meisha pulled out her Sidekick. "I'm a busy man, Meisha. You know if I could stop time, I wouldn't need this Rolex."

Chanel sucked her teeth. "Plllease. You need to stop your bullshit."

"Here she go again," Candy mumbled to Leah. They had seen Chanel and Rich go at it regularly. Rich once had his eyes on her until she and Rich"s friend Chase got drunk and woke up in each other"s arms after a night of sex.

Rich spun around in his chair and faced Chanel with a smile. "The lovely Ms. Chanel. You sure look good, girl. I ain't even gon' lie." He shook his head. "But not good enough for me."

Chanel gave him the finger. "You wish you could have this." She shifted her butt toward him.

"Just tell me how much," Rich said. "A Gucci bag? Louie? No, no, no, no. You big time. Hermes Birkin bag, right?"

Chanel pinched her tight jeans. "You can't afford what's in these True Religions."

"No, no, no, no, baby. You got it all wrong. Rich don't pay for pussy. I need to know what it's gonna cost me to get you off my dick?"

"No, he didn't," Leah whispered.

"Yes he did," Candy said.

"Fuck you, Rich!" Chanel spat, turning around.

Almost on cue, Meisha returned and began prepping Rich. She loosened his braids and shampooed his hair, as more customers entered the shop. Within 10 minutes, all the chairs were full. The flat screen TVs at each end of the shop were on and Mary J. Blige was crooning through the sound system.

At one o'clock, the ladies went out to lunch, and then returned 45 minutes later. The ladies were seated in the shop joking about Rich and Chanel

"Chanel, look me in the eyes and tell me you don't wanna

fuck Rich," Meisha said.

Chanel spun around, stared into Meisha's doe eyes and calmly replied, "No, I don't wanna fuck—" She burst into laughter before completing her sentence.

"I knew it," Meisha said, biting down on her bottom lip. "It's okay, girl. I know how it feel. When I be doing his hair, sometimes I just wanna jump on him and take the dick."

"He's so picky with who he mess with," Chanel said. "Conceited bastard."

"Just like you," Leah added.

"That's why y'all will never get together," Candy interjected. "You looking for somebody to drink your bath water and he looking for somebody to hold his dick when he piss."

Chanel jumped from her seat and began posing in front of a mirror. She held one of her breasts. "D-cups, all natural." She ran her hands through her long curls. "Real hair." She pointed at her hazel eyes. "No contacts." She shifted her hips. "And I got ass for days. Not conceited, I just know for a fact that Chanel Dennison is the shit."

"Candy's right, though," said Leah.

"Come on, Leah. I know you're not buying that bullshit. Not from Candy, anyway," Chanel said. "She get more pussy than Rich."

Candy laughed. "Now you know I didn't always have my lickin" license." Everyone in the shop knew Candy had once dated some of the most notorious guys in Harlem. One hustler, Dez, had run in the same circles with Rich until he was murdered five years earlier at a dice game on 135th Street. Candy had always liked women, but never acted on her desires until after Dez's death. People speculated whether Dez's lesbian sister Sheena had turned Candy out, but Candy denied it.

"All right, Candy," Chanel said. "We know you used to get up under a dick, but you been out the loop for a minute."

"I still know you and Rich will never work."

The women continued talking, but had changed the topic by the time clients began trickling in. Meisha was busy removing tracks from a woman's hair and Chanel was twisting another woman's curly 'fro. Leah was plugging in a curling iron and Candy was shampooing a client's hair.

Leah glanced at one of the TVs and noticed President Obama was speaking. "Y'all think Barack ever cheated on Michelle?" she asked.

"Hell, yeah!" Chanel blurted.

"Only one thing can stop a man from cheating," said the middle-aged woman in Leah's chair.

"What's that?" Leah asked.

"Attica."

The ladies erupted in laughter.

"You put Barack behind bars," the woman continued, "and he'll be faithful, because Michelle is the only woman that can come on them trailer visits. My sister was married to a man in prison. Only faithful man she ever had. You know they only let them jailbirds go on them conjugal visits with their wives. A trailer will slow Barack up. His ass cheat just like the rest of these trifling men out here. Think he ain't got him a black Monica Lewinsky, if you want."

"That's right," said Chanel. "God designed man's body for cheating."

"What?" Meisha was puzzled.

"The clothing designers too," Chanel said. "See, a man can unzip his pants, slip his dick through his boxers into your mouth, bust a nut, zip up his pants and be out the door in less than five minutes."

"She right," another woman said.

"It takes me damn near five minutes to pull down my pants and my panties," Chanel continued. "Then at least another twenty minutes to cum. And that's only if the brother knows how to work his tongue right. By the time I'm dressed and out the door, we talking thirty minutes easy. In that time, my man done had his dick sucked by at least four more hos."

"She's got a point," said the woman in Meisha's chair.

"Come on, now. Y' all know Leah just got engaged," Candy said. "She don't need us making her second guess her future husband."

"I'm fine, Candy. Anything is possible, but I don't base my life on possibilities," Leah said.

Chanel sucked her teeth. "Shit, we ain't talking 'bout possibilities. A man's dick turning up where it don't belong is a fact of life."

The women talked about infidelity for a little while longer, until Candy switched the conversation to her idea for opening a hair care business. Everyone in the shop vowed to support her if she did. They felt developing hair care products was a natural progression from owning a hair salon.

Clients began trickling out of the shop. Others with appointments, who had been waiting, took their seats. The cycle of exiting and entering clients replayed a few times. Then, a slim bohemian-looking sister with a large black and brown curly 'fro stepped inside. The young woman sported beaded bracelets that wrapped her neck and wrists. She donned a long denim skirt and a plaid button up shirt that fell below her waist. It was loose fitting, but there was a shapely petite frame that could be seen beneath it.

Candy had been watching every move of the unfamiliar woman since she entered the shop. *She is so sexy,* Candy thought. She wondered whose client the woman was.

"Excuse me," the light-complexioned woman said in a gentle tone. "I'm looking for Candy."

"Sookie sookie. PYT alert," Chanel mumbled with a smile.

Candy saw the same serious look on Leah"s face that followed Vera"s exit earlier.

Candy's client was just sitting down. "Go ahead," she said in her thick Spanish accent. "Speak to her. I'll be waiting." Candy stepped over to the sexy young woman with the angelic glow. There was innocence about her that Candy was not used to. "I'm Candice Johnson, but everybody calls me Candy."

The woman shook Candy's hand. "I'm Vanessa. Vanessa Denay. I read your help wanted ad on Craig"slist."

"So you're interested in the job?"

Vanessa smiled. "Yes. I've been doing hair for six years."

"Hold on." Candy looked at her watch. "We run a tight schedule around here. Appointments only.
That means I have to tend to my client." She rolled her eyes toward the Latina in her chair.

"I can come back later if you'd like."

"We close at eight."

"I'll be back at seven-thirty."

"Perfect." Candy shook Vanessa's hand again and fantasized about her body in the nude, as she walked off.

"Snap out of it," Leah said. "You're lusting already."

Candy snapped out of her daze.

"That heifer is at it again," Chanel said. "One clit just ain't enough, huh?"

"Me and Vera got a understanding." Candy giggled. "Nah, she's just interested in the job."

"Oh yeah?" Leah sighed.

"Look like you interested in putting in some work too," Chanel said.

"She is hot." Candy licked her lips. "Slim, but sexy."

"Should've never got her started, Chanel," the woman in Chanel's chair said.

"For real," Meisha sucked her teeth.

Candy said, "Y'all sit around here complaining about men all day. Y'all need to quit bitchin' and start lickin'."

"You know that's a sin?" Meisha said.

"Having some fool beat your pussy up until it's sore and you don't even cum, that's a sin. Or some inexperienced asshole scrapping his fangs against your clit like he Jeffrey Dahmer, that's a sin for sure," Candy snapped.

"It's nasty," Meisha said.

Chanel turned to Candy. "The shit just ain't natural."

"And you fucking every hustler in Brooklyn with a BMW is?" Candy laughed. "Get off the pulpit with the bullshit."

"You know you gonna burn in hell, right?" Meisha asked.

"Go on," Candy said. "Tell me what hell feel like. 'Cause these trifling ass men you mess with been putting your through hell for years. Shit, you must be a hell expert."

"Okay, ladies," Leah interjected. "It's time to change the channel."

Meisha turned to Leah. "Candy know I'm just fucking with her. I don't care who pussy she eat, as long as it ain't mine."

"Yeah, Candy," Chanel said. "You one freaky-ass heifer, but I'll slap the shit out a ho for violating you." She pulled out a razor. The clicking sound resonated as she pushed it out of the orange plastic casing. "That's that East New York loyalty."

Candy smiled. She had been in far more heated debates about her sexuality with the women in the shop. The ladies always ended up agreeing to disagree on certain issues. Candy used to tell herself that she didn't care what people thought or said about her desire for women. But that changed after her family disowned her and the women at the shop became her family. She had never been in a serious relationship with a woman. The intimacy she shared with women was purely sexual, born through shared passion and raw lust. It was the women at the shop who Candy was close to. They were the people she went shopping with, hit clubs with and discussed her personal problems with. Candy did not doubt the love the women at the shop had for her.

Time drifted by until 7:30. p.m. when Vanessa stepped back into the shop and took a seat. Candy watched the young woman observe what was going on in the shop. After laughing at a few jokes, Leah invited Vanessa into a conversation in progress. Vanessa was reserved, assertive about her views on life and seemed very open to the opinions of others. She told the group that she was a twenty-two-year-old poet and writer who lived in Greenwich Village and was pursuing an MFA online.

"I'm a pretty liberal thinker and I let people be," Vanessa told Chanel. "I'm not going to school to be a judge."

Candy liked her style almost as much as she liked her sexy body. After the shop was clear, she took Vanessa into her office for a formal interview.

Vanessa sat on a seat in front of Candy's desk.

"So why should I hire you?" Candy asked bluntly.

"Because I'm experienced, I'm dedicated and I can make you a lot of money." She smiled.

"Money is definitely a good thing." "They say business is about the bottom line."

"You are aware that we work ten-hour shifts? Ten in the morning 'til eight at night. Lunch is from one to two."

Vanessa nodded. "I'm aware."

"Days off are Tuesdays and Wednesdays. We work weekends, because clients want their hair done on Fridays and Saturdays. On Sundays, we're getting them ready for work on Monday."

"Tuesdays and Wednesdays off, fine with me," Vanessa said.

"If you want your hair done, it has to be between nine and

ten in the morning. I'm always here an hour before we open."

"No problem."

"Before I decide whether to hire you, I need to see you in action, plus know that you get along with the staff. We're a family here."

"That's cool," Vanessa said.

"So I need you to bring in five clients, and I'll be observing." Candy paused, thinking before staring directly into Vanessa's eyes with a serious look. "Under no circumstances will I allow anyone to compromise the reputation of the shop."

"Understood."

"You gel with the staff and you impress me five times, the job is yours."

"That's cool. I have a list of clients."

"Six years in the business, you should." Candy smiled. "One more thing, do you have a problem working with people who are gay?"

"Not at all," Vanessa said emphatically. "Virtually every shop I've worked in has had a guy who was gay."

"How about lesbians?"

"I've never worked with one, but it's not a problem."

"Good, because I am very much openly gay." Candy looked for any sign of apprehension, anger, or some other hint signaling a lack of tolerance. There was none. She analyzed Vanessa's demeanor and facial expression in hopes of spotting an indication of her some intrigue about girl-on-girl action. Again, there was none. *But I can change all that,* "Candy thought. "So you don't have any hang-ups?"

"I'm applying for the job of a beautician. I have no aspirations of being a judge," Vanessa said with a grin.

"I like that." Candy stood, shook Vanessa's hand, then handed her a business card. "As soon as you're ready to bring your clients in, e-mail me, call or whatever. I'll arrange a date and we'll see what you're capable of."

"Will do." Vanessa smiled, before stepping off.

Candy's eyes zoned in on Vanessa's strut. *I gotta have her.* Candy envisioned Vanessa's legs wrapped around her neck. She imagined what she tasted like, what aroma her slippery insides generated when stimulated.

Although Vanessa did not know, the job was hers the second she applied for it. Candy knew if she hired Vanessa, she would be one step closer to making her visions a reality and finding out the answers to her erotic questions.

CHAPTER TWO
VANESSA

Vanessa sat in her dining room eating a soy burger and a salad with croutons for lunch. She had been a vegan for two years. It was a health decision spawned by the death of her mother from complications due to high blood pressure. Her father suffering two heart attacks had also helped push Vanessa toward eliminating meat and meat byproducts from her diet.

Vanessa's father was a wealthy real estate investor who lived on Park Avenue. He owned the building in which she had lived in rent-free since her 18th birthday. He also footed the bill for her education. Her Nissan Altima was a graduation gift from her brother who was a successful marketing executive in California. With her family financing her most expensive possessions, Vanessa had managed to save much of the money she earned as a beautician and writer.

Dozens of articles and poems had been published in magazines, online and in anthologies with Vanessa's name listed as author. Writing was her passion and way of life. It helped her grow through questioning her thoughts on paper and challenging the things she learned during the research process required for her writings. She also enjoyed being able to create something from nothing. It also provided a vehicle for her to freely express herself without fear of being criticized or judged in person.

Throughout high school and college, Vanessa never seemed to fit in. It was part of the reason she began taking classes online instead of attending school on campus. Her style of dress, the way she thought and her desire to question norms was something most people she met could not relate to. Her relationships with men were short-lived and her friends were few. Although people were not usually accepting of Vanessa, she always remained open to others. She had a thirst for learning and she knew she could learn from anyone.

After Vanessa finished her lunch, she went into her second bedroom, which served as her office. The walls were decorated with a couple of abstract paintings, an African mask and a Chinese astrological chart. Vanessa was a Scorpio who believed her life was guided by the stars.

She sat behind her desk and sparked lavender-scented incense. She folded her legs in the lotus position and closed her eyes. Breathing in deep, while closing one nostril shut, she started a breathing exercise in which she alternated inhaling and exhaling through each nostril. It was a yoga practice she learned as a freshman in college. After five minutes, her heart rate slowed and her mind was calm.

Vanessa opened her eyes and turned on her Mac. After the computer screen lit up, she clicked on her playlist of india arie and then opened the most recent writing she had been working on. It was the manuscript for her first novel, an erotic tale of a young woman who was attracted to powerful men. The men ranged from government officials to drug dealers. The young lady found herself in an intricate maze of street drama and love triangles. The story was semi-autobiographical. Vanessa often fantasized about submitting to the sexual prowess of men who commanded authority. She was intrigued by their dominance in public and yearned to learn if their forceful reign extended to their performance between the sheets. But Vanessa had never attracted a powerful man and she was too afraid to approach one.

As she began to type, her iPhone rang.

"What's up, Nessa?" her best friend Mimi greeted her.

"Nothing. Just started working on this book and I'm listening to some music."

"Erykah Badu, Maxwell or Floetry?"

"india arie."

"Same difference. Girl, you gotta stop this mother earth, incense-burning bullshit, you feel me?" Mimi laughed. "I bet you burning frankincense."

"Lavender."

"Same shit. You stay cramped up in your crib like a damn monk in a monastery."

"My spirit moves me, not the other way around."

"Yeah, yeah. You need to come up with a better one liner than that, too. You been running that shit in the ground."

"Blame it on the stars."

"You're gettin' better."

"I don't dictate the truth, I just live. It's all in the stars."

"Yeah, yeah, yeah, Miss. Astrology. Anyway, I called to see if you wanna go bowling tonight?"

Vanessa looked at the computer screen. "Depends on how I do with this writing."

"Girl, you ain't gon' be writing all day, and definitely not all night. It's Saturday and Bowlmor is open 'till three-thirty in the morning, you feel me?"

"Call me back at nine and I'll let you know."

"Listen, Nessa. At nine o'clock I'm gonna be knocking on your door like a Jehovah's Witness."

Vanessa giggled, picturing her best friend's facial expression and hand movements. Mimi was the most animated person Vanessa knew. She seemed to do more talking with her hands than her lips, sort of like she was a sign language expert and everyone in the world was mute.

"You heard me, Nessa?"

"Okay. Now leave me alone so I can take care of my business."

"I'm gone," Mimi said, before hanging up.

***

It was 8:00 p.m. and Vanessa was typing away when she got an e-mail from Mimi that read: BCNU @ 9. Not a Second L8. C 50 Cent's sex tape attached. CU L8R.

"Fifty Cent sex tape?" Vanessa was fascinated. She turned off her music and clicked on the video attachment. Her eyes and mouth opened wide. *It's not him, but it sure looks like him, muscles and all.*

Vanessa sat in awe, watching a 50 Cent look-alike plow himself into a young dark-skinned woman. She was bent over a glass table in a large dining room. Vanessa stared at the close-up of all nine inches of the man ramming away. The woman's buttcheeks jiggled as she screamed like she was being beaten to death.

Vanessa's finger tapped on her desk, while her juices began flowing. She had always been easily aroused, and her long-standing crush on 50 Cent was overpowering her mind. She began visualizing the look-alike as the real thing and the unknown woman as herself. In minutes, Vanessa's hand was inside of her sweatpants and creeping beneath her panties. She let out a deep moan, as she slipped two fingers inside of herself. She let her legs fall to the floor.

Her body fidgeted. She grabbed the desk with her freehand,

while shifting in her chair. Her breathing accelerated, undoing the tranquility that came from her earlier breathing exercise.

"Ahh, shit." She stared at the contorted look on the woman, wishing it was her being manhandled. The 50 Cent look-alike turned the woman over on her back. Her ankles stretched up against his shoulders. He reached down, slid inside of her gently, and locked his arms around her legs. He began a few slow strokes, and then started ramming her ferociously. The woman yelled. Her huge breasts bounced wildly.

"To hell with this!" Vanessa stripped naked. She turned the volume on the computer as loud as it could go. The moaning and screaming of the on-screen couple roared like they were getting it on live inside Vanessa's office. She snatched one of the desk draws open and removed a large neon dildo. Leaning back in her chair, Vanessa cocked both legs up until her feet were on the edge of the desk.

"Yeah... ahhh," she purred, while sliding the dildo in and out, staring at the video. She moved faster in a turning motion, while rubbing her clit with her finger.

Vanessa closed her eyes and focused on the moans and panting of the woman on the video.

"Fuck me. Come on," Vanessa whispered with each lunge of the dildo. "Come on, Fifty. Hurt me, baby." Vanessa's whispers grew louder and her breathing sped up. She could feel her blood pumping harder into a boiling passion. A surge of energy flowed inside of her as the bald slit between her legs exploded with wetness. She took her slippery fingers and massaged her small, hardened nipples.

"Damn, shit." She opened her eyes, as she caught her breath, gazing at the ceiling with her head tilted back. She thought about her ex-boyfriend Troy. She had broken up with him two weeks earlier and she had not had sex since. Even during the times she had sex with Troy, he never satisfied her needs. No man had. The only time she had ever climaxed was when she pleased herself. But she still craved a man's touch. She needed to feel firm hands grip her body. Her problem was that she had trouble finding Mr. Right, and often settled for casual sex.

Her mind suddenly flashed on Mimi as she remembered that they would be going bowling soon. Perhaps her search for Mr. Right would end then.

* * *

Bowlmor Lanes became a New York landmark in 1938, but it became the second home of Vanessa and Mimi in 2007. Forty-two lanes, glow-in-the-dark bowling with neon bowling pins, music while they bowled, music in the Pressure Lounge upstairs, lively crowds—Bowlmor had everything they needed to unwind. As Vanessa and Mimi sat in the dimly-lit Pressure Lounge, Vanessa was hoping Bowlmor had the man she needed in her life.

Mimi had been sipping on a lemon drop martini in between taking bites of one of her turkey club wraps. "You need some meat in your life, Nessa."

Vanessa frowned. "There's so much better things to do in life than eat animals."

Mimi removed the lemon slice from her glass and offered it to Vanessa with a smile. "Here you go, Earth Lady."

Vanessa laughed, staring at her best friend. Mimi was wearing a pair of tight white jeans with a striped blue and white button-up shirt, both by Polo. She was the assistant director of public relations at Ralph Lauren, so her wardrobe consisted of everything from Polo and Chaps to Rugby and Black Label. Mimi was Chinese, but had more soul than the average sister and far more experience than Vanessa with black people in the 'hood. While Vanessa was growing up in the comfort of a Park Avenue condo with a doorman and concierge, Mimi was carving out a space for herself as the only Asian girl in Queen's crime-ridden Baisley Projects. While Vanessa was in private school with personal tutors and dedicated teachers, Mimi was running with crowds of future dropouts inside the halls of August Martin High School. But when the pair met at NYU, they gravitated to each other like family. They were intrigued by each other's backgrounds and struggle to fit in.

"You holler at that chick from the salon yet?" Mimi asked.

"I e-mailed her yesterday, but I didn't hear anything yet."

"Don't sweat it. You gonna get that job."

"Mimi the psychic."

"I don't gotta be Cleo to know what you capable of, you feel me?"

"Tell that to Candy." Vanessa shook her head, rolling her eyes across the dance floor in search of Mr. Right.

"I thought you said she seemed impressed with you?"

"Yeah, but who knows." Vanessa sipped her club soda. "Tell you one thing, I'm sure she'll cut to the chase with her decision."

"What makes you say that?"

"She sure didn't have a problem telling me she liked being licked."

"Who doesn't?" Mimi chuckled.

"Oh, excuse me. I forgot, I'm talking to 'Ms. I-experimented-once-while-I-was-tipsy.'"

"Hell of an experience. Toes curled up like a Cheese Doodle." Mimi rubbed her hands together and grinned. "But Mimi likes pee pee. Strictly dickly, you feel me?"

"Hard to tell."

"I just understand how a chick could get caught up. It's like crack—very addictive." She laughed.

"To each his or her own."

Vanessa and Mimi strolled around Bowlmor after leaving the Pressure Lounge. They flirted with a few men before heading home. Vanessa drove through Manhattan, craving to have the itch between her legs scratched by a man. The two weeks that had passed since she had sex felt like two years. She wanted the real thing…fast. But she would have to settle for the fake 50 Cent waiting on her computer screen at home.

* * *

The following week, Vanessa stood in front of her bathroom mirror applying lip gloss. It was merely an enhancer of her natural beauty. Makeup had never touched her face. Her flawless skin was the product of Shea butter, tea tree oil and organic soap from the Body Shop. Vanessa knew she was naturally beautiful and she felt her body deserved only the best "nature" could produce. She slipped on some loose-fitting slacks and a long silk wrap over her tank top. Turning off the light, she headed out her apartment.

She got in her black Altima and steered into Harlem. She had not been in the neighborhood since she and Mimi saw Anthony Hamilton perform at the Apollo months earlier. She now parked in front of Candy's Shop and looked around, expecting to see Mimi's car. "Damn," she whispered. It was 10:00 a.m. and Mimi was scheduled to be the first client that Candy would observe Vanessa work on in the shop. Vanessa had stressed to Mimi the importance of her arriving at 10:00 a.m. sharp. The plan was to leave a good impression on Candy in an effort to secure the job. Frustrated, she pulled out her iPhone and called Mimi.

"Don't worry," Mimi said. "I'm two minutes away. I got you, Nessa. Be easy."

"Okay." Vanessa smiled and hung up. She stepped out of her car and into the shop. She was surprised to not hear music playing like the first time she had been there. All the ladies greeted her.

"You'll be working here," Candy said, pointing at the second chair. Leah was working the first, Candy held down the third, then came Chanel and Meisha in the row of large chairs. Candy opened the drawers in front of Vanessa's chair. "There's everything and anything you need in there. Combs, curlers, curling iron, blow dryer, you name it" Candy pointed to the cabinets, which contained assorted hair care products.

"Okay," Vanessa said.

"Money to blowww. Gettin' it innn," was blasting from a car stereo.

"Damn, that shit loud," Meisha said, looking through the shop windows to see where Drake's singing was coming from. She pointed at the shiny black Audi A4 parking in front of the shop. "Is that Rich out there?"

Chanel peeked outside, followed by the rest of the women. "I don't think so," she said. "But that shit is hot." She paused as the music ceased and the driver's side door of the Audi opened. "Oh, shit. An Asian broad pushing a kitted A-Four, rocking hip hop. Ain't that some shit?"

"That's my friend," Vanessa said.

Mimi stepped inside the shop donning a gold Black Label halter and matching skirt with a black Prada bag and shoes.

"Hey, Mimi. Right over here." Vanessa's eyes lit up like a child with a new toy.

"Nessa, what's good?" Mimi hugged Vanessa. "It's bakin' out there." She pointed outside. "Shit hotter than Jamaica, Queens after that cop got murdered back in the days."

Vanessa noticed everyone staring at Mimi in awe. It was a look she had seen many times when people first got a glimpse of Mimi's swagger. "Everybody, this is my best friend Mimi," Vanessa said."

"Hey, girl. I'm Leah."

"Candy." Candy smiled.

Chanel also introduced herself.

Mimi was smiling and nodding her head as she returned

their greetings. "All right, I want y'all to know off the rip, Vanessa's my heart, you feel me? But that shit don't mean nothing when it come to this `do?" She pointed to her silky hair. "So since I'm letting her touch my hair, you know she get busy, you feel me?"

"I feel you, girl." Meisha clapped her hands, grinning and pointing at Mimi. "You the truth."

"Shit, I'm just keepin' it a hundred. I gotta be at work with these crackers when I leave here. So I gotta talk like a white girl, hair gotta be right, everything. „Cause they be just looking for a reason to fire yo" ass if your eyes ain't blue. And Mimi is not gettin' rid of her A-Four and moving from SOHO back to Baisley Projects, you feel me?"

Everyone burst into laughter. Chanel asked Mimi if she knew a guy whom she used to date from Baisley. Mimi started telling war stories about the guy, who she had grown up with. Then Vanessa and Mimi began reminiscing about their college days and the men they dated. Everyone in the shop started rehashing tales from their past. By the time clients began trickling inside the shop, hip hop was banging from the speakers and Mimi was rapping faster than Twista.

After Vanessa was done styling Mimi's hair, Candy stood, inspecting the style from different angles. She was impressed. Vanessa had transformed Mimi's straightened burgundy hair into a black French bun with gold streaks that complimented her outfit.

After finishing with Mimi, Vanessa completed three other clients perfectly. She converted one woman's afro puffs into micro braids. Vanessa styled another woman's Shirley Temple curls into a short Anita Baker 'do. The third woman left the shop with a weave that hung to the small of her back.

"I see you puttin' it down, Vanessa," Chanel said.

"Since I was sixteen," Vanessa responded, sitting down to

wait on her last client's arrival. "How old are you?" asked Chanel.

"Twenty-two," Vanessa said proudly. Her eyes drifted to the man waltzing up to the shop in a crisp Armani suit. *Damn, he's handsome. His body looks kind of toned underneath that blazer, too.*

Chanel noticed Vanessa's roaming eyes. "That"s Rich," she announced.

Vanessa watched Rich. He sat on one of the chairs in the row reserved for clients awaiting service. He folded one leg over the other, like a business professional in an executive meeting. His green Maury alligator shoes shined under the bright lights in the shop. He began reading *The Wall Street Journal.*

"Hey, Rich," Meisha said. She was trimming a woman's hair. "You got about five minutes before I'm done."

"I know I'm a little early," Rich said, peeping over the newspaper.

"How you doing, Rich'?" Leah yelled.

"Leah, how you, baby?"

"Can't complain."

"Ain't you supposed to be switching your last name?"

"Just engaged, for now. Two more months and I'll be in that long white dress."

"Just give me the date and the address. You know I gottta watch you walk down that aisle"

"You know you're invited."

"All right, all right." Rich smiled, then looked at Candy. "Big Candy, what's going on in your world?"

"Progress. I think I have a new stylist," she said, putting her hand on Vanessa's shoulder. Vanessa turned to her with a wide smile.

"You got the job," Candy whispered.

"Thanks."

"Don't sweat it."

Rich's eyes were sizing up Vanessa. "And what might this lovely new lady's name be?"

Vanessa responded with her name.

"Well, Vanessa, I'm Rich." He grinned. "Let me rewind that. My name is Rich, but I am fairly wealthy." He chuckled.

"Tsss," Chanel sighed.

Rich turned to Chanel. "Somebody get a spare, ,cause ol" girl got a flat tire."

"Not tonight, Rich." Chanel waved her hand.

"Not tomorrow morning, afternoon, or night either. It will never be nothing between us but air."

"What. . .ever," Chanel said, rolling her eyes.

Rich pointed at Chanel. "I'll take that as a cue that I can continue talking to this lovely young lady." He turned back to Vanessa.

"Vanessa, right?"

"Correct," she answered.

"Well, Vanessa, I wish you success on the new job."

"Thanks."

"Thank yourself, 'cause you made it happen. It's all about you, baby." He smiled.

"That's one way to look at it," Vanessa said, as she sized up Rich. Her eyes took in everything from his trimmed mustache and sideburns, to the diamond stud in his right ear and the bulge between his legs. She could tell that Rich was the type of man who women feared introducing to their friends. He had a strong presence and sense of style that could cause the most loyal woman to cross her best friend. He was a smooth talker, not just because of what he said, but how he spoke. Words rolled off his tongue with an air of confidence and preciseness that Vanessa had never seen. She was itching to know if he handled himself as smooth in the bedroom.

"What's up, Vanessa?"

Vanessa looked up, spotting her last client strolling through the door. She helped the young man to his seat. Vanessa started by shampooing his 'fro. Next, she dried his hair and greased his scalp, before braiding his hair into cornrows. When she was finished, Rich was walking past her.

"You have a good night." He winked at Vanessa and was out the door before she could respond.

"Girl, you don't want to mess with him," Candy said.

Vanessa turned to Chanel. "So what's it with you and Rich?"

"Nothing," Chanel said.

"She thinks she's God's gift to this world and Rich thinks he is God," Candy said.

Chanel huffed. "You know when you were little and a boy liked you, so he was always messing with you? Pulling your hair and all type of crazy shit? That's Rich. He want to be a part of the Chanel Legacy, but he don't know how to approach me."

"Don't forget the part about you wanting to give him the pussy," Meisha said, laughing. "And everybody know you fucked his homie Chase."

"I didn't fuck Chase; he just ate my pussy. But that's another story. You like him, Vanessa?" Chanel asked.

Vanessa shrugged her shoulders. "I don't even know him."

"And you don't want to. Trust me," Candy said, emphatically.

Vanessa listened to the ladies rehash stories about Rich dogging women. They told her that he was one of Harlem's most celebrated drug dealers. Vanessa learned about the rumors of people found dead after Rich had ordered them killed. There were tales of family members who had been kidnapped and held for ransom by Rich's henchmen. Vanessa heard the chronicles of crooked cops who turned a blind eye to Rich's criminal enterprise, because he had lined their pockets. The narratives never involved Rich getting his own hands dirty. The stories always pertained to Rich ordering that dirty work done.

Vanessa interpreted that as him being the ultimate boss. The more she heard, the more she was attracted to him. By all accounts, Rich was the dominant man who reigned with power. He was the man Vanessa had been writing about, the man she fantasized about, the man that could now become hers if things worked out how she wanted them to.

CHAPTER THREE
RICH

He was born Jamel Thomas in 1975 at Bronx Lebanon Hospital. But the thirty-five-year old had earned the name Rich as a kid who ran drugs for Rich Porter—a legendary Harlem hustler who was murdered in 1990. Rich had studied the game and learned from the mistakes of others, especially his dead mentor.

Unlike the average hustler, he was an investor. Instead of opening barbershops, grocery stores and other businesses like many drug dealers, Rich purchased stock in companies like Microsoft, McDonald's and Wal-Mart. These were blue chip stocks—stocks that were essential to the American economy and had a long history of generating money. His smallest investment was in his uncle"s company, which rented luxury cars. Rich worked in the company"s promotions department. It was virtually a no-show job that made him a tax-paying citizen with free access to any car he wanted. So the spotless BMWs, Bentleys and other cars he was praised for in the streets were not his. That was a secretRich used to his benefit. He knew the importance of image and he capitalized off of it every opportunity he had. It was a tactic he learned from Free, a squeaky clean co-worker of his who often attracted women of the strength of Rich"s street credibility.

Rich walked through the door to the roof of the Polo Grounds Housing Project in Harlem. Two of the young goons who worked at one of his dope spots had a man hemmed up. Another of Rich's goons stood by observing. The man's wrists were tied behind his back with duct tape and his head was covered with a filthy pillowcase. Rich slipped on his Versace shades as the sun beat down on the gravel-covered roof. He stepped over and snatched the pillowcase off the man's head. He smiled, looking into the teary eyes of the stickup kid who had robbed one of his spots weeks earlier. Rich ripped the duct tape from the man's mouth.

"Yo, Rich. I ain't have nothing to do with this shit," the man pleaded.

Rich grinned. "You know the streets is always talking and my ears stay open."

"Shit, the streets be lying. Dudes got this shit all wrong."

"I thought you would've came up with something better than that."

"Huh?" the man mumbled, his lips quivering.

"Your life is on the line and you can't even think of an excuse to save it?"

"That's word to my dead grandmother, I'm telling the truth."

"That's fucked up."

"What?"

"You lying on your dead grandmother, knowing you about to go see her." Rich pointed to the ledge of the roof.

"Come on, Rich. This shit ain't gotta go down like this." The man begged, struggling to free himself from Rich's goons, as they dragged him to the edge of the building.

Rich followed them, along with his third goon. The fearful robber stood frozen in front of the ledge, as the two goons backed away. Rich winked his eye and flashed an evil grin at the third goon, who pulled a .44-caliber automatic from his waist. He pointed the huge blue steel handgun at the man.

"Mouthpiece," Rich ordered.

Instantly, Rich's goon jammed the semi-automatic into the robber's mouth, breaking a tooth, before squeezing a single round. The back of the man's head exploded. Rich peeped over to the ledge and viewed the brain tissue and skin dropping twenty-four stories down, followed by the lifeless body that added to the list of murder victims who had felt Rich's wrath. As he watched the man's body fall, it seemed to get smaller and smaller.

Rich was growing tired of the drama that came with the game. But he knew it was an inevitable part of fast money and the streets. He liked fast money more than he liked life itself. It gave him a high that was as potent as the product he pushed throughout Harlem. Yet, he had been thinking about making his exit and entering the legal world. But there was always something pulling him back in.

* * *

Later that night, Rich pulled into the garage of his penthouse and parked next to a midnight blue BMW 650 Coup. He exited the Bentley Continental G and hopped inside the BMW. He adjusted the mirror and pulled off, driving down Lennox Avenue until he double parked next to a black Mercedes.

The tinted window of the Mercedes slid down. "What's good?" said Chase, as his hand gripped the wheel. Chase was a stocky roughneck who had left a trail of blood and bullet shells throughout Harlem before his 18th birthday. He served five years for manslaughter after he disarmed and shot a man to death, a man who had attempted to kill Rich. Chase slipped past 25 to life, because of a slick-talking lawyer that Rich hired with money he and Chase generated from their dope spot in Wyandanch, Long Island. By the time Chase came home, Rich had expanded their operation to every borough in New York City. Neither Rich nor Chase ever had any more legal trouble. Part of their success came from their decision to never sell drugs in Harlem, where they lived, and never show their faces at any of their dope spots.

"You still wanna hit Club Dream?" Rich asked Chase.

"Yeah. Free coming?"

"He said he'll meet us there."

Chase ran his hand over his bald head and down to his goatee. "All right."

"Hold on," Rich said, answering his cell phone. His face grew solemn. Through clenched teeth, he spoke in an assertive low tone. "We not gonna keep going through this!" He hung up the phone and shook his head, then let out a deep breath."

"Danella?" Chase asked.

Rich nodded.

Danella was a high-class model who had been stalking Rich since he dumped her two months earlier. She was looking for love; all Rich ever knew was lust.

"Chicks like Danella ain't used to gettin' shitted on," Chase said. "Ain't too many dudes from the 'hood can even bag her. And you probably the only dude around that kicked a chick to the curb, knowing she one of the only black chicks that"s been on the cover of *Sports Illustrated*. *I* would've kept her just off the strength of how she looked in that swimsuit."

"That's the difference between me and ninety-nine-point-nine-percent of dudes in the world. Anyway, what you doing here?"

"Waiting for this broad to bring down my chain. I left it on her dresser."

Rich's eyebrows arched. "What broad?"

"Some little ho I bagged at the Knicks game last night."

"Yeah? But on some real shit, I took care of that."

"What's that?" Chase asked.

Rich replayed the incident that happened earlier on the roof.

"I'm glad that shit is out the way," Chase said. "Always gotta make examples out of heads, no matter how long we been in the game."

"You only as good as the last person you killed," Rich said.

* * *

It was almost midnight when Rich and Chase pulled up in front of Manhattan's Club Dream. There were two long lines extending the length of the long city block—one for women and one for men. Rich and Chase exited their rides and exchanged hugs and pounds with the valet, before handing him their keys. Chase pulled up his droopy Red Monkey jeans and twisted his fitted Yankees cap backwards.

Rich looked at Chase's Nike ACGs, and then his own ostrich shoes and grinned. He and Chase had always dressed opposite. Rich was usually in designer or tailored suits and hardbottoms, but occasionally he sported slacks and moccasins or gum soles. Chase was famous for urban fashion—Timberlands, sneakers, jeans, sweat suits and any other garments or accessories made famous by latest hip hop videos.

The bouncers greeted Rich and Chase, ushering them inside as if they were artists set to perform. A TI song flowed throughout the club, as Rich took in the scenery. He and Chase stopped at the coat check room. A young white guy gave Rich a pound and hug. They exchanged a few words and then the guy handed Rich three VIP passes. Rich and Chase stepped off.

"There go Free," Chase said, pointing at a light-skinned pretty boy seated at the bar, kicking it to a thin white woman with auburn hair.

"Yeah, that's him," Rich added, stepping toward the bar. Free was short for Dexter Freedman. He was a silver spoon fed baby from Jamaica Estates in Queens. He had never been arrested, never been in beef, never sold drugs and had no idea what it felt like to have a gun tucked beneath his belt on his waistline. Blood money was foreign to him, but he knew all about making legal money. That's where he and Rich saw eye-to-eye. Rich used Free to get himself and Chase into doors that were closed to thugs with rap sheets and street credibility. Virtually every lawyer, accountant and investor with ties to Rich and Chase met them through Free.

Rich and Chase nodded at Free as they walked past. They sat a few stools away. Rich ordered a gin and tonic and Chase ordered a bottle of Cristal.

Rich shook his head, resting his hands on the marble bar counter. "Can't take the 'hood out you."

"Last time I checked, they ain't make Cristal in Harlem," Chase said.

"No Kool-Aid and quarter waters either. And that's classic ghetto shit."

Free walked over and gave Rich and Chase some dap. "What's going on, fellas?"

"Jungle Fever in the air," Rich said.

"That's what's going on." Chase grinned.

"I'm blind," Free said. "All I do is smell pussy and hit it."

"I hear you. But a brother like me got a sweet tooth and a taste for chocolate," said Rich. "As a matter of fact, I see a nice little chocolate bunny I wanna get to know."

Chase's eyes followed Rich's. "Yeah, she bad."

"That's the truth," Free said.

The thick woman in stiletto heels and a mini skirt sat two stools away from Rich.

"Excuse me, gentleman." Rich handed two VIP passes to Chase and Free. "That young lady is hungry and I got all the meat she need."

With that, he walked over and sat beside the woman, getting a close-up of her full lips and round eyes.   She was sipping a margarita. "Excuse me, Miss. I don't mean to invade your space, but I like what I see. And when I see something I like, I got for it."

She turned her body toward Rich, her thick thighs showing as she crossed them. "So you like what you see?" she said, seductively gazing into Rich's eyes.

His pupils veered down between her legs, then back to her eyes. "I want what I see."

"Sometimes people bite off more than they can chew."

"Listen, baby," Rich eased his arm between himself and the woman, looking at his Rolex.

"Every minute I waste, I'm losing money and getting older. And we're both adults. So let's skip the preliminaries and get to the main event."

He stood and held his hand out. When the woman grabbed it. Rich helped her from the stool.

* * *

Minutes later, Rich and the woman were inside a stall in the club's unisex bathroom. His blazer was slung over the wall of the stall. He had just slipped on a condom, pinned the woman against the wall and pressed his dick against her round butt. As she pulled up her short skirt, a plump cheek popped out. Rich moved her thong to the side and slid into her.

She grunted.

Rich grabbed her shoulders and thrust himself in and out of her with forceful strokes. Her cheeks began a rhythmic clapping. They grew louder as Rich dug deeper into her with each plunge. He lifted her leg. "Put your foot on the toilet."

"Huh?"

"The toilet!" he barked.

She complied and stepped her right foot on the toilet. Rich placed his foot behind hers. Then he grabbed her left shoulder with both hands and rammed deep inside of her on an upward angle.

"Shhhiit!" the woman's voice rose.

Rich was literally jumping inside of her with each stroke. "This what you want, right?"

"Yeah. Like that." She reached her hands up as high as she could, as if she was trying to climb the wall to escape Rich's plunging. Suddenly her leg slipped. She and Rich fell from the toilet. She turned around and asked, "You okay?"

Rich nodded. He backed up and grabbed her skirt, lifting it all the way up in front. He tore her thong apart and tossed it in the toilet.

She smiled and grabbed his dick. "Put it in."

"Calm the fuck down." Rich paused a second. "Take them shoes off."

"Huh?" She frowned, looking confused.

"Just do what I say."

She smiled and removed her heels. Rich stepped forward, slipping into her. He grabbed her butt with both hands and lifted her up, pressing her back against the wall. "Put your feet against the wall behind me." Her feet hit the wall behind him. Her knees were bent in the cramped stall, as Rich stood between them, pumping. She wrapped her arms around his neck, clinging to him.

"Yeah, take this dick," Rich said.

She clutched him tighter, shifting herself into his strokes. "Give it to me."

"Yeah, come on." Rich sped up, as her tightness pulled him into a climax. He slowly caught his breath and stopped stroking. He let her down from the wall. Backing up, he removed the condom and tossed it into the toilet, before grabbing some tissue and wiping his dick. He adjusted his tie and carefully put on his blazer. Rich grabbed the handle of the stall.

"You ain't gonna give me your name, number, nothing?" the woman asked.

"I gave you enough for the night." Rich grinned before making his way to the sink. He washed his hands and face. Seconds later, he was strolling out of the bathroom.

Rich hit the bar and bought two bottles of Krug Rosé on a bucket of ice. As he turned around, a thin extremely light-skinned woman in a tight miniskirt strutted toward him. Her almond-shaped eyes beamed at Rich. She held a virtually empty champagne flute in one of her hands.

Rich sighed. *Danella. Here she comes with her bullshit.*

"It's not nice to hang up on people," she said, stopping in from of Rich and smiling. "Especially someone who loves you."

"Love can make people do crazy things, and for every action there's an equal and opposite reaction."

Danella smiled. "The laws of physics according to Sir Isaac Newton. Your intellect has always been a turn on for me. You're so much more than the average guy from the 'hood.'""So much more than you deserve." Rich chuckled. "Baby, it's the type of bourgeois shit you just said that's stoppin' you from staking your claim in the wonderful world of Rich."

"You don't really mean that."

"Baby, Rich always mean what he say." He walked away without another word.

"Richhh!" Danella screamed over the music in the club and slammed her champagne glass on the floor.

Rich turned around, spotting the crowd of people gathering to watch Danella's antics.

"Who the fuck do you think you are!" she yelled, storming toward Rich.

After a few steps, a bouncer snatched her. Her legs were swinging wildly, as the huge bouncer picked her off her feet with one arm while she screamed every curse word imaginable. The bouncer, who had known Rich for years, turned to him and said, "What do you want me to do with her?"

"I think she's had too much to drink and she's ready to go home."

The bouncer nodded at Rich, then carried Danella off toward the front door.

Rich noticed the looks in the eyes of the people who crowded the scene. Some foreign eyes projected disgust for Rich. Familiar eyes displayed astonishment. Rich assumed these people, who knew his status, expected more of a man with such a smooth demeanor and reputation that prevented people from challenging him. Rich now questioned whether Danella had left a chink in his armor. Although he had not overreacted to the situation, people were aware that he had a situation. That in itself was a problem for a discrete man who had mastered the art of keeping his personal life private. Danella's status as a famous model increased the probability of Rich's problem being publicized. *This shit ain't good. I can't have no freaks playin' me in public.*

Rich neared the VIP area, surprised to see the women from Candy's Shop. While he watched Leah filling glasses with champagne, he recalled that days earlier in the shop he had heard Leah mention that she was treating the women to a ladies" night out. The women were seated with Chase and Free on a large U-shaped couch that surrounded a table. Rich gazed at Candy. *Perfectly good piece of pussy going to waste.* She was sitting beside Vanessa. But she always stood out, because she was tall. Even in the dim VIP lounge, her long yellow legs seemed to light up the area.

"What's up, Rich?" the VIP bouncer asked.

"My stock, hopefully." Rich gave the short Dominican man in front of him a pound. Rich flashed his VIP pass. The man removed the velvet rope, allowing Rich admittance to the large area.

He walked toward Vanessa, who was seated closest to him. He adjusted his tie, a little nervous that his bathroom fling minutes earlier may be visible from his disorderly clothes.

"Hi, Rich," Vanessa greeted him with a smile.

"Can you please stand up for a second?" Rich gently grabbed her hand, helping her up. "Umph, umph, umph. You looked so good sitting down, I just needed to see you in totality."

Vanessa giggled. "Thank you."

"No, thank you." Rich kissed her hand and then sat her down. He greeted everyone else, before sitting next to Vanessa. He placed the bucket of ice and champagne on the table, before filling an empty glass.

"Yo, Rich, how was that?" Chase asked with a smirk, obviously referring to Rich's fling with the woman.

"Yeah, what's up?" Free added.

"In and out," Rich responded. "Just an appetizer. I'm waiting on the main course." He nodded discretely toward Vanessa, who was talking to Candy.

"I hear you." Chase flashed a smile.

Rich grabbed a bottle of champagne and popped the cork. He turned to Vanessa and Candy and then offered them some. Candy grabbed a flute and Rich filled her glass. "How 'bout you, Vanessa?"

She smiled. "No thank you."

"You sure?"

"I don't drink."

"Oh, excuse me. Didn't mean to infringe," Rich said.

"Not a problem."

As Free sparked up a conversation with Candy, Rich made his move on Vanessa. "You mind if I inquire why you don't drink?"

Vanessa told Rich about the health problems that plagued her family, including her mother's death. She mentioned her vegan diet and interest in nutrition. She said she also tried to live as simple as possible, and that drinking champagne was bit extravagant for her.

"You're making me think over here, Vanessa." Rich leaned back.

"A little food for thought is always good."

"Yesss, feed me, baby. I'm hungry. Give me some of that vegetarian food for thought." He laughed.

Vanessa laughed too. "You're crazy."

"That may be a good thing. We got a lot of sane people that got us into a recession, two wars, you name it." The look in Vanessa's eyes told Rich that she was impressed and surprised to hear him speak on such topics. He was almost certain that her mind had been molded in the shop to see him as an ignorant womanizing criminal. So he started building off of her "crazy" comment. He talked about the dynamics of Barack Obama being President, while only two of the 100 U.S. Senators were black. He expounded on his view that hip hop had helped race relations, because white children were embracing the hip hop culture, which is predominantly a black culture. He even added on to Vanessa mentioning health, noting that childhood obesity was at an all-time high. He expressed that children were glued to their seats playing video games and that the hormones and steroids pumped into food were adversely affecting their growth.

"So how do you change the world, Rich?" Vanessa asked.

"It starts with self. That's why I'm always growing mentally." He paused and leaned forward. "But you know what I really need?"

"What?"

"You." He gently grabbed her hand. "I need you to help me grow."

Vanessa blushed. "Me? You're sure about that?"

"Malcolm had Betty. Martin had Coretta. Barack got Michelle. Shit, even Jay got Beyonce."

Vanessa giggled.

"You know the cliché, 'behind every strong man is a strong woman.'"

"I'm sure you got enough of those."

"Not at all."

"Why me?"

"Why not you?"

"You can't answer a question with a question."

Rich grinned. "According to who?"

"Vanessa Denay."

"Okay, Ms. Thang. I'll play by your rules."

"That's good, because I feel I deserve an answer." Vanessa looked into his eyes with a slightly seductive stare.

"How 'bout I answer with this." He slowly leaned toward Vanessa and kissed her. His tongue swirled around her mouth just a second, enough time to leave a smile on her face and shock on the faces of the rest of the group.

"Ohhh, shit," Meisha blurted, covering her open mouth with her hand.

Rich looked around, noticing that Leah was smiling too. Then he saw hate in Chanel's hazel eyes. He imagined that she was wishing it was her mouth that his tongue had just probed. He expected her anger and jealousy. But the disappointment in

Candy's eyes startled Rich. He was sure Candy was upset that Vanessa was falling for him. With that in mind, he was motivated to treat Vanessa like a queen, just to prove Candy''s view of him wrong. But that was just one thought within the mind of a man who saw all women as nothing more than objects of his lustful desires.

* * *

After spending hours in the club talking and dancing with Vanessa, Rich was zooming down the FDR Drive with one hand on the wheel of his BMW and his other hand planted deep within Vanessa's 'fro, as she slurped all ten inches of his rock-hard dick. She massaged the shaft, while her lips and tongue worked the head. She was taking Rich to a new level. He could feel his entire body radiating.

Vanessa began gently rubbing Rich's balls. She looked up at him. "You like that, right?" Rich nodded, peeping at her, but trying to keep his eyes on the dark expressway ahead of him, while keeping his foot steady.

Vanessa ran her tongue around the head of his dick, and then down and up the length of his. "Yeah, I know you like it." She went back at it.

Rich's foot went down on the gas. "Damn, girl." Before he knew it, he was pushing 90 in the Beamer and sirens were flashing behind him. "Fuck!" he barked.

Vanessa looked up. "Oh, shit."

Rich pressed down on the gas more, passing 100. He grabbed Vanessa's head. She went back to work. Rich zipped pass a Suburban and cut in front of a Porsche. It was almost 3:00 a.m., so the road was relatively clear. The dial on the Beamer read 115 and that was the end of the cops behind him.

"Damn," Rich moaned. He slowed the car and turned off the FDR at 96th Street. As he headed up the street's steep hill, he climaxed. Vanessa had sucked him dry.

"How was that?" she asked, leaning back in her seat.

"I'm speechless." Rich had experienced some wild oral adventures, but none like what had just taken place with Vanessa. Her sexual expertise surpassed his expectations. That, coupled with the high-speed chase, gave him an adrenalin rush that drove him over the top. There was still plenty of time left, and he was eager to see what else Vanessa was capable of.

***

Rich and Vanessa raced to undress as they stepped through the door of his penthouse. Clothes dropped on the Persian rug and the chairs, tables and the loveseat in his living room. The couple ended up on the terrace that overlooked Central Park. Vanessa's body was bare and the only thing on Rich was a condom. Vanessa's back was pinned against the huge glass sliding door that separated the terrace from the spacious living room. Rich was determined to outdo Vanessa's raceway episode. He felt challenged by her prowess. He needed to prove that he had more sexual skills than she did. That meant more than a quickie. He had to give her the balance between love and raw sex.

Rich sucked on her neck, making his way down to her breasts. They were barely a handful, a perfect fit for his mouth. Back and forth, he worked her erect nipples in between taking in mouthfuls of her entire breast.

"That feels so go, Rich," Vanessa whispered.

Rich slipped his finger inside of her, pulling at her g-spot with the 'come here' motion.

"Rich." Her body tensed. "Please," she moaned. "You don't know what you're doing to me." Her body began squirming in between Rich's grip. "It feels so good."

Rich lowered his head and applied just the right amount of pressure to her clit with his tongue, while still fingering her.

Vanessa hoisted her leg over Rich's shoulder. She grabbed

the back of his head, pulling him into her as she came and her body went limp.

Once Vanessa regained her poise, Rich walked her to the ledge of the terrace. He took a few pillows from the nearby couch and situated them on the floor. "Get down there," he ordered and Vanessa complied. "Grab the gate."

As she clutched both hands on the three foot high gate on the ledge, Rich gripped his dick, standing over her. He salivated over her small naked frame, as she kneeled on the pillows. He eased down behind her on the last pillow and began hitting her doggy style.

Her back arched and she leaned forward, before screaming, "God, Rich."

Rich started a slow rhythm. His firm hands gripped her waist, as they both stared over the twenty-one stories down to Central Park. "How that feel?" he said, grunting.

"It hurts so good," she cried.

Rich sped up a bit, stroking from an angle.

"Yeah, you're working it."

He looked down at her pint-sized body, amazed that she could produce so much pleasure. He could feel her love muscle pulling him deeper into her as she rocked back into his strokes. He could feel himself going deeper and deeper into her wetness.

"Yeah, Rich. You're fucking me right!" she screamed.

He began plunging harder.

"Come on, dick me down!"

He grabbed her tighter and rammed harder.

"Harder, Rich!"

He plunged in and out. Her body bounced back and forth, her pussy tightening, becoming wetter and more sensational for Rich. "Damn, girl. Shit," he blurted.

"Harder," she begged. "You gotta fuck me harder!"

This little broad is wild. Straight freak. Rich strained his dick with each stroke. "Yes, like that, Rich. Yes. Yes. I'm coming!"

Rich slammed into her more forceful each time he stroked until Vanessa came seconds before he did. He fell back on the pillows, exhausted, his dick sore.

Vanessa crawled on top of him and kissed on his neck. "I don't know where you been, but I'm not letting you go anywhere," she whispered in his ear.

CHAPTER FOUR
CANDY

Candy was inside of her office the following morning when Leah walked inside carrying her laptop.

"Hey, girl." Leah said, hugging Candy. She pointed at Candy's desk. "Can I sit down? I need to show you something."

"Go 'head," Candy said.

Leah set her laptop on Candy's desk and sat down. She began browsing the Internet. "When I woke up this morning, I had an idea for your business," she said as she logged onto a website dedicated to entrepreneurship and labor practices. She began pointing out statistics about the field Candy was considering.

"This is gonna be hell trying to really get this business up and running, while I'm holding down the shop," Candy said.

"You know I'm always here to help."

"I know. Thanks."

"But believe me," Leah looked up from the computer

screen and into Candy's eyes, "if this new business gets up and running how I predict, you'll be making so much money, you're gonna wanna get rid of this shop. It'll just be slowing you down."

"Maybe—"

Leah cut her words short. "There's no maybe. I'm telling you. Numbers don"t lie."

"We'll see." Candy looked at her watch. "Everybody should be up front by now." She stood up and Leah followed suit. They went to the front of the shop and began conversing with Meisha and Chanel. A minute later, Vanessa strolled inside. Although Candy had not known Vanessa long, she knew the look on her face well. The smile that displayed more teeth than usual, the glimmer of her eyes, the glow of a woman whose heart and mind were reenergized—it was a look that came from good sex, love or a combination of both.

"How's everyone doing?" Vanessa asked.

Meisha sped over to her. "Girl, have a seat, breathe slow and let it out."

"You act like she's having a baby," Candy said, as Meisha sat Vanessa in her chair. "Calm down."

Meisha looked at Vanessa. "Last night. Give it up. Size first. Can he fill out a Magnum?"

"All the way," Vanessa said, with a smile. "I didn't know if I was gonna be able to take it all."

"Well, you was limping a little bit when you walked in here," said Meisha with a laugh.

"I take it he pleased you," Leah stated matter of factly.

Vanessa closed her eyes and nodded. "He just took control, giving orders. I loved it."

"I hope you be careful. Don"t get sprung," Leah said.

"Been trying to tell her ass that since she met him," Chanel shook her head, like a mother upset with her child.

Meisha turned to Chanel. "You need to stop hatin'!"

Chanel rolled her eyes. "Heifer, you just talking shit 'cause you got lips."

"Anyway," Meisha said, turning back to Vanessa. "Did he take you to the penthouse?"

"The terrace. Twenty-one floors, stars in the sky, just beautiful. It went down while we were looking down on Central Park."

"Oh my, God." Meisha began jumping around, her curly hair swinging wildly, as she covered her mouth with her hands. She closed her eyes briefly, then opened them wider. "I ain't never seen Central Park from that high, and you had your back dug out from up there? Bless your soul."

Candy fumed silently as she listened to how Rich had begun destroying the hopes she had of her and Vanessa. She had managed to gain Vanessa's trust through conversations they had during Vanessa's two weeks in the shop. But Candy had not moved in on the intimate level it would take to make Vanessa hers. She was still feeling her out and waiting for some personal time alone with her. Despite the women in the shop knowing that she was attracted to Vanessa on first sight, Candy had been downplaying her interest in Vanessa. Anything that developed between them would have to be a private affair. The gossip that went on in the shop could destroy the strongest relationship. And Candy was determined to be with Vanessa, uninterrupted by he say-she say or any other external influence.

As clients began to trickle into the shop, Candy kept her eyes on her crew. Meisha was still probing Vanessa about Rich. Candy could see Chanel's blatant jealousy was developing into hate for Vanessa. Besides a pretty face, Vanessa was nothing like the females who were fabric addicts with big hips that Rich was known for having, women like Chanel. The more Candy thought about Rich's womanizing, the more she assumed his use for Vanessa would run out quickly. That would leave Vanessa broken hearted, giving Candy the perfect opportunity to make her move while Vanessa was vulnerable.

"Chanel," Leah called.

"What?" Chanel responded over the sound of the TVs.

"Who was that fine young brother that was all over you last night?"

"Fine young brother on me all last night?" Chanel snapped her fingers, trying to remember. "You gotta be specific, because every brother with two eyes and a brain wanted to be a part of the Chanel Legacy last night."

"The one with the Knicks jersey on."

Chanel sighed. "Some college ball playing ass dude. He was pissin' in my ear all night, talkin' 'bout he about to go pro."

"Better grab him before he blow up," Meisha said.

"Shit, every damn dude in the 'hood that's not hustling think he gonna be the next Lebron or Jay-Z," Chanel said.

"She ain't lying," said a client, waiting to have her hair done.

"I told that fool last night that he need more than a hoop dream and a hard dick to be a part of the Chanel Legacy. You gotta be doing A-Rod numbers just to get a whiff of this pussy," Chanel said.

Candy turned to Vanessa. "So, you're serious about Rich?"

"I don't know yet."

"So you just wanna see where it goes?"

"That's all you can really do with any man. Hope for the best and expect the worse," Vanessa said.

Candy liked what she was hearing. She interpreted the slightest frustration with men as a signal that Vanessa might be fair game.

"I don't understand them," Vanessa said.

"Exactly why I switched lanes," Candy said. "Well, part of the reason."

"What's the other part?"

"I never met a man that could make me feel like a woman."

"I hear that." Vanessa smiled, slightly shaking her head.

"I don't expect you to understand. It's something that requires experience to comprehend."

"That rules me out," Vanessa quickly replied.

"I used to say the same thing."

Vanessa"s eyes widened. "What happened?"

"It's a long story. I'll tell you one day." Candy needed to slow down. She was becoming aroused by just breaching the topic of lesbianism with Vanessa. It was hard for her to talk to Vanessa without fantasizing about sexing her. So she reserved her conversation for a future day when they were alone, because words could easily lead to actions. Candy wanted to make sure that if she lost control of herself, no one was around to witness it.

Vanessa was interested in hearing what drove Candy over the top, and Candy took that as a sign that Vanessa could be reeled into her world. Experience had taught her how quick the transition from straight to gay could be.

Candy turned to Leah. "I did some research on the business," she said.

"That's good." Leah picked up a curling iron.

Candy told Leah about a few figures and details she had uncovered about the hair care industry. She said her niche would be starting small with a few organic revitalizing scrubs. "My cream will help you with that dry itchy scalp feeling. You know, when you're hair gets all flakey?"

Leah's head bobbed. "Yeah, girl, especially when you're wearing braids. In between those times they get redone it can be hell on your scalp."

"Exactly. My cream will be like that Carita Cream, but all natural." Candy said. "I downloaded some stuff off the internet for you to look over for me. It's in my office."

"I got you. This may be the foundation you we're talking about. The hair care industry is the next level for you moving on from the shop, maybe."

"I don't wanna just abandon the shop," Candy said, thinking of the time and energy she had put into, making Candy"s Shop into a profitable business that was respected in Harlem.

"I'm just saying," Leah's eyes widened. "Think about it."

"I'm capable of doing two things at once," Candy said. She wondered why Leah was so adamant about her leaving the shop. Could it be that Leah was possibly harboring ill feelings because of Candy"s interest in young women? The funny looks and comments that Leah had been making about Candy's sex life had become questionable since the day her eyes beamed at Candy after she met Vanessa. But Candy did not want to make assumptions or begin interrogating Leah. She couldn't risk a misconception destroying a friendship with one of the few people she valued having in her life.

"Also, you may wanna explore some other options for research instead of just going online," said Leah.

"Yeah, I was talking to Free last night. He said I should contact SCORE."

"Service Corps of Retired Executives," Leah uttered the meaning of the acronym. "It's a subsidiary of the Small Business Administration. I learned about them in school. They're retired bigwigs from different companies. They give you business advice for free."

"Yeah, that's what Free said. He told me to have them help me with putting together a business plan."

"Leah," Chanel interrupted. "That heifer still beatin' you in the head with them Bill Gates dreams?"

Leah laughed.

"What the hell you know about business, Chanel?" Candy inquired.

Chanel grinned. "The truck I drive? Escalade." She pointed at her red open-toe shoes. "You see these pumps? Gucci. My handbag in the back? Gucci. Skirt and blouse? Dolce and Gabbana."

"What's your point?" Candy asked.

"Everything I just mentioned is promotion and advertising to a target market of ballers with money to blow." Chanel slowly waved her hand over her body, from head to toe. "The Chanel Legacy is the fastest growing business in the 'hood."

VANESSA

Vanessa was strolling through Midtown, Manhattan with Mimi during their lunch break. She was giving Mimi a blow-by-blow visual of her night with Rich. She even revealed the car episode—part of the sexually explicit story that she didn"t tell the women in the shop. She had yet to gain complete trust in them, like she did Mimi. So exposing that she had given a man she hardly knew a blow job while he was driving was something she was sure would tarnish the perception the women in the shop had of her. Had she not been so engrossed in Rich and left the club with him, she would not have mentioned anything about them having sex. Mimi was the one person she could trust with her deepest secrets.

"You got a winner," Mimi said.

"Yeah, I never had a man do me like that. I'm telling you, Mimi, it was amazing."

"But you gotta watch them hos at that shop, you feel me?"

"What do you mean?"

"Candy and Chanel."

"I don't get it." Vanessa shrugged her shoulders.

"Come on, Nessa. Quit the Stevie Wonder routine. I know you saw the hate in the eyes of them hos when we was up in the club and Rich was on you like a cheap suit." Mimi mentioned Candy being virtually silent after Vanessa left the club with Rich. "And Chanel," Mimi shook her head, "she was so heated that she broke out right after you and Rich left."

Vanessa explained how Meisha accused Chanel of hating earlier in the shop. She also said that she could feel Chanel's jealousy, no matter how hard she tried to mask it. But in the club, she had not detected anything unusual or felt any bad vibes from Chanel or Candy. She thought Candy had her best interest in mind. "She's a lesbian. Why would she be jealous of me being with Rich?"

Mimi shrugged her shoulders. "Maybe she go both ways and she wanna fuck Rich. Damn if I know. What I do know, is how hos act when they jealous. I seen 'em a hundred times in the `hood. And Candy was jealous last night."

Vanessa tried to make sense of what Mimi was saying. Maybe Candy *was* interested in Rich? Everyone in the shop agreed he was a good catch sexually. Maybe Candy had not totally abandoned men? *Mimi's straight, but she's admitted to enjoying her experience with a woman.*

"Just keep your eye on Chanel and Candy," Mimi said. "I'm telling you. So when you gonna see ol'' boy again?"

"I don't know." Vanessa realized that she did not have Rich's phone number or e-mail address. She actually knew very little about him that was substantial. Shortly after their sexcapade, he had driven her to pick up her car parked near Club Dream. During the drive, most of their conversation revolved around their sexual experience together and sexual desires. She was amazed at how comfortable she felt discussing sex with Rich. She had never been with a man who was so open about what he wanted and desired, or whether she was satisfying in bed. She knew that if she could freely discuss sex with him, they could easily talk about any topic. Their discussion inside the club had proved that he was quite the conversationalist. But as it stood, she and Rich had communicated much more sexually than verbally.

Vanessa began speculating if her interaction with Rich was just a one-night stand? If not, did he want anything significant to develop between them? Would he be only seeking a bond between them based on sex? Everything that she had learned in the shop about Rich suggested that he specialized in sex, not relationships and love. Vanessa would be content for now with his strong sexual presence in her life. But she knew she would eventually need more from Rich. She thrived off mental stimulation almost as much as she did sex and she felt that Rich could provide her with both.

"On another note, what's up with your book?" Mimi asked.

"Halfway done. Got something to draw on now, after last night." Vanessa flashed a sneaky grin.

"Nessa, I know you not gonna be putting your penthouse fuck scene in that damn book."

Vanessa laughed, but she had definitely planned to rewrite her experience with Rich into the book. He reminded her of a character in her book and the main character was based on her, so she could easily weave their sex-filled night into the story.

Vanessa and Mimi stopped at the parking lot where their cars were. "Call me later," Vanessa said, getting into her Altima. She pulled off, weaving through traffic.

Rich was on her mind as she made it back to the shop in record time. She had thirty minutes left for her lunch break. The door to the shop was open, but she didn't see anyone inside. She figured only Candy was inside somewhere. Vanessa walked in and headed to the back when she noticed Candy's office door slightly open.

As she stepped toward the door, she heard moaning coming from inside the office. *What the hell?* She crept softly past the lockers over the tiled floor, and then peeped through the slim opening of the doorway. "Oh my God." She covered her mouth. It was the second time Vanessa had seen Vera, but the first time she had seen her naked. Her face was between Candy's legs, which hung from the edge of her desk as she laid back. Candy whined, squeezing her own breast, her eyes and mouth open and shut sporadically.

Vanessa could tell that Vera was very experienced at eating pussy. Vanessa knew that two women were not supposed to be together, but Candy's high-yellow complexion and Vera's chocolate skin tone was a contrast that seemed to complement each other perfectly.

This is unbelievable.

Candy and Vera switched positions. Vera was now on her back on the desk. Candy was on top, slowly grinding her pussy into Vera's mouth. Candy's huge breasts jiggled as she gyrated her hips.

"Yes, put it in," Candy cried as Vera inserted a finger into her asshole. Candy grinded harder and called out Vera's name louder, until she reached a climax and collapsed on Vera. Her eyes blinked as she stood, turning toward the door.

"Oh shit." Vanessa whispered and crept off quickly. She hoped that Candy did not spot her playing Peeping Tom. In seconds, she was outside of the shop, walking down Lennox Avenue. Her heart was racing. She tried to digest the reality of what she had just witnessed. She looked down, realizing her nipples were hard, visible through her tank top. She could feel a slippery wetness between her legs as she walked. *This is not supposed to be happening.* She stepped inside of a McDonald's bathroom and washed up. For the rest of the lunch hour, Vanessa walked throughout Harlem, fighting the feelings and curiosity that made her question her sexuality.

She nervously made it back to the shop, slowly stepping inside. Everything seemed to go in slow motion and her mind blacked out the music blaring. The only thing she thought of and viewed was Candy, who was setting up her station.

"What's up, Vanessa?" Candy smiled at her.

Vanessa didn't know how to respond, how to interpret the smile. Paranoia was dominating her mind.

After a moment of silence, Candy asked, "You All right?" She stepped over and put her hand on Vanessa's shoulder.

Candy's touch felt different than the normal contact Vanessa had with her. An eerie sensation flowed from her shoulder throughout her body. She grew tense, trying not to appear disturbed. "Just had something on my mind," she replied and slid over to her station.

Vanessa kept her eye on Candy while she flat-ironed a customer's hair. She was trying to see if Candy would reveal any signs that she had noticed Vanessa spying earlier. But Candy was her normal self, so Vanessa assumed that her roaming eyes had gone unnoticed by Candy. She must have made her exit from Candy's office doorway just in time.

While Vanessa was observing Candy throughout the day, she could not help but gaze at her body in a way that she had never looked at women. Candy's creamy skin and Amazon curves had a new meaning since Vanessa had seen them nude. She tried not to allow her mind to wander, but it was hard not to think of what it would feel like to be with Candy. She and Vera had seemed so passionate and their bodies worked in unison, satisfying each other in ways that Vanessa didn't think a man could. The wetness between her legs and her hardened nipples that resulted from the sight of the two women was something that Vanessa could not ignore. But although she could not control her thoughts, she could control her actions. She had no plans of acting on the visions that flowed through her mind.

RICH

Rich paced back and forth in front of the tall window behind the mahogany desk in his office. He had been engaged in a conversation with Free about Danella. After the club scene with her, Danella had left a message on his phone that she was going to have him arrested. "This freak is a on some fatal attraction shit. And when people start talking badges and cop cars, the game get a little too dangerous for me."

"You're smarter than her, Rich. The last thing you should be worried about is the police. Those days are over for you, right?" Free said.

"Yeah, man."

Earlier Free had questioned Rich about Chanel referring to him as a drug dealer, so Rich convinced Free that he had retired from the game. It was a lie that Rich planned to soon make good on. Rich knew that he could not sell drugs forever. But at the moment he was a hustler at heart. That meant he did not need any heat from the police courtesy of Danella or anyone else.

"You need to reevaluate how you treat these women, though," said Free. "When a famous professional woman like Danella starts making scenes in public like she did at the club, it's because you really hurt her deep."

"These freaks just go berserk when I hit 'em with the big skin payoff." He laughed, grabbing his crotch. "Women are emotional. They need discipline. That go for the famous ones too. Danella ain't no different than Naomi Campbell or Foxy Brown. You know how they act up in public."

"If you know that, I'm sure you know a woman scorned is not

a good look."

Rich's speakerphone rang and he pressed the answer button. "Cindy called," said Rich's assistant. "She left you a message that she wants to meet you after work."

Rich shook his head. "Thanks." He clicked the phone off and flopped down on his leather swivel chair, staring at Free. "I'm about to cancel Cindy."

"You only been dealing with her a hot month."

"That's thirty days too long. One night and one nut. That's all she's worthy of." Rich grinned. "I don't even know how Cindy got my work phone number. It's a reason I ain't been dialing and her phone ain't been ringing. But some of these freaks need a magnifying glass to see I'm moving on to bigger and better things."

"Vanessa."

Rich pointed at Free. "Now, you—Mr. twenty-twenty vision. You need to let Cindy borrow your eyes." He chuckled and stood up. "Let's get something to eat."

Both men stood up and walked into a long hallway. As they passed the water cooler and proceeded to get on the elevator, the receptionist called Rich. She was signing a clipboard as a delivery man stacked a large box on the floor. He placed a bouquet of flowers on top of the box.

"This is all for you, Rich," the young white receptionist said, smiling. "Somebody's really thinking of you."

Rich stepped over to the receptionist, trailed by Free. He read the card. "From Danella, with love." Rich shook his head and looked at Free. "She don't know when to quit."

"You gonna open the box or what?"

"You look more interested than me. Go ahead. Open it."

"All right." When Free opened the box, a sickening smell overtook the area. He dropped the box. What appeared to be at least one used roll of shit-stained paper spilled out along with a large sheet of paper that read:

You're not the only one who knows how to shit on somebody. I just have the decency to wipe my ass. Danella.

"Oh my God," the receptionist yelled, holding her nose.

"She violated," Rich mumbled.

"Somebody actually mailed you a box of shitty paper?" Rich's supervisor asked. "This is unbelievable."

Rich was silent. He looked around the area. Close to a dozen people seemed to surface from nowhere. There was some laughter, but most people looked on in disgust. A couple of women were fanning their noses as they walked away.

Rich huffed. *This fuckin' freak is outta control.* He thought of Free challenging him minutes earlier about his womanizing ways. Infidelity was a way of life for Rich. But Danella's continuous embarrassing acts were forcing Rich to analyze the impact of his actions. The extent to which Danella had gone—in the club and at Rich's job— demonstrated how much he had hurt her. Rich was not moved much by women's feelings. But when the feelings he created in women caused his life to become unmanageable, Rich knew he had a problem he needed to solve.

* * *

The shop was closing up that night as Rich strolled inside with his eyes on Vanessa. She had been on his mind since the night before. She stood beside Leah, engaged in a conversation and his eyes were transfixed on her small breasts protruding from beneath her yellow tank top. The taste of her nipples was still on his tongue. He needed to have her again. And again, and again, and again. The newness of sex with a different woman was what usually attracted Rich to a woman. But he felt it was more than the newness. Vanessa's small body and sexual skills was something different than the norm, something he had to have.

He walked over and kissed her, then greeted the women.

Moments later Rich and Vanessa walked outside and stood next to Vanessa's Altima.

"First things first," Rich said. "That yard of tongue I just put down your throat was for two reasons."

"Oh yeah?" Vanessa smiled.

Rich slipped one of her hands in between both of his. "It was to let you know I want every night to be like last night."

"And the other reason?"

"To let every one of them freaks inside that shop know that I'm not no one-night stand man playing hump 'em and dump „em with Ms. Vanessa."

Vanessa grinned.

"I'm serious, baby. Rich been in a lot of women's beds, but he just don't go around putting his lips on any woman. And I know my name done came up in that shop so much you might think I work there. Them jealous freaks in there probably pissing in your ear so much you might have an infection. Let me see." He gripped her ear between his fingers.

"Stop." Vanessa giggled. "You are crazy."

"Listen, where you on your way to?"

"Wherever you wanna go."

"It's not about me, baby. This your world. I'm just trying to live in it."

"This is our world," Vanessa said before kissing Rich. "But I'm gonna get in my car, you get in—" She looked around and paused in silence for a few seconds. "I don't see your car."

"It's right behind yours."

Vanessa looked at the Aston Martin DBS parked behind her Altima. The pearl white paint job glistened underneath a streetlamp. Rich laughed to himself as he watched her eyes expand at the sight of the customized sports car with its chrome rims. He knew she was expecting to see the Beamer that he sped down the FDR in with her head in his lap.

Vanessa's non-materialistic persona had vanished. The car with the six-figure price tag appeared to reduce her to the same status as the women who Rich usually overwhelmed with his money-making image.

"Follow me," Vanessa said, before jumping inside her Altima.

Rich drove behind her, thinking of what their next sex scene would be like. His fantasies had been saturating his mind since their mind-blowing rendezvous. Rich was seeing five other women, and he occasionally scrolled through the 100-plus numbers in his Sidekick to spark an episode with an old flame. His routine had been the same for years and no new strategies were in his game plan because of Vanessa. She had simply earned a space as number six on the list of starters he kept in active rotation. And she would need more continuous performances like her first in order to maintain her position.

"I know this freak ain't planning on going in there," Rich mumbled as Vanessa parked in front of Washington Square Park. He pulled up behind her. He had not taken a woman to a park since he was in junior high school. His dates spanned from dinner at exclusive French restaurants to Caribbean cruises. He stepped out of the Aston Martin after Vanessa exited her Altima.

She held her hands out and smiled. "So what do you think?"

"You made the call and I picked up the phone."

Vanessa grabbed his hand. "I know this is probably different for a man of your taste, but you'll be surprised how fun a park can be. When I was young my parents used to take me to Yellowstone Park every year," she said. "There's nothing like the outdoors, even if it's a city park."

Rich walked into the park with Vanessa, and sat on a bench. He listened to her life story. She told him about her always being the strange person in the crowd, and how people did not understand her. She told Rich about her history with Mimi and the bond they shared. Rich also listened to her speak passionately about her love for writing. He liked the ideas she mentioned about the novel she was working on. As she continued talking, Rich realized that she was holding in many things that she seemed anxious to get off her chest. She had a unique style that was growing on Rich. He had not been with a woman who so openly disclosed her frailties, like having her heart broken and dying without having found true love. He assumed that most women feared that their weakness would be exploited. It was that rationale that caused Rich to keep his personal weaknesses bottled up. So he was impressed, because Vanessa was displaying courage that he did not have the heart to show.

"Vanessa, you're obviously not bent on material things," Rich said, although he knew she was moved by the fact he had driven two cars with a combined cost of over $200,000 in less than twenty-four hours. "What do you value in life?"

"Life itself."

"That's real specific." He chuckled.

"Everything. The good, the bad, people, animals, our planet, the sun. Everything that comprises our universe. That's why I'm open-minded and willing to hear people out, because I respect their views as part of the bigger picture of diversity in our universe that makes everything complete. Even if I don't agree with people's views. There is no one thing in life that I can point to in terms of what I value, because I view things holistically."

Rich nodded. "For every job outsourced to India, someone in the States is unemployed."

"Yes, exactly. The moon affects the tides in our oceans. Everything, no matter how distant or seemingly insignificant, plays a role in the larger picture."

"I got you."

"But let me ask you something, Mister. How did you come to be so comfortable with your sexuality? I mean, discussing it?"

Rich laughed.

"I'm serious." Vanessa pinched his arm. "I've been thinking about our sex talk since I left you. I've never discussed sex with a man in such a detailed manner like we did. It was liberating."

"First, you gotta understand that there's nothing more natural than sex. If our parents weren't freaks, we wouldn't be here."

"True." Vanessa giggled.

Rich told her about his first experience with a girl at twelve years old. It was a girl in her late teens, and for the next four years, each girl he had sex with was older than him. This was the result of him being practically raised by older hustlers in the streets who kept a flock of groupies around that Rich had access to. Sex was talked about daily in the circles he rolled in, and the women he dealt with knew exactly what they wanted and weren't afraid to voice it.

"I think I can understand you."

"I keep it simple. I'm not a complex man, and I hate when people make a science project out of something simple."

"I must admit, sometimes I like to make things hard." Vanessa looked around, then eased her hand into Rich's pants and began sucking his neck.

Rich looked up at the bright lights beaming through the trees around him. Glancing around, he saw a few people about 200 feet away.

Vanessa lifted her skirt and slid on top of Rich's lap, while unbuttoning his pants. "You just like taking that dick, don't you?"

"Get used to it." Vanessa grinned as Rich palmed her butt.

He pulled a Magnum from his pocket and gave it to her.

"Don't forget this."

She ripped the wrapper off it with her teeth, like a pit bull locking on a poodle and shaking it. Rich rolled up her tank top, just enough to reveal her golden breasts. She eased the condom on Rich"s manhood and straddled him in one swift motion. *This freak is a pro.* Rich pulled her close to him, taking one of her small breasts into his mouth.

"Suck 'em." She slowly rode him, her body melodically grinding against his.

Rich could feel the summer breeze on his skin as Vanessa's warmth wrapped him. He switched breasts, gentling stimulating her nipples with his teeth and tongue.

"Rich, I feel you deep inside of me."

Rich came up for air, leaning back. Through his peripheral, he noticed an elderly couple about 80 feet away. They were walking in his direction at a turtle's pace. "We got company coming," Rich whispered.

Vanessa glanced at the couple. She turned back and kissed Rich, before speeding up her pace.

"Yeah. Hurry up." Rich looked toward the couple. They had not noticed he and Vanessa. Yet it was exciting knowing that he could be caught having sex in public. It gave Rich a rush like their car chase sexcapade.

"Yes," Vanessa moaned.

Rich could feel the muscles of her pussy choking his dick. That was the thing that impressed him most about her sex game during their first encounter. She was an expert at working her insides. "Damn, you know how to work that pussy, girl."

Vanessa rode him faster, rocking front to back."

"Come on, girl. Hurry up. Ahh." Rich came, his energy leaving his body. The couple was about fifty feet away. Rich pulled down Vanessa's tank top. "Get up. They right there."

Vanessa stood quickly, fixing her skirt.

Rich zipped up his pants, the condom still on. "You a straight freak, girl." He grinned.

Vanessa laughed and sat beside him, wrapping her arms around him and kissing him.

When the couple got closer, they smiled at Rich and Vanessa admiringly. The sixty-something black man sporting an applejack hat said, "Excuse me, but you two make the perfect couple. I was just telling my wife that it's nice to see that young brothers still take sisters out to the park. Have a good night."

"You too," Rich said.

Vanessa smiled and waved. She turned to Rich as the couple walked off. "Told you that you"d be surprised how much fun you could have in a park."

CHAPTER FIVE
CANDY

Themansion... he sprawling twenty-room mansion in Florida sat on fifty acres of land. It was the perfect place to get married, so Leah and her fiancé Moses had rented it for their special day. Candy watched the couple salsa dance after Moses had placed the ring on her finger minutes earlier. They danced on a large white circular stage surrounded by chairs and tables that accommodated 100 people in the backyard of the mansion.

Candy sat at a long rectangular table with the women from the shop, along with Mimi, Rich, Chase and Free. But her mind was on Vanessa, who had been under Rich's spell for two months—way beyond Candy's expectation. She knew that waiting for him to dump her was no longer an option. Vanessa was slipping further out of her reach by the day. Therefore, Candy had developed a plan that she intended to enact before they left Florida.

Chanel stood up. She was draped in a silk Chanel dress and a pair of white patent leather Christian Louboutin stilettos that added four inches to her short sexy figure. She picked up her champagne flute. "I would like to make a toast to somebody very special." She gazed around the lengthy table. "Somebody that we all love. Somebody that's real. Somebody that deserves all the best that life has to offer." She held up her flute and the rest of the table followed suit. "I'd like to give a toast to the one and only, Chanel Dennison."

"Girl, sit your ass down," Meisha said.

Chanel sipped her Moet. "Thank you very much, everybody. Please disregard Meisha's outburst. She's one of the few fools who still don't understand the Chanel Legacy."

"Yeah, yeah," Meisha said.

"Excuse me, I have to use the ladies" room," said Chanel.

"Me too. Hold on, girl," Candy called out and joined Chanel. They trekked through the grassy lawn lined with exotic flowers and multi-colored roses. Walking through two large white pillars of the Colonial mansion, they stepped inside.

"This shit is exclusive," Chanel said.

Candy scanned the glass staircases, fireplace and windows that spanned almost from the floor to the thirty-foot ceiling.

"Now, if a man don't think your pussy is worth this, what good is he?" Chanel asked.

"Shit, you couldn't even get into Rich's penthouse," Candy spat, initiating her plan to make Vanessa hers.

"Rich is just intimidated by strong women."

They began walking through a corridor to the restroom.

"You taking shots at Vanessa, huh?"

Chanel smirked at Candy. "Now, you and I both know Vanessa can't walk in Chanel's designer shoes. But you," she pointed at Candy, "you want Vanessa to walk into your bedroom. Think I don't know."

Candy stopped, clutched Chanel's hand and stared into her hazel eyes. "So I want Vanessa and you want Rich. What are we gonna do about it?"

Chanel was silent for a few seconds. "You tell me."

"I gotta plan. You down?"

"What's good?"

Candy shared her plan for making her move on Vanessa. She was confident that she could turn Vanessa out, and she was going to videotape them having sex. She would then give the video to Chanel. Chanel would find a way to give the video to Rich. "Then you use it as leverage to get him to leave Vanessa."

Chanel's eyebrows arched. "Heifer, is you crazy? You think he gonna get rid of one of the hundreds of chicks he slingin" pipe to, because she got her pussy licked by one of the baddest hos in Harlem? That motherfucker will be happy to have that tape. Shit, I can see his ass smiling now in front of a eighty-inch flat screen."

"You missing the point," Candy said.

"Then help me not miss it."

"Everybody and they mother in Harlem know Rich for getting any chick he want."

"And?" Chanel frowned.

"You see how he be coming in *my* motherfuckin' shop, kissing and hugging all on Vanessa? He never did that shit with no other woman. You know what all that's about, right?"

"Yeah, he tryin' to piss me off and let everybody else know we couldn't convince that heifer not to slide up under his dick."

"Exactly. Now he comin" in the shop to get his braids done three times a week all of a sudden."

"So? What's your point?"

"You think he would be able to face everybody in the shop, let alone me, if we all knew he couldn't handle his woman? Think about it. Big Rich the Mandingo who couldn't stop a woman from taking his woman."

Chanel smiled and snapped her fingers. She pointed at Candy. "That's why I fucks with you. You a thinker, girl. We put Rich business on front street like this, that motherfucker will move outta Harlem before he faces us or anybody else in the 'hood. But you gotta turn Vanessa out and get her on tape."

"Don't worry about that. I got her. But you gotta do something too."

"What it is? Holler at your girl?"

"You gotta throw the pussy at him so he'll think he's getting back at us and Vanessa by fucking you."

"Yeah, that's how he'll save face, saying even though his chick got loose, he moved on and fucked another one of us anyway."

"Exactly. But we're gonna keep the video just between us. You only tell him that everybody knows, so you can fuck with his head and get him to mess with you."

"What if he mentions the video in the shop?" Chanel asked.

"That's not his style. As long as we're cool, he'll be cool. I've known him for years. Trust me."

"How 'bout Vanessa? What if he mentions it to her, or shows her the video?"

"You just let me handle that."

Chanel took a deep breath and shook her head. "You playin' with fire."

"I don't give a fuck if I go down in flames. Vanessa gonna eat this pussy. Mark my words.

VANESSA

A couple of months after Leah's wedding, Vanessa sat in Candy's chair. It was early in the morning before the shop opened. Vanessa had just had her hair dyed brown and Candy was now blow-drying it. While Vanessa had managed to fight off the strange feelings she had after seeing Candy and Vera have sex, she was still curious about the cause of Candy's first experience with a woman. She knew that Candy had a long history with some powerful hustlers and that they probably handled their business in the bedroom, just like Rich did.

After Vanessa asked a conversation about Candy's ex-boyfriends, Candy asked, "Wasn't I supposed to tell you that story about me *after* Dez died?"

"Oh, yeah. You switching from men to women." The words felt awkward rolling off Vanessa's tongue.

"Well, there was a girl that used to work here named Sophie. Everybody knew Sophie liked girls. Anyway, one day she came out of the shower in the locker room butt naked."

"Nobody uses that shower," Vanessa said.

"Exactly. Sophie was advertising. And I happened to be coming out of my office and I saw this beautiful body. She was lotioning herself. I was stuck there, just watching her."

"Oh yeah?" Vanessa caught a flashback of when she was stuck, watching Candy and Vera getting it on. She could identify with appreciating the beauty of a woman's body. She couldn't logically explain why, but she understood.

"I was getting aroused just by how she slowly massaged that lotion into her smooth skin," Candy said.

"Yeah." Vanessa closed her eyes, imagining. She didn't want to, but she couldn't control her wandering mind. She couldn't stop the burning sensation between her legs that came with the thought of another nude woman. She couldn't stop herself from envisioning Candy and Vera going at it.

"She was massaging that lotion in so gently, like only a woman could," Candy said. "Before I knew it, we were both naked and she was massaging me."

Vanessa felt Candy's soft hands rubbing her neck as the warm air from the blow drier graced it. She was in a zone that would not allow her to tell Candy to stop. Her body froze, her lips immobile.

"So soft." Candy turned off blow drier and began massaging Vanessa's neck and shoulders with both hands. "So soft, like only a woman could," she whispered into Vanessa's ear. "It felt so good that I couldn't fight it." Her lips gently touched Vanessa's neck, then her ear. Candy slipped her tongue inside.

"Ahh," Vanessa moaned, her panties becoming wet. She could feel the cotton soaking between her lips. Vanessa's nipples hardened. A warm feeling engulfed her skin, just from the touch of Candy's tongue. It was an unusual sensation that felt so good, as if Candy's tongue was designed solely for Vanessa's skin. Vanessa was in another world. She was someplace where no one or nothing existed. Just her and the exhilarating feeling that she wanted to last forever.

Candy worked her hands down to Vanessa's breast. She gently rubbed them, slightly pinching Vanessa's stiff nipples, causing Vanessa to fidget and moan.

Vanessa's eyes opened. Reality set in. She was a straight woman being fondled by a gay woman. She pulled away, jumping to her feet. Vanessa was breathing heavy. Gazing at Candy, she was not certain what to think about what had just happened.

"It's okay," Candy said. "You know you want this." She stepped toward Vanessa. "I saw you peeking through my door, watching me and Vera in my office that day. It's okay."

Oh, shit. I knew she saw me. Damn!

"When you saw me and Vera, you felt the same thing I felt when I saw Sophie." Vanessa thought she was going to melt from the delicate touch as Candy pulled her. "All you have to do is stop fighting what's inside of you. Let yourself go. Free yourself."

She softly kissed Vanessa's hand, and then sucked a few of

her fingers.

Vanessa's body was on fire. Candy led her to the back of the shop. With each step, Vanessa's anticipation grew stronger. She could feel her clit throbbing from just the thought of Candy and the feeling of her soft hand guiding her. When Vanessa stepped into Candy's office, the desk in front of her evoked visions of Candy and Vera. Vanessa was eager to feel the pleasure they shared the day she had watched them.

Candy closed the door. She began slowly undressing Vanessa, gently caressing each unclothed portion of skin. Vanessa was frozen, goose bumps flooding her skin, her heartbeat increasing. She was hungry for the experienced woman to guide her into the foreign world that had only been a dream to Vanessa. Each time Candy's hands touched her Vanessa could feel a sensation shoot from her skin to her clit. She was becoming overly anxious and nervous at the same time.

"Don't worry," Candy said, after Vanessa was naked. She stripped nude and stood in front of Vanessa.

Oh my God. Her body is perfect. Vanessa took in every inch of Candy's flawless frame. Her light skin and dark brown areolas were topped by small hard nipples. A flowery scent resonated from her silky skin. There was a mole on her flat stomach and baby hair that trailed from her waistline to the thin strip of hair above her pussy.

"This is what you wanted. Now it's yours," Candy said.

Vanessa closed her eyes as Candy leaned forward and their lips touched. The kiss was slower and more passionate than any kiss Vanessa had ever experienced. It reminded her of the kisses she had watched in romantic movies as a child. Candy's lips were softer than Vanessa anticipated. Their tongues danced to a tune only they could hear. It was perfection. Candy's tender body wrapped hers. The thin hairs of Candy's arms stimulated her back as Candy caressed her. Her breasts touching Vanessa's were a unique sensation for Vanessa. Candy was soft and gentle. She knew all the right places to touch and she had the perfect pace for Vanessa to savor the moment. Vanessa moaned as Candy's tongue began working her neck.

"Feels good, don't it?" Candy asked in a seductive whisper.

"Ump, humph," Vanessa moaned.

Candy worked her way down to Vanessa's breasts.

Vanessa's back arched forward. Yes," she mumbled as her hardened nipples were stimulated with Candy's tongue, lips and teeth. She could feel Candy working the other breasts with her hand, gently squeezing it and applying the perfect amount of pressure to her nipple.

Candy slowly pinned Vanessa against the wall, slurping away at her nipples.

"Take me," Vanessa panted.

Candy lowered to her navel, sticking her tongue inside of it.

Vanessa's body tensed up, her stomach thrusting forward from the wall than backward, until Candy gripped her firmly.

"Ahh, yes." Vanessa screamed.

Candy had discovered her erogenous zone. Vanessa cuffed Candy's head, pulling her closer as Candy licked her hotspot and palmed Vanessa's small butt cheeks. "Candy," Vanessa called out.

Candy parted Vanessa's legs slightly, kissing between her thighs. She had to hold Vanessa up as her knees buckled. She made her way to Vanessa's meaty wet lips.

Vanessa's back arched deeper. She palmed Candy's head tighter. Her heart rate was traveling at warp speed. She bit down on her bottom lip as her legs got weak. "I'm about to cum." Candy pulled away.

Vanessa opened her eyes, staring down at Candy kneeling. She grabbed Vanessa's waist and turned her around. The air conditioner sent a gust of cool air in between Vanessa's butt cheeks as Candy parted them. Her tongue trailed from Vanessa's pussy to her asshole. Vanessa screamed, crying tears of joy. She had never felt such an intense pleasure. She balled her fists as tight as she could as her body began to vibrate. Candy worked her lips and tongue until Vanessa exploded in ecstasy.

Vanessa turned around with tears streaming from her eyes past her smiling lips. "Thank you," she mumbled. She reached for Candy's breasts.

Candy took her hand and kissed it, before sucking her fingers.

"Another time."

Vanessa was silenced by the awkwardness of the moment. She had just experienced sex that satisfied her on another level. But the reality that a woman's tongue had roamed her body sent her a mixed message. She wanted Candy more than anything, but she didn't know what to make of that burning desire. Staring at Candy, she imagined the taste her flesh, her skin, her clit, the lips of her pussy, her asshole. There was no place on Candy's body that Vanessa did not yearn to explore. She wanted to please Candy, to return the unique blessing that Candy had bestowed upon her. But Vanessa was rendered immobile by her own inexperience and Candy telling her "another time."

"It's almost time to open the shop. Go in there and clean yourself up." Candy pointed to the bathroom door behind her desk.

Vanessa leaned against the wall, watching Candy's flawless figure. She wanted to cradle her breasts. She needed to feel them in her mouth. Vanessa wanted Candy to ride her face like she had done Vera's. Vanessa felt like a junkie experiencing withdrawals. She was liberated, but frustrated that what was started could not continue immediately. She regretted that she had waited so long to do what she now felt was so right. But she knew there would be many future opportunities to make up for lost time.

RICH

It was a Sunday afternoon and Rich was seated inside Manhattan's Kellari Taverna. The exclusive restaurant was filled with people who would leave the eatery if they knew Rich was a drug dealer. Even the woman sitting across from him would flee if she knew his real occupation. Her name was Linda and she was a media consultant from New Rochelle. Free had set Rich up with her. Linda was the product of a Japanese mother and Trinidadian father, so her exotic eyes and skin tone attracted Rich immediately. He was determined to slide between her slim thighs as soon as possible.

"I just love this restaurant," Linda said. She had been mouthing off about the eatery since she and Rich arrived twenty minutes earlier. She boasted about being there several times before for power brunches with executives from FOX News.

Rich was more concerned with the cleavage underneath her sleeveless dress. It was hard for him not to gaze at it. He knew Linda had spotted his wandering eyes more than once. From the smiles she responded with, he was certain that it was not a problem. He interpreted her blushing as a hint that he would get his chance to see a full view of her breasts before the night was over.

"You haven't touched your Solmos," she uttered the Greek word for avocado-dusted salmon with grilled asparagus, baby carrots and finger potatoes served with blood orange vinaigrette.

Rich had practically eaten the entire side dish of onion rings and flirted with the vegetables, but he wasn't moved by the sight of the fish. He had been cutting back on eating food with a face since Vanessa was an excellent chef, but meat was never on her menus. She had been stuffing Rich's stomach with meatless meals at her apartment, where he had been spending a good amount of time.

After Rich did not respond to the food comment, Linda said, "I love salmon. You should see the buffets they serve at NBC before the executive meetings. I've been to several of them. Linda's shallow conversation had also contributed to Rich losing his appetite. Everything out of her mouth was work-related, as if they were on a power brunch instead of a personal dinner. She wore her work on her sleeve, replacing her individuality with business jargon and the job title *media consultant*. She lacked the free thought and carefree nature that Rich had begun to value in Vanessa.

"You okay?" Linda asked. "The last time someone sat silent at one of these tables with me, I lost out on a major deal that could've boosted my career tenfold."

It's time to turn it up on her. "Excuse me, baby. My mind is just wrestling with the reality of sitting here with such a beautiful woman."

Linda smiled. "Thank you for the compliment."

"I'm curious. What is it that you do to unwind after those long work hours?"

"Well, I enjoy theatre. I spend a good deal of time shopping at Saks, of course." She grinned and patted her chest. "This Isaac Mizrahi piece happens to be one of my most recent purchases."

Rich squinted his eyes seductively. "Clothes can only do so much. It's your beauty and your body that bring out that dress."

"Flattery is one path that leads to my heart."

"Then maybe I should admit how your eyes mesmerize me."

"Maybe I like a man who's not afraid to admit the effect a woman has on him."

"Your skin tone is so perfect and smooth. The way your dimples glow each time your sexy lips pave the way for that picture perfect smile." Rich closed his eyes, slowly shaking his head, before opening them. "Every second I look at you, it becomes harder and harder for me to be a good boy and keep my hands to myself."

Linda was speechless. Her eyes were glued to his. She was clearly surprised, in a good way. Her mind seemed to be rationalizing her next statement. "I can see where this is going," she said.

"You ready for the ride?"

"I like to ride."

"Life in the fast lane?" Rich licked his lips.

"Or sometimes nice and slow."

Rich laughed to himself at the tic-for-tat flirtation of wordplay he and Linda were engaged in. Free had told Rich that Linda had a very sexually driven persona that she hid behind her air of professionalism. Free had been introduced to her by an old friend who said she was practically a nymphomaniac. Rich continued the conversation for a few more minutes, before their sexual tension led to them expressing direct desires. They left the restaurant and headed to Linda's room at the Plaza Hotel.

Linda tossed her Chanel bag on one of the end tables. "I'm telling you now," she said, stepping out of her dress, "I wanna be fucked right."

I like this freak here. Rich was naked, slipping on a condom. He thought of the many women he met that transformed from angels in public to animals behind closed doors and lust guided their actions.

"No nice and slow tonight," Linda said. "We're not in love."

Rich tore her panties off and pushed her onto the bed.

"Yeah," she looked up at him with a smile. "That's how I like it."

He turned her over and slipped a pillow underneath her, propping her butt up. Staring at her tan complexion, he leaned down and climbed inside of her. *What the fuck?* He felt as if his ten inches of thickness was fighting to find friction in an endless tunnel. The walls of her insides had been demolished like a building at a construction site.

"Go deeper," Linda panted as Rich stroked.

He plunged and pounded, shifted and stroked, ramming into her in search of stimulation, only to find five minutes of frustration. Refusing to waste his time and energy, he removed himself from her. He grabbed a small bottle of lotion from the end table and lubricated her ass and his condom.

"You better fuck my ass right," she said. "Or don't even go there."

Rich parted one cheek and guided himself inside.

Linda grunted like a cow being prodded on a farm. Then she screamed, "Fuck my ass!"

Rich worked in and out. Her tightness pleasured him, but he could tell that her ass had been worked out regularly. He had been through enough anal adventures with women to know when a female kept her backdoor shut, open on holidays or twenty-four hours a day. Linda was definitely the twenty-four seven-type. Business was never closed for her.

"Harder," she demanded.

Rich pulled the pillow from underneath her. He commanded her to get on her knees. Once she did, he put her hands against the wall, and rammed into her ass, grabbing a handful of her hair. She screamed and thrust her ass back into Rich's strokes. He began slapping her ass.

"Yeah. Like that. Take this ass."

Her voice turned Rich on. He slammed into her harder and faster, grabbing her waist with both hands. The soft flesh of her butt clapped against his thighs. His palms grew sweaty as his body heated up until he came, overflowing the condom. He slapped her ass one last time, then rolled over on the king-sized bed.

Linda turned around, glaring at him like a cop who had just run a crook down and arrested him. "Don't tell me you're finished."

Rich chuckled, removing the condom and tossing it in the nearby trashcan. He grabbed her panties and wiped his dick dry. He slid off the bed and began getting dressed.

"Fuck this. Where's my bag?" Linda looked around like a detective searching for clues at a crime scene. She pulled an extra large vibrator from her handbag and began jamming it inside of herself."

This freak is something else. Rich specialized in women with high sex drives and the desire for experimenting, but Linda"s sexual craving left him disgusted. He was still irritated about the warped pothole between her legs that he had sunk into. It was a symbol of what he perceived to be the force of countless men who had pillaged her sanctity. He assumed all women he dealt with were sexually active with other men. But he rarely felt physical reminders of those men on the women's bodies.

Rich walked out without a word and thought of Vanessa. She was becoming the model for his expectations in women. Linda clearly existed in another world as far apart from Vanessa as the sun and earth. Linda made Rich think of everything he hated about women and liked about Vanessa. It had been years since he was in a relationship with a female he appreciated as a person and not just a tool for sexual pleasure. But one of Rich's past experiences was preventing him from giving Vanessa the commitment he felt she deserved. Yet, his feelings for her were causing him to ponder if she was capable of helping him overcome his past.

CHAPTER SIX
CANDY

I gave up hope on men," Candy said as she lay in Vanessa's bed with her. She was explaining the depth of her transition from men to woman and why she would never involve herself with a man again. "There's nothing like a woman."

"I admit that you make me feel sex on another level, but I just love men. When Rich is fucking me and handling me, shit." Vanessa closed her eyes and let out a deep breath. "They call it manhandling for a reason."

Candy gently ran her hand between Vanessa's legs. She could feel her vibrate as her hand traveled to Vanessa's breasts, then into her mouth.

Vanessa sucked on Candy's fingers.

Candy asked, "Does Rich make you feel like that?"

Vanessa twisted her head. "No." She guided Candy's hand back between her legs. Candy slowly swiped two wet fingers back and forth around Vanessa's clit, bringing her body to a rumble. Vanessa's lips quivered and her eyes blinked uncontrollably. Even her hands were trembling. Candy kissed her passionately, while Vanessa began humping her hand. Candy trailed her tongue into Vanessa's ear and moaned. "Rich make you feel like this?"

"Please," Vanessa begged. "Please."

Candy leaned back and smiled when she felt Vanessa's juices flow onto her fingers and down her leg. She eased her wet fingers back into Vanessa's mouth, watching tears trail from her eyes as Vanessa suckled her fingers. "Rich make you cry with just a touch?"

"No," Vanessa whispered.

Candy wiped Vanessa's tears and kissed her. It was one of the many episodes that occurred between them within the past month since Candy had begun sexing Vanessa into submission. Candy had worked every move on her that she knew and used every sex toy she had, several that Vanessa did not know existed. After each encounter, Vanessa confessed that Candy brought feelings out of her that she did not know she had. But Vanessa had seven years of sex with men that peaked with a versatile stud who had the biggest dick she had seen and was more experienced than any man who had ever sexed her. So while Candy knew she had a hold on Vanessa, she understood that Rich did also.

Candy knew she could not compare to Rich and Rich could not compare to her. They were experts in the same field who used equally powerful tools in different ways. Candy wanted Vanessa for herself, but she did not mind settling for the position that Vanessa played in her life. The video of their first swing at sex was just another recording to add to the collection of porn she owned. She had no intentions of revealing it to Chanel as they had planned. Just as she had no intention of revealing her relationship with Vanessa to anyone.

"That was good," Vanessa said, getting up.

"It's always good, ain't it?"

"Yeah. Now I'm ready for some dick." Vanessa giggled.

"Good for you."

"You don't know what you're missing, girl."

"I'm eight years older than you, Vanessa. When you was humping boys in the school staircase, I was in bed with grown men."

"But you admitted that a man never made you cum with his dick."

Candy reflected on that reality. She had often flaunted it as a justification for why she began experimenting with women. She had only experienced orgasms from men through oral sex. There were times when she had wondered if her body was somehow sexually dysfunctional. She eventually realized that she was simply involved with minute men, inexperienced guys and selfish sex partners. So with that curse, and the pain of losing the only man she had ever loved, Candy took a shot at the world of women.

"I've got the best of both worlds," Vanessa said. "What more could you ask for?"

Candy noticed the clock on her wall. She had an appointment in two hours with a representative from SCORE. They were scheduled to discuss her business idea. "I gotta go take care of this business," Candy said.

"The meeting Leah set up for you?"

"Yeah."

"She might as well be your business partner," Vanessa said.

"She has been helping me a lot."

"She gave you the business idea and pretty much rewrote your business plan from just a few ideas you had."

"That's why I like her. She's professional and that's why I let her run the shop when I'm not around. She's about her business and pretty quiet."

"Sneaky," Vanessa said.

Candy assumed Vanessa was critical of Leah because Leah was known to get on Candy about her love for younger women. Candy wondered about Leah's comments sometimes. But Leah had been consistent in helping her. Plus Leah was the most respectful woman in the shop. It was Chanel's jealousy of Vanessa that Candy hoped would not cause a problem in the future.

* * *

After showering and getting dressed, Candy stepped outside, jumped into her BMW and started the engine. As she was about to pull off, she thought of Vanessa and all the praise that she gave Rich. Although Candy didn't feel there was a competition between her and Rich, she felt that Rich did not deserve to be worshiped. Not just by Vanessa, but by any of the countless women that put him on a pedestal. No man deserved such treatment in Candy's eyes.

Candy drove downtown and walked into the building that housed the Small Business Administration. She took in the ogling eyes of men who stared at her as she stepped through the building. The Yves Saint Laurent business suit she wore highlighted her sexuality with an aura of professionalism. One man flirted with her, walking beside her, saying all the right things that would have impressed her years ago. Candy brushed him off with a lie about her being in a relationship.

"That's not a problem for me," he countered.

Candy flashed a smile as the elevator door opened. She stepped inside, leaving the man behind. *He was fine.* Candy had never ridded herself of the ability to recognize handsome men. Occasionally, she even felt her heart flutter or that tingling sensation between her legs when she saw a man's bare chest or a bulge in his pants. But her days of acting off her impulses were over. She had developed a level of discipline that countered the control men had once wielded over her.

Once Candy stepped off the elevator, she spoke to a receptionist, who directed her to the office of the SOCRE representative she came to see. Candy walked into his office and introduced herself.

"I'm David Rosenberg," the aging Jewish man responded with an inviting smile. He adjusted his glasses and sat in his leather executive chair.

"It's good to finally meet you," Candy said.

"Likewise. Have a seat," he instructed her.

Candy sat in the chair in front of his redwood desk. She began expounding on her proposed company. "Nature's Beauty is the next wave of organic hair care products." She handed him a copy of the research she had conducted and a synopsis of her company. She said she planned to introduce "Candice Cream" as her first product. She projected that she would produce several shampoos a year afterwards, depending on the sales of Candice Cream. She expected to begin turning a profit within her second fiscal year in business.

Rosenberg read the pages that Candy handed to him. He nodded a few times, approvingly. He grabbed a highlighter and marked several places on the paperwork, before lifting his head and facing Candy. "Well, Ms. Johnson, you seem to have a pretty firm grasp on your consumer demographic and your target market. But I believe that we can do some additional research with an emphasis on international sales." He explained that Candy should take advantage of the global reach of the Internet.

"A friend of mine suggested the same thing," Candy said, referring to Leah. "But I've had a difficult time locating information on the global market."

Rosenberg smiled. "Don't worry yourself. We'll take care of it. When we're done, you'll have a comprehensive business plan to help guide you through your first three years and to help you secure additional funding, if necessary."

Candy listened to Rosenberg for half an hour. He explained in depth what SCORE would help her with and he gave her a broader insight into her business idea.

"It was a pleasure meeting you, Ms. Johnson." He shook Candy's hand. "I look forward to helping Nature's Beauty become a profitable company."

Candy thanked him and left his office with a smile on her face. She was pleased about the thought of owning a second business. Besides her pockets becoming fatter, ownership had its psychological benefits. It was an ego booster for her. During her younger years, she had depended on the profits of the drug trade in Harlem to trickle down to her through the hands of hustlers she dated. But after Dez was killed and Candy gave up on men, she became obsessed with having control of her life and her finances. Opening the shop was the result of that obsession. Being a boss and having financial freedom became her drug of choice.

RICH

Rich smiled as Candy entered the elevator. "Well, well, well. How sweet you look in that business suit," he said, standing with his briefcase. He inhaled her Donna Karan perfume and followed her into the elevator. "It's a rare occasion I get to see you in a suit."

"Speaking of rare occasions, I wouldn't expect to see a drug dealer in the Small Business Administration." She turned her back to him and pressed the button for the first floor.

"Still underestimating me," Rich said, his eyes shifting down to her butt.

"Still? What's that supposed to mean?"

"Means I defied the odds."

"Odds?"

"Yeah, Rich versus Candy, Chanel, Meisha and Leah. The deck was stacked and y'all tried to deal me five funnies."

"You should've been a prophet, because you love speaking in parables."

"Let me be clear. Y'all was shittin'' on my name so much in that shop that I can smell it every time I walk in."

"You know the world doesn't revolve around you, Rich." She turned and faced him. "There's enough things to gossip about in the shop other than you." She turned back around.

"Hard to tell from all the stuff you told Vanessa about me being a dog." He laughed. "Well, the dog got his bone."

"I could care less where you put your dick."

"I don't believe you." Rich stepped forward, pressing his dick against her butt. He immediately became erect. He planted his lips on her neck, causing her back to arch forward as she gasped.

"Get the hell off of me!" She moved away and turned around. Her eyes zeroed in on the huge bulge in Rich's pants. Then she looked into his eyes. "You playing yourself!"

"It took five seconds of this dick on your ass and my tongue on your neck for you to figure that out? A delayed response say a lot." Rich grinned.

"Vanessa gon' find out a whole lot quicker."

"Vanessa so hypnotized by this dick that she wake up with it in her mouth and go to sleep with it in her hand. She ain't gonna let this thing go if you beat her with a bat."

Candy's eyes shifted back to Rich's erection.

"My grandmother used to tell me the eyes don't lie," Rich said with a smirk.

Candy looked up as the elevator door opened. She stepped

out and turned back to Rich. "Fuck you."

"That's exactly what you wanna do and you know it." He stepped out the elevator, following behind Candy. He wondered if she was switching her hips for his visual enjoyment, because she had some extra swagger in her step. Staring at her butt, he thought of how soft it felt against him. The scent of her lingered in his nostrils. He could still taste her skin on the tip of his tongue. He had been thinking about sexing Candy for a while. But his mind had begun wandering more after his sexual catastrophe with Linda. His mental vision of Linda's worn out womb and the gang of men that he assumed caused it made him see Candy in a different light. She was the exact opposite—a woman who had not been with a man in years. Rich wanted to feel the tightness he knew he could only find between Candy's legs. He knew there was the potential she had been using dildos. But there was no tool that could compare to the natural stroking and weight of a man's body. With all these thoughts of Candy, Rich still had no plan for approaching her. It was simply the solitude of the small elevator, her sex appeal, erotic aroma and slick mouth that nurtured the sexual tension that pushed Rich to act.

Rich made his way to his Porsche Carrera after Candy pulled off in her car. He needed to relieve himself after being riled up by his move on her. He pulled out his Sidekick and texted Vanessa. She sent him a message that she was at Mimi's house and would see him later that night. She mentioned having some good news. Rich then texted Jasmine one of the top hotties he kept in rotation. She texted him back, telling him that she was in her pool waiting for him.

Rich put the Porsche in drive. He stopped by his penthouse and dropped off his briefcase. In it was some information he had gotten from a friend in the Small Business Administration before he ran into Candy. There were a few hundred pages about a technology company he was considering investing in.

Rich left his home and jumped back in the Porsche. He drove Uptown, through the Bronx and into Westchester County. He soon found himself parked in front of a white villa on a quiet tree-lined street in New Rochelle. He got out of the Porsche and walked up the cobblestone path through the lawn. He stepped on the porch, flipped through his keys and opened the front door. Walking through the large living room, Rich began unloosening his tie. He went to a bedroom, and peeped out the window.

"She a bad motherfucker," he spoke under his breath.

Jasmine was sporting a pair of Gucci shades, lying on a beach chair. She was reading a *King* magazine with a picture of her gracing the cover. The young video vixen had the face of Meagan Good and the body of Beyoncé. But she stayed in more drama than Wendy Williams. Rich had met her at a strip club that she used to work at, before shaking her body in hip hop videos became more profitable than spinning on poles in the nude.

Rich began undressing, carefully laying his clothes on Jasmine's bed. He grabbed a pair of his Calvin Klein trunks from the closet, slipped them on and headed outside. His bare feet trailed the wet tiles on the sun baked patio. He leaned down and planted a kiss on Jasmine's lips, then laid on the lounge chair beside her. "How many times you gonna look at that magazine?" he asked.

"How ever many times it take for me to understand why these rappers' wives is beefing on my blog every fuckin' day about my interview."

"It could be them tig old bitties," Rich said, palming one of her large silicone-filled breasts." He laughed.

"Stop," she swatted his hand. "Broads just hatin'. That's what the fuck it is!"

"That's the logical outcome of admitting in the pages of a national magazine that you had a married rapper's face between your legs."

"A million motherfuckers is calling theyself MC-this and MC-that. I fuck one motherfuckin' rapper and I'm a ho. Broads all scared of me and shit."

"Them pictures of you posing damn near naked in front of this house he paid for on that Mercedes old boy gave you can easily make freaks nervous."

"Fuck 'em all." Jasmine dropped the magazine and her shades on a small table and stood up. She walked to the edge of the pool, her butt cheeks jiggling with each step. She slowly eased out of her bathing suit, then turned to Rich. "Come and get me." She dove into the water.

"This freak got me chasing the pussy, literally," he mumbled. "Watch when I catch her ass."

He quickly peeled out of his trunks as he stood up. His dick rose while he was staring at Jasmine's breasts. She was leaning in the corner furthest from him in the pool. Even with 15 yards separating them, he could see the sun glistening off her wet body.

Rich dove into the pool and swam toward her. As he closed in on her, she took off.

He swam after her.

She circled past him with a smile.

Rich pursued her, but she went under water and slipped past him again, popping up in another corner. *This fucking freak got me going in circles.*

"Guess I'll just let you get it," she said, climbing up on the edge of the pool. She spread her legs wide, her feet dangling beneath the cold water.

Rich focused on her thick thighs. He saw the thin layer of hair covering her pussy glowing with droplets of water as he got closer to her. She laid back. Rich stood on the steps that lined the entire wall at the bottom of the pool. He grabbed her thighs and planted his face between them.

Jasmine let out a moan and her body jerked.

Rich slithered his tongue around her clit, then inside of her. Her legs wrapped around his neck as his tongue overpowered her. Her body began to quake. Next came the flow of her juices into his mouth, then her legs fell from his neck back into the water. Rich looked up, gazing at her flawless frame. He was laughing inside. He always found it comical how easy it was for him to subdue Jasmine's 32-22-38 physique with a few swipes of his tongue. He had never met a woman he could make cum so quickly.

"You the motherfuckin' man, Rich," she whispered as she leaned up on her elbows. She inched forward and wrapped her arms around Rich's neck, while slipping into the pool.

Rich eased inside of her. He grabbed both butt cheeks as her legs wrapped around his waist. Then he suddenly pinned her to the wall and began pumping. Water splashed violently with each of his strokes. He winced when her long fingernails dug into his back.

"You the motherfuckin' man," she yelled.

Rich rammed harder. He was about to cum. Her legs clenched him tighter as he released a load. She squeezed her legs tighter around him as his body went limp.

"Damn," she moaned. "Your shit strong. I can feel your nut up in me."

Oh shit, Rich thought. As they parted, he grabbed his dick. *What the fuck!* Until then, he had not had sex without a condom in over a year. The last time he did he had to coax an old flame into having an abortion. Children meant commitment, potential baby mamma drama and child support cases—all things Rich hated more than cops and snitches.

"You hungry?" Jasmine asked. "I'm about to make me something to eat. You sucked all the damn energy out me, so I need to re-up."

"I gotta go."

"Motherfucker, you just got here!"

Rich's mind was so focused on a possible pregnancy that Jasmine's tone of voice didn't upset him. He climbed out of the pool and walked off.

"So you just bust a nut and break out? I ain't one of them hoodrats from Harlem, Rich!"

"I gotta take care of something," Rich responded. He had been seeing Jasmine for almost a year. Her home was his second residence and her cooking was something he craved each time he was there. He spent the night in her villa at least twice a week. He had his own key, a closet full of clothes, plus a towel, rag and toothbrush in her bathroom. He had practically moved in. But it was the first time he was leaving after staying less than a few hours.

Rich sped up his pace, entering the villa. He made his way to the bedroom, where he had undressed and put on some fresh clothes. He had just finished lacing his brown Salvatore Ferragamo shoes, when Jasmine burst through the door like a stickup kid in a drug spot.

"This is some real bullshit." She pointed at him. She flailed her arms aimlessly as she barked about Rich treating her like a ho. Her eyes were bulging and her head was bouncing like a bobble head doll. She was naked, still dripping water from the pool.

Rich jumped up. "Look, baby. I ain't walking out your life, I'm just walking out the door. Good thing about a door is you can go in and out of it, so I'll be back."

"Nah, fuck that!" She jumped in front of the door and folded her arms. She twisted her head back and forth. "You ain't walkin' out this motherfuckin' door."

Rich stepped toward her. He put his hand on her shoulder. "Why you playing, girl? Games is for kids and athletes. And neither one of us play with toys or balls, so let's stop the bullshit."

Jasmine gritted her teeth and slapped Rich's arms, knocking his hand off her. Before his hand fell to his side, his other hand had instinctively slapped her. Jasmine flew into a nearby dresser. She scrambled to her feet, knocking her jewelry box and bottles of perfume off the dresser to the carpeted floor.

Oh shit. What the fuck did I just do? Rich's heart sunk into his chest. He wanted to apologize, but that would do little to change what he had unintentionally done.

Tears trickled down Jasmine's face. She stood up, silently. Her mouth was open, her upper lip bleeding. Like a frightened animal, she slowly backed into a corner away from Rich. She was curled into the fetal position.

Rich walked out of her room and her house. As he drove home, he regretted that he lost control. He was a womanizer, but not a woman beater. He had trained himself to control women with a slick tongue and stiff dick. His violent outburst was a sign that he had lost all control. Just like him chasing after Jasmine and sexing her without a condom. Just like him making a move on Candy. Rich was realizing that his lust for multiple women was creating problems for him. His life was slowly becoming unmanageable. He knew that he would have to get to the root of the problem to prevent any future drama.

VANESSA

Later that evening, Vanessa answered her doorbell. She greeted Rich with a kiss and let him into her living room. Sandalwood incense burned and Anthony Hamilton's vocals provided a backdrop inside Vanessa's cozy home. She sat beside Rich on the plush couch. "Remember when I texted you back earlier and told you I had some good news?" She smiled as Rich nodded. "Well, I got a book deal."

Rich kissed Vanessa and hugged her. "Damn, you doing your thing."

Vanessa had already explained that an agent had taken an interest in her book proposal—a few chapters, synopsis and outline. He had shopped it to a publishing company. She had learned today, that the company was interested. The contract offered to Vanessa required her to complete the manuscript within a year. It was ample time, considering that she was halfway done, but needed time to complete her college assignments and work at the shop.

"I'm proud of you," Rich said.

Vanessa sensed some discomfort as she looked into Rich's eyes. She began rubbing his neck. "What's wrong, baby? Something's bothering you. I can see it in your eyes."

"I'm good. Cooler than a fan."

"Damn it, Rich." She shook her head. "Please, don't lie to me."

Rich sighed. "I'm good."

"You're talking to me, Rich. I know you. When I walk into the shop, I can smell your cologne before I see you. I can tell your walk from almost a block away. I know everything that you hate about politics and love about investing. I know you sleep with your mouth slightly open, because some nights I've sat up and just watched you rest so peacefully. I know when you're about to cum just by looking into your eyes while we're making love."

"Love?" Rich's eyebrows rose as his eyes widened.

Vanessa stood and began pacing. The word love was not supposed to come out of her mouth. She leaned against the wall next to the window. Her heart rate was accelerating, while Rich stood and walked toward her. She took his hands into hers, staring into his eyes. "What are we doing?"

"Damn near all day, I've been asking myself, *What am I doing?"*

"We've got this open relationship going. I don't question you. Sex with you is unbelievable. But it's become more for me," Vanessa said. "Lately, you've been having sex with me, while I'm making love to you."

"That's deep."

"It's the truth. Sure, there is the physical aspect of what we share, but it's about the spiritual reality that spawns from the physical act. When you're inside of me, I feel like our bodies are one. Literally. I've never felt that way before. And when we're not having sex, but we're together, like now, I can feel your aura. It's kind of creepy, but in a good way, if that makes sense."

"I think I understand."

"Rich, I've never felt this way about another man. I don't wanna feel this way about another man, because I don't want another man. And you don't need another woman."

"You laying it on a brother kind of thick, baby."

"I need to know where you stand."

Rich was silent. He did a poor job of masking the fact that something was troubling him. "There you go again. Is it me?"

"What?"

"Something was on your mind earlier. And something is on your mind now."

"It's not you, baby."

"Then what is it? You said you've been questioning yourself all day. Talk to me."

"I went through a situation today."

Vanessa could see an emotional side of Rich emerging that was new to her. A lump rolled down his throat. Nervousness was in his eyes. Those were signs that fell outside of the calm, controlling demeanor she had always saw Rich display. She reached up, delicately placing her palms on his cheeks. "What kind of situation did you have?"

"A female situation," he said.

Vanessa's hands slipped down to his waist. "It's okay. You can tell me."

"The details are not important. What matters is I realized I got issues."

"What do you mean, baby?"

"Long story."

"We got time." Vanessa was anxious. Her mind was everywhere, speculating the issues that Rich had to reveal. She had made up her mind that she would not allow anything to push her away from him. He had become a person she needed in her life.

Rich took a deep breath and frowned.

"It's okay." Vanessa rubbed his leg.

Rich took another deep breath and exhaled slowly. His eyebrows arched and he gritted his teeth. "Listen, baby," he spoke slowly. "I don't want them freaks down in shop all in my business."

"I would never share anything personal about you to them."

"Mimi either. Nobody. If you gonna be my woman, I need absolute trust in you that you can hold water."

Vanessa nodded. "You can trust me, Rich. I love you."

Rich froze. It was as if he was assessing the depth of Vanessa affirming her earlier proclamation of love.

Vanessa hugged him and whispered in his ear, "I'm gonna love you no matter what."

As they parted, Rich gently ran his hands over his face and focused. "I can't believe I'm about to tell you this. We only been knowing each other for like five months."

"I don"t want you to feel pressure. It can wait, baby,"

Vanessa said. "I'm not going anywhere."

"Nah, these bones been buried in my closet for too long. If I don't get this off my chest, my ribs might cave in. I'm telling you because you're the only female I ever saw as a real woman."

"You're the realist man I've ever known."

"Remember in Club Dream when you asked me about changing the world and I said 'it starts with self, but I need you to help me grow?'"

"I remember it like yesterday."

"I done had this monkey on my back for years and I knew I needed a woman to help me get him off. When I saw you for the first time, I knew you might be that woman. You was in the shop with a bunch of high-maintenance freaks in designer clothes and more weaves than Wendy Williams. But you was standing firm— no Prada bag, your afro everywhere and not a spot of makeup on your face. And I could see the confidence in your stance. I knew right there, if you could be yourself in the middle of that shop, you could help me deal with the issues I need to help me be me."

"I'm here for you, baby." Vanessa kissed Rich on the cheek and hugged him. She was overwhelmed. No man had ever truly understood or accepted her individuality.

"Remember I told you about me being raised by older hustlers?"

"Yeah."

"Well, I ended up meeting those hustlers in Harlem at nine years old, because I ran away from my mother in the Bronx." Tears began to well in Rich's eyes. "She used to—"

"It's okay," Vanessa said when Rich paused for a few seconds. "Whatever happened, it's okay for you to say it. I love you and nothing in your past can change that."

Rich looked down for a second, then took a deep breath. He gritted his teeth and hissed. There was a rage on his face that gave Vanessa nervous chills. She knew Rich had no reason to be mad at her, but he was furious about something or someone. Something or someone had scarred him so deep, he had hidden his wound from the world. He stared into Vanessa's eyes for a few seconds, then said, "My mother used to rent me out to men."

"I'm sorry" Vanessa hugged Rich, cuffing the back of his head in her palm. "It's okay, baby. That was a long time ago. You're okay, now." She could feel the tenseness inside of him as she rubbed his head and back. She had no idea that Rich would tell her anything remotely close to the trauma he had been experienced. She was thankful that he had entrusted her with such a personal secret, a secret he had not disclosed to anyone else. But Vanessa was torn apart. She could not help but envision a helpless young Rich being taken advantage of by sexual predators old enough to be his father.

After a few minutes of the couple embracing, Vanessa listened to Rich explain that he had hated women. He didn't trust women because of what his mother had done to him. He saw his mother's face in each female he met. Vanessa began to understand why Rich was a womanizer, because he enlightened her and expressed how he had consciously detached himself from women as a defense mechanism.

Rich took one of Vanessa's hands into his. He pressed it against his heart. "You feel that?"

"Yes."

"The strongest man can be reduced to a weakling if he lets the wrong person inside of here."

"I promise you, I'm the right woman."

Rich was silent for a few seconds. "And I wanna be your Mr. Right. I really do. But I can't promise you that it ain't gonna be no bumps in the road and we gonna ride off into the sunset to live happily ever after. My life ain't never been no fairytale. You gotta understand, I'm thirty-five years old and I have never been faithful to a woman."

"I understand." Vanessa believed that she could be the woman to help Rich transcend his past and emerge as a new man. She knew she could satisfy him on every level. But she felt guilty because she was having an undercover affair with Candy while she stressed to Rich that she wanted him to commit solely to her. As Vanessa hugged Rich, her heart pressed against his, she was certain that there was no way she was going to end the passion she and Candy shared.

CHAPTER SEVEN
CANDY

Candy was naked. She had just stepped out of her shower. She wrapped her hair in a towel and gazed into the mirror. Suddenly she had a vision of Rich. It had been a few weeks since she and Rich had their elevator scene. Neither of them mentioned it to Vanessa. In fact, when in each other's presence, Candy and Rich acted as if nothing had happened between them. Candy found if awkward that Rich had not so much as winked at her since their encounter. Even more strange was that each time she saw him, an unusual feeling overcame her. It was a mix of anger and intrigue. She was angry with him for having the audacity to press her, but she was also intrigued by him. Their brief encounter in the elevator was the closest she had come to a man in years. She hated to admit it, but it felt good. But Candy wasn't ready to trade a sure thing for a possibility. She had been satisfied with every woman she had experienced. The possibility of Rich completely satisfying her would make him the single success among the many men she encountered.

As Candy stepped into her bedroom, Vera was sitting on the bed. She turned to Candy with fire in her eyes and a remote control in her hands. "What the hell is this?" Vera asked, pointing at the flat screen TV. In high definition was the video displaying Candy's face between Vanessa's legs.

"Turn it off, now." Candy walked toward Vera.

"After you answer me." Vera popped up from the bed, fidgeting and tapping the remote against her thigh. She was still in her thong and bra that she had slept in. "I want some answers."

"I don't owe you no damn answers." Candy's jaw was tight with anger. She reached for the remote and Vera threw it across the room.

"Who else pussy you sucking on down in that shop?"

"You better go pick up that motherfuckin' remote control!"

Vera sucked her teeth and turned to walk away. Candy grabbed her, pulling her back.

Vera tried, with both hands, to pull Candy's forearm from around her neck. She had no wins against Candy's 171-pound, five foot ten body.

"I can't breathe," Vera managed to squeeze out.

"Should've thought about that when you was disrespecting me in my own motherfuckin' house." Candy yanked down Vera's thong and brutally jammed three fingers inside her pussy.

"Ugh. You're hurting me!" Vera cried.

Candy bit down on her neck like a rabid dog.

Vera screamed for help and tried to wiggle away to no avail.

"You better fuckin' recognize then next time!"

"Please, Candy," Vera begged while tugging harder at Candy's forearm.

Candy loosened her grip just enough for Vera to breathe adequately. She bit Vera again, then began sucking her neck. Candy's forceful fingers started caressing Vera's clit. Soon, Vera stopped pulling at Candy's forearm. Her fight was over. Pain turned to pleasure. Vera began moaning.

Candy turned her around and immediately saw the fear in her eyes and the trail of tears. Unmoved, she grabbed Vera's neck and forced her to the floor, on her knees. Candy strained her eyes at Vera, as if she were her worse enemy. Vera cuffed Candy's butt, still crying. She slowly leaned in between Candy's legs and began working her tongue. Candy closed her eyes and palmed the back of Vera's head.

After a few minutes, Candy grabbed a fistful of Vera's dreads and pulled her to the floor. She stood over her, staring into her eyes as she descended. Candy grabbed the edge of her bed, squatted over Vera and rode her face. Vera's head thrashed against the floor until Candy climaxed.

Candy rose to her feet. Her eyes never left Vera. She extended her hand. Vera nervously took it and Candy helped her up. They stood face-to-face in silence. Candy began wiping the tears from Vera's eyes.

"I'm sorry," Vera whispered. She leaned forward and passionately kissed Candy. When their lips parted, Candy playfully slapped Vera's butt and smiled. "Now put that video away and go get dressed. I gotta open the shop."

Vera grinned and walked away.

It was the first time Candy had ever gotten violent with Vera. It frustrated her having to hurt Vera, but she knew that it was necessary. Yet, she hoped that Vera did not push her to the point of violence again.

Candy stepped back into the bathroom and washed up. She got dressed and walked out of the door with Vera at her side.

"I'm gonna call you later," Vera said meekly.

Candy smiled at her, hopped into her BMW and drove off. She whipped through traffic for ten minutes, then pulled up in front of the shop. "Hey, Chanel," she said once she got out of the car.

Chanel was leaning against her Escalade. She glanced at her iced out Jacob's watch. "'Bout time," she hissed. "You all late. We only got ten minutes 'til it's time to open, so you gon' have to stay after we close to do my hair."

"Yeah, yeah. I got you." In the midst of the drama with Vera, Candy had forgotten about her appointment to do Chanel's hair before opening the shop.

"I hope so, because my man is coming back from outta town tonight and my shit gotta be tight."

Candy and Chanel walked inside of the shop and started preparing for work. Candy's mind was still on Vera. She had never seen Vera act out like she did. They both had agreed that they were in an open relationship, free to see whom they pleased. And Vera had never gotten angry with Candy dealing with other women.

"I see your master plan with that heifer ain't work, huh?" Chanel asked.

"I'm done with her," Candy lied about Vanessa.

"So just fuck me, huh? You can't catch the cat, so Chanel don't get Rich."

"I just had a plan and the shit ain't work. But since when you need me, pussy-eatin' Candy, to get a man?"

"The Chanel Legacy is an independent entity. I was just trying to do a little networking." Chanel grinned. "But give me a minute. I'll show you how it's done. I got my own plan to get Rich."

The shop was packed later that day. Vanessa was sitting in her chair waiting for Mimi to arrive for her appointment. She was discussing her book to Leah.

"So you're telling me the main character is a twenty-year-old girl that's creeping with her pastor?" Leah asked.

"Yeah," Vanessa said as she picked her 'fro.

"You know preachers got dicks too," said Chanel. "And

they money longer than train smoke. Shit, I let T.D. Jakes hit this and his ass will go crazy. Have him convert his big ass church into a mansion for me. His ass will be so happy, he'll be on the Internet givin' sermons about this pussy."

"You wild, Chanel," Leah said.

"How 'bout you, Meisha? What preacher you'll give the pussy to?" Chanel asked. "Reverend Run," Meisha said.

"I think Farrakhan is sexy," Vanessa said.

"Girl, you playing a dangerous game," said Chanel, shaking her head. "That man is watched by the FBI and protected by the NOI. Ain't no dick worth doing time over or getting stomped out by a hundred motherfuckers in bow ties."

Mimi entered the shop and took her seat. She exchanged greetings with the women and began listening to the conversation.

"So what it's gon' be, Mimi? Who you gon' let hit it?" Chanel asked.

"The Pope," Mimi responded.

Chanel nodded. "That's why I fucks with you. The Pope is a baller for real. He ain't claiming no blocks. He locked down a whole city and ride around in a bulletproof car. Shit, Frank Lucas, Supreme Team, World, none of them street legends had nothing on the Pope."

"And I'm bringing his ass in the 'hood, too," said Mimi. "Put some rims on that Pope Mobile."

"Some twenties." Chanel laughed.

"That's right," Mimi continued. "Take that Yarmulke-type shit off his head, too. Hit him off with a Yankee fitted and have him in the projects blowing 'dro, you feel me?"

The shop lit up with laugher. The women continued talking, switching to a list of what celebrities they would sex and what rumors they had heard about them. Afterwards, Vanessa and

Mimi left for lunch. After they ate, they headed to Morningside Park where they sat on a bench and Vanessa sparked a discussion about Rich. She had told Mimi about their commitment to each other the day after they made it.

Vanessa had not revealed Rich's secret to anyone. But the intimacy that they had shared that night had reinvigorated their relationship. They were becoming closer by the day. Vanessa was moved by him exposing his vulnerabilities. She had developed a view of his life that the women in the shop had never seen. Each bit of exclusive information she learned made her feel special.

"So things really picking up for y'all?" Mimi asked.

"The more I learn about him, the more I love him, Mimi. And there is so much more to him than people know."

"Oh, yeah?"

"Yes. Take yesterday, for instance. I've been waiting to tell you this one in person." Vanessa smiled. "Rich is taking me to lunch, but I ask him to stop by my agent's office. So we're in the waiting area—"

Mimi interjected, "He went inside with you?"

"He needed to use the restroom. Afterwards, I asked him to keep me company."

"Okay, I thought you had a stalker on your hands." Mimi giggled.

"Come on, Mimi. So anyway, we're waiting inside and in comes this short white guy who looks like Jack Nicholson. He and Rich make eye contact, smile and the next thing you know they're hugging like high school buddies at a class reunion. My agent opens his door and tells me he's ready."

"Rich knows your agent too?"

"Just listen. My agent sees the Jack Nicholson guy and shakes his hand. Jack Nicholson introduces Rich to my agent. Then my agent and Rich call me over and introduce me to Jack

Nicholson. Turns out the Jack Nicholson look-alike is really Ted Evens, the owner of my publishing company."

"How's he know Rich?"

"They're both part of the same investment club. Rich has known him for years. A guy who owns one of the largest publishing companies in the country knows Rich. It's unbelievable."

"And you givin' what, fifteen percent of your money to your agent? Rich could've got you the deal for free."

"Same thing I thought. But it's my fault, because I told Rich I had a powerful agent who was sure to get me a good deal. Who would've known that a man of the streets of Harlem would've known Ted Evans?"

"Small world, Nessa." Mimi smiled and rubbed Vanessa's shoulder. "I'm happy for you. The deal, Rich, things are looking up for you."

Vanessa was happy to have Mimi's approval of Rich. Mimi had seen her aggravated in sour relationships and she had seen her frustrated as a single woman who could not find the right man. Vanessa talked with Mimi for a few more minutes about the happiness Rich had brought her. She admitted to being amazed that she was able to maintain a relationship with a man of Rich's caliber. Powerful men like him usually walked past her without a second look. They typically sought out arrogant fashionistas who spent hours in the mirror making themselves up before leaving home. She knew that Rich could have any woman he wanted, but he chose her. It was something that made her proud and something that she hoped would not change.

* * *

Later that night, Vanessa was greeted by Rich, as she stepped through the door of his penthouse. She was tired from work, so Rich gave her a hot bath and cooked dinner for her. After they ate, they curled up on the couch and watched Comedy Central. A comedian was telling sex jokes.

"He gonna be the next Dave Chappelle," Rich said, laughing along with Vanessa, as she lie on top of him.

The comedian began telling a joke about every man wanting to have sex with two women at once.

"How would you feel if I asked you to bring another woman into our bed?" Rich asked.

"How would I feel?"

"Yeah."

"How am I supposed to feel?"

"That's what I'm trying to find out?"

"I would feel like I'm not satisfying you."

"You do understand that a woman would benefit both of us, right?"

"Assuming I wanna be with a woman," Vanessa said.

"You ever thought about being with a woman?"

If only he knew. "Thinking and wanting are two different things. Moral of the story is I never thought or wanted to share my man. Can we talk about something else? Or better yet, let's finish watching TV."

"All right," Rich said.

* * *

The topic was sparked by a comedian, but Vanessa knew Rich was considering it. She also knew that if she did not please her man, another woman—or women—would. It was a fact of relationships she had learned years ago.

Her mind flashed to Candy. As much as Vanessa enjoyed being with Candy, she had never contemplated bringing a woman into her relationship with Rich. The two people were separate entities. But she was now exploring, within her mind, the possibility of uniting both entities. Candy would actually be the ideal candidate for a threesome. *But she would never deal with a man, especially Rich. The only reason she stopped slandering him is because she knows that I love him. And even if she was willing, she's too close to me and Rich. That could easily destroy my relationship with him.* She began rationalizing that one threesome with Candy may be enough to shut Rich up. *I already have the best of both worlds with each of them. But what if I could convince Candy to join us, just one time? Candy and Rich—that would be a hell of an experience for me!*

RICH

The following morning, Rich opened his eyes after a peaceful night of rest. Vanessa was staring at him, as she sat on the bed beside him. She leaned down and kissed him on the cheek. "I love you, Rich."

"I love you more." He grinned.

Vanessa kissed him again, then left the room.

Rich went into the bathroom, brushed his teeth and took a shower. He stepped back into the bedroom, thinking of Vanessa. He had awoken to her staring at him before, but that morning the look on her face was different. He left the bedroom in search of her and found her on the terrace, gazing over Manhattan. He hugged her from behind and kissed her on the neck. "What's up, baby?" he whispered in her ear.

She turned around. "You know I love you, right?"

"I question a lot of things in life, but that's not one of them."

"I didn't get to sleep until four o'clock this morning."

Rich remembered turning off the lights and cuddling with Vanessa, before he fell asleep at around midnight.

"And I woke up at five," Vanessa continued. "I came out here to the terrace for an hour, and then watched you sleep for two hours. The whole time I was thinking about what you said last night."

Rich's eyebrows rose. "Refresh my memory."

"The other woman."

What other woman? Oh, I know she ain't talking about that threesome conversation. I wouldn't mind a threesome, but I was just fucking with her.

"Is that really what you want?"

"What?"

"A threesome."

"What I want you to know first and foremost is that I love you. I'm completely satisfied with you on every level. That means mentally, physically, spiritually, sexually, emotionally, intellectually and every other thing with a L-L-Y at the end of it," Rich said.

Vanessa's face lit up with a smile.

"But I want both of us to share something different. And I know we'll both enjoy it," Rich said."This ain't gotta be no permanent affair, just a one-time adventure."

"Only under one condition," Vanessa said.

Oh shit, I got her. Rich refrained from smiling. "What?"

"I choose the woman."

"Now, baby, you know I'm allergic to bearillas."

"Bearilla?" Vanessa's face was puzzled. "What's that?"

"A woman that looks like a bear mixed with a gorilla," Rich said.

Vanessa burst into laughter. "You know if I bring a woman into our bed, she"s, gonna be clean, beautiful and down for whatever."

Rich kissed Vanessa and she walked off the terrace. He envisioned them having a ménage a trois. He had been in a few, but each with women that he hardly knew. Now he would be in a threesome with the woman he knew better than any other female. He was certain she would choose a woman who would meet the level of attractiveness he desired. He felt it would be good that he had no ties to the other woman. That would assure that he was emotionally attached to only Vanessa during their sex session. He was trying hard to be faithful, and the last thing he wanted was to become attracted to another woman.

* * *

Later that day, Rich parked a Lincoln Navigator in front of Chase's Harlem home on Striver's Row. He honked the horn. Seconds later, Chase came down stairs and climbed inside the SUV.

"What's good, Rich?"

"You tell me."

"We gonna have to go check the connect. The spot in the BX is damn near outta work. Shit pumpin' over there way more than usual."

Rich nodded. "Yo, some funny shit happened to me the other day."

"Holler."

Rich told Chase about crossing paths with Ted Stevens.

"New York City ain't as big as people think it is."

"Vanessa couldn't believe that this rich-ass white dude was praising me like I was the second coming of Christ."

"Next level. You always say that's where we gotta take shit."

"We already there. That's what that situation showed me," Rich said.

"What you mean?"

Rich turned to Chase. "The cards been playing my way for a long time and I got a nice stack of chips. I'm ready to cash 'em in before the Feds or one of these fools on the street stack the deck on me."

Chase was silent. After a few seconds, he strained his eyes to see beyond Rich's face and into his mind.

"This ain't no poker face. I'm sitting on a full house. The game is over, but we still hanging around the table."

"So you actually serious about this shit?"

"I couldn't bluff you if I tried. It's only two people in these streets that really know me, and both of "em is sitting inside this truck." Rich had never told Chase, but he felt he owed Chase something that he could never repay him. Killing a man to save his life and losing five years of his life in prison was priceless.

"You sure?" Chase asked. "You really wanna leave all this behind?"

Rich said he was certain that Chase should consider leaving the game also. He stressed that they had been on top for years, watching hustlers come and go, entering the game with ambition and leaving in caskets and handcuffs. "It's only a matter of time before karma catch up to us."

"We sitting on a empire that generate more paper than *The New York Times*. And all we do is pick up bricks from our connect, drop 'em off with the lieutenants and we done. This shit is a goldmine that run itself. Even the money get delivered to us. The whole operation is a moneymaking machine. All we do is push buttons, damn near risk-free."

"*Damn near.* That's the key word. A lot of things done happened to hustlers in the streets on them trips to drop off and pick up work."

"You really serious about this shit, ain't you?" Chase said.

"Dead ass."

"So you comin' with me to get these bricks tonight, or what?"

"Of course. You don't just desert your suppliers without saying good-bye after years of good business relations. But this is my last dance."

* * *

Rich returned home that night after he and Chase met with the connect. He walked through the door and found Vanessa sitting Indian style on the couch. She was tapping away at her laptop. On the coffee table in front of her, were a dictionary,

thesaurus and a manuscript marked with notes for revisions.

"Hey, baby." Vanessa puckered up and kissed Rich as he sat down.

"You serious about this book, huh?" Rich picked up a few pages of the manuscript.

"Best seller," she said. "Although writing is not really about the money to me; it's about creating. But the more people who enter the world I create, the better."

Rich read two pages and handed them to Vanessa. "Some of this is not adding up."

"What?" Vanessa asked, analyzing the pages.

"First of all, this little freak got the pastor eating her pussy and a drug dealer dicking her down."

"What's wrong with that?"

"Be easy, baby." Rich rubbed her leg. "Let me fuck this cow, you just hold the legs. Now this little freak's boyfriend is slinging dope, right?"

"Ump humph."

"Well, you can't have him calling dope 'girl',"

"Why not?"

Rich laughed. "Because dope is called *boy*. *Girl* is coke."

"Oh, I see."

"Now you also got this drug-dealing boy loading up ten shots in a three-fifty seven revolver." Rich shook his head. "Now, baby, this type of gun only holds five or six shots, depending on the model and brand."

Vanessa sighed. " Mimi was supposed to do a fact check on the street stuff, but she let all of this slide by."

"Mimi may be from the projects, but that don't make her no expert on the 'hood. Most cats creeping through the streets on a regular never seen the half. I know dudes who killed people, but never seen a dead body."

"That makes no sense, Rich."

"Makes plenty sense."

"How?" Vanessa asked.

"You put three bullets in somebody's head in broad day, you don't need to check they pulse to see if they breathing. Before they hit the ground, you stepping off, looking for cops, witnesses and the quickest route to a getaway. You don't got time to see what the dead body looks like."

"I never looked at it like that."

"That's a good thing. Because knowing this stuff from firsthand experience ain't nothing to be proud of. A lot of pain and regrets and bad memories come with being educated on street corners and back blocks. That's one of the reasons I walked away from it all today."

"What do you mean?"

Rich explained to Vanessa that his days in the drug game were over. She had previously expressed to him that she had heard the stories of him selling drugs. But she wasn't interested in the details, because she was confident that Rich would eventually leave the streets behind. He had told her he appreciated her attitude. Her sentiment was that a man would be a man. Part of that motto meant that she was in no predicament to dictate how a man lived.

"What does Chase think of your decision?"

"Doesn't matter what he thinks." Rich held back the truth that he and Chase had an extended argument after leaving the connect. Chase felt that Rich was abandoning him. He said what made him upset most was that he felt Rich's decision to leave the game was based on Vanessa. He accused Rich of siding with a woman he had known only for a few months instead of standing firm with a comrade he'd known for years. Truth was Rich's decision was based largely on seeing Ted Stevens again and realizing Ted's wealth and prestige was something Rich was worthy of. Chase and Rich settled their debate before Rich left, but Rich had a bad vibe about Chase. He knew their friendship had taken a blow that had changed it permanently.

Vanessa set her laptop and the manuscript pages on the coffee table. She turned to Rich. "I'm really proud of you, baby." She kissed him.

"I understand I'm not just living for me no more."

"We should be celebrating."

"I got a better idea. Put some shoes on." Rich stood. "And bring your laptop.

Within minutes, Rich was driving Vanessa down Lennox Avenue in a Bentley Flying Spur. He pointed to the housing project they slowly drifted by. "That's Foster Projects. I got shot in there over a dice game when I was thirteen." He pulled over. "Open your laptop. I'm gonna take you to school. Give you some inspiration and facts for that book."

"So this is a 'hood tour?" She grinned.

"You wanna write about a hustler, the best place to learn about the game is Harlem. And I ain't talking Nicky Barnes, Frank Lucas and these other lames in the game that was getting bread but snitching to the Feds. I'm talking 'bout the Rich Porters and Fritzs."

Rich pulled off. He stopped at a few drug spots, old crime scenes, restaurants and gambling spots where thousands of dollars in drug money had circulated. He told Vanessa stories from his personal experience and mythic tales of street legends that were talked about everywhere from project halls, jail cells and rap songs to street DVDs and magazines. He answered Vanessa's questions as she typed away on her laptop.

While they rode home reality set in. Rich realized he had actually given up the streets that raised him. He was feeling the bittersweet dynamic of transcending the drama that had nearly cost him his life, while the same drama had given him life. His very being had been molded by hustlers, crime, street wars and fast females.

His actions and achievements were based on his observations. Careless drug dealers had inspired him to become an investor in an effort to avoid their downfalls. His image, molded by the streets, is what attracted Vanessa. And it was Vanessa and the day outside of her agent's office that sparked the end of the game for Rich. His life had come full circle. The factors that led him into the game had led him out of the game. And he had picked up wealth and a woman he loved in the process.

But in the back of his mind, Rich felt he could not escape karma. He was certain that a new life came with new drama.

CHAPTER EIGHT
CANDY

It was almost closing time at the shop. The scent of hair scorched was everywhere. Candy was putting the finishing touches on a weave of one of her clients. She had been getting hot all day as she stared at Vanessa's butt clenched by a pair of white spandex. She could see Vanessa"s panty line beneath the thin fabric. Vanessa was the first woman Candy had been with who made her horny while she was clothed.

She's so small, but she sure knows how to work that body. Candy looked at her watch. *Fifteen minutes 'till closing. I gotta get her home with me tonight.*

"Vanessa," Meisha called out. "How the hell you manage to tame Rich? I been meaning to ask you that shit. I don't see no more broads in his whips. I don't even see him driving through Harlem too much no more like he own the motherfucker. What, you got him a job?"

"His job is selling drugs and breaking hearts," Chanel interjected.

Vanessa rolled her eyes at Chanel. "My man always had a

job. And these materialistic divas," she cut her eyes at Chanel, "that was trying to get laid in one of the cars he drives, didn't even know they were company cars."

"Must be a pharmaceuticals company," said Chanel. "Distribution and sales or import-export."

"But how did you transform his ass?" Meisha said. "That's what I need to know. 'Cause I watched him chase pussy like a linebacker going at a quarterback."

"I just gave him what I know for a fact he couldn't get from any other woman...me."

Candy watched as Chanel sucked her teeth. The more Rich showed his face in the shop to pick up Vanessa, the more jealous Chanel had become. For weeks, she had been making sarcastic remarks about Rich in the presence of Vanessa. Most times, Vanessa simply ignored Chanel.

The shop began to empty out, as closing time neared. Candy turned to Vanessa. "I need to speak to you in the office, if you got time."

"All right," Vanessa said.

Chanel was the last person leaving the shop. "Chanel," Candy called. She caught up with her and they stepped out of the shop together.

"What's up, Candy?"

"You gotta be easy with Vanessa."

"What?" Chanel's hazel eyes squinted. "Who you? Captain Save-A-Ho?"

"You got clients looking around at you makin' a scene. And you know I'm business over bullshit," Candy said.

"You got a point." Chanel shook her head. "Shit, I thought you was takin' that heifer side over me. I been knowing you too long for that shit."

"Just be easy in the shop."

"All right," Chanel said. She walked off to her car.

As Candy stared at her, she thought about the years she had known Chanel and all they had been through. Chanel had been a friend after Dez was murdered and Candy became trapped in an emotional whirlwind from being disowned by her conservative Christian family. Chanel had been there for her. Now, Candy had just lied to her for a second time because of Vanessa. The first lie was about the video she made of her and Vanessa. Now, she lied about not taking Vanessa's side over Chanel's. Business was definitely a priority for Candy. But sometime between when Vanessa first made her cum and the last time Vanessa made her laugh, she had become Candy's top priority. Unlike Vera, Vanessa was someone Candy could talk to about a range of topics, and she enjoyed her presence even when they weren"t having sex. The work week at the shop had given all of the employee"s time together to bond. But what Candy and Vanessa shared was something that exceeded what the rest of the women shared with Candy.

Candy left Chanel and walked inside of her office then locked the door. Her first sight was Vanessa's butt. She was bending down lacing her sneakers. Candy's nipples instantly got hard. She stepped over to Vanessa and hugged her from behind, as Vanessa rose. Her hands explored Vanessa's breasts.

Vanessa let out a slight moan, as Candy began sucking her neck. "Feels so good," Vanessa whispered. She began fingering herself and stimulating her clit at the same time.

Candy's tongue rolled into Vanessa's ear. "Damn, you taste good," Candy mumbled, as Vanessa fingered herself quicker, moaning louder by the second. Candy slipped her hands underneath Vanessa's shirt and began gently caressing her breasts.

"Ahhh," Vanessa moaned with pleasure.

Candy could feel Vanessa's body sink back, her knees buckling and her legs wobbling. She held Vanessa up, as she let out an extended moan while she came.

Vanessa slowly turned around, finding Candy unbuttoning her blouse. She slipped her tongue into Candy's mouth. Vanessa back peddled, as Candy led her to the couch and spread one leg over the couch.

"Sit down," Candy instructed. Vanessa complied. Candy laid her back and spread her legs. She sat facing Vanessa. Slowly she inched toward Vanessa and slid one of her legs between Vanessa's.

Vanessa moved forward until their wet pussies were touching.

"Yeah," Candy instinctively responded to the tingling sensation that jolted from between her legs throughout her body.

Candy and Vanessa began grinding their pussies together. Their bodies sensually swerved together like a couple dancing to reggae music. They were panting and moaning harder and louder until they climaxed simultaneously.

Candy laid back, her eyes closed. She had come so hard that she did not have the energy to move. She sat still until Vanessa began to sit up. "You wore me out," she told Vanessa.

Vanessa wiped the wetness between Candy's legs, and then reached up and began stimulating Candy's nipples.

"Don't start me back up," Candy warned.

Vanessa leaned over and kissed Candy, before lying on top of her.

Candy slowly caressed Vanessa's butt, staring into her eyes. "How far would you go to please me?" Vanessa asked.

"I'll suck your pussy 'till you come right in the middle of Times Square," Candy said, laughing.

"Stop playing." Vanessa kissed her, then ran her hands through Candy's hair. She gently sucked on Candy's neck for a second, before planting kisses on her neck and cheek. She gazed back into Candy's eyes while stroking her hair. "I'm serious. How far would you go to please me?"

"You know it's no limits between us."

Vanessa stared at her for a few seconds. "None?"

"We did everything together."

"Not everything."

"Name it."

"I wanna have a threesome," Vanessa whispered in a sexy voice.

"I knew you had your eye on Vera."

"Not with Vera," Vanessa said seductively. "With Rich." She eased her tongue into Candy's mouth before she could respond.

The passionate kiss felt so good that it lessened the impact of Vanessa's words. Candy opened her eyes as Vanessa's lips left hers. Her hands were still on Vanessa's ass. The office was so quiet that Candy could hear the clock on her wall ticking. Every thought she had of men raced to the front of her mind. Dissatisfaction, anger and frustration were only a few of the feelings that men had stirred within her.

"Talk to me," said Vanessa.

"I can't do it."

Vanessa's eyes grew sad. "Why?"

"You know why."

"I thought you cared about me. What happened to there being no limits between us?" The hurt etched on Vanessa's face made Candy want to cry. "I care about you more than anybody I've ever been with, man or woman. But—"

"There is no buts. The most precious thing I have is between my legs and I gave that to you. Something I never dreamed of doing. I've never been with another woman and you're the only woman I'm gonna be with. But I love Rich just as much as I love myself. And I'll do anything I have to in order to make sure he's happy. All I'm asking is for you to do something for me one time."

"I can't—"

Vanessa silenced Candy with another kiss. As her tongue left Candy's mouth and she pulled her face away, she placed her index finger over Candy's lips. "Just consider it and get back to me later. Please."

Candy watched in silence as Vanessa stood up and got dressed. She reminisced on all of the comments that Vanessa had made about how good Rich was in bed. Then she remembered the day with him in the elevator and how hot Rich made her. "Vanessa."

Vanessa looked at Candy. "What?"

"Did Rich tell you to ask me this?"

"He wants a threesome. He has no idea who's coming home with me. And you know he doesn't know about us. I asked you because you're the only woman I wanna be with."

Candy walked over and kissed Vanessa. "Stop looking so sad. You're breaking my heart." She hugged Vanessa, rubbing her back, while Vanessa's hands palmed her butt. "I think I'm falling in love with you."

* * *

"You a fucking freak," Mimi said, smiling. "I can't believe this shit."

Vanessa had left the shop and headed straight to Mimi's home. She told her everything about her and Candy, including their first experience and Candy's falling in love comment. "So you told her you care about her a lot after she said she was falling in love?"

"Basically."

"I can't believe this shit," Mimi repeated.

"I like her a lot. I love Rich."

"If you care a lot about somebody, you can end up fallin' in love. It's not rocket science. And you can be in love with two people."

"You're not helping me any."

"Remember I told you I understand how a chick can get caught up 'cause I been through it?"

"Yeah."

"Well, ya girl Mimi recovered. You, my friend, are strung out."

"Come on, Mimi. You gotta do better than that."

"I can tell that you that during that three-way, they both gonna be competing for you. ol" boy don't know that ol" girl tongue been in your pussy for months. So he gonna want to make sure she don't turn you out. Only if he knew." Mimi laughed. "Then ol" girl falling in love, so she gonna wanna take you from him."

"Impossible. I love Rich way too much. Plus, Candy respects that."

"We'll see."

"No, I already see that."

"So you should be okay. You got a night to remember coming up."

"But she didn't even agree to do it."

Mimi sighed. "See, you on that Stevie Wonder shit again. She told you she's fallin' in love with you for a reason."

"You're right."

"But I'll tell you one thing, you better lay down your best fuck game. The last thing you want is Candy stealing Rich from you."

***

The following morning, Vanessa stepped into the shop minutes after Candy did. Ever since Leah got married, she was no longer the first person at the shop, so they were the only two inside. Vanessa entered Candy's office and found her seated behind her desk.

Candy stood and walked around to Vanessa. "About yesterday, I know you love Rich. I respect that. I just felt I had to tell you what was on my mind. I can't control how I feel, especially when it comes to you."

"It's okay. I'm glad that you told me."

"And you know I'm gonna do it, the three-way."

Vanessa's face lit up and she hugged Candy. "Thank you so much."

"But I'm letting you know now, it better go down on that terrace," Candy said. "I wanna see that Central Park view."

"I can arrange that." Vanessa looked at her watch. "But right now, I gotta go to the health food store. You want something?"

Candy put her arms around Vanessa and palmed her butt. "I got what I want right here." Vanessa pecked her on the lips and walked toward the door. As she reached the door, she heard a knock. She opened the door and spotted Vera.. "Hello," Vanessa said, smiling.

Vera sucked her teeth and frowned, as she brushed past Vanessa.

What the hell is all that about? Vanessa turned around and Vera was halfway through the spacious office. *To hell with her.* Vanessa exited the shop and walked down the street, predicting what the threesome would be like and how it would affect her relationships with Candy and Rich.

Vanessa turned the block and met Leah on her way to work. The two women stepped into the health food store together. Vanessa ordered a strawberry and kiwi smoothie along with a pound of cashews. Leah purchased a fruit salad. The women sat down at one of the tables in the lounge area.

"So how's the book coming along?" Leah asked.

"A lot better since Rich gave me some perspective on what really happens in the streets."

"So you and Rich are really serious?"

Vanessa smiled. "Yeah."

"I'm happy for you. Actually, more happy that he actually loves you. It proves that everybody is capable of change."

"He's really a good man when you get to know him. He's just very guarded. But thank God I was able to penetrate the armor and get to the real man."

"I think you should have a talk with Chanel, privately. Everybody in the shop has a view of Rich, which we actually need to reassess since he's growing. But we both know that Chanel is overdoing it."

"You can look at me and see I'm no drama queen."

"I understand. And the last thing you want to do is get into a shouting match or a cat fight with Chanel. You're a smart woman. I'm sure you can be diplomatic about it."

"I'll think about it. Thanks for the advice."

"Anytime."

The two women chatted about Vanessa's book, then the topic changed to Leah's marriage. Vanessa was not ready for marriage, but she had thought about it a few times. She never discussed it with Rich, though. He had made it clear that he was still learning to love.

"You ready?" Vanessa asked.

"Yup."

The women stood and stepped out of the establishment into the summer sun. They strolled down 125th Street through crowds of people in the shopping district. As they neared the corner, shots rang out. People on the sidewalk parted.

"Look," Vanessa pointed in front of them.

"Get down!" Leah pulled Vanessa behind a parked Acura TL.

Vanessa watched Chase running through the crowd as it continued parting. Behind him was a teenager with a large handgun. Vanessa flinched, as the youth took aim and fired five more shots. Chase was a moving target that cut across the street, weaving in between moving cars. Bullets shattered the windows of a parked Chevy Envoy, as Chase dipped behind it, picking up speed on the sidewalk across the street.

"That young boy tryin" to gun down Chase, for real," Leah said.

Vanessa was frozen, shocked. It was the first time she had heard live gunshots or witnessed life-threatening beef. The only guns she had ever seen fired were gripped by actors on television and movie screens. All the violence that Rich had told her about during their tour of Harlem was now vivid in her mind. She thought of Rich. What would have happened had he not left the streets behind? Would he have been with Chase, fleeing for his life?

"Come on," Leah said, tugging on Vanessa's arm. "Let's get out of here before the cops pop up and start asking questions."

They made it to the shop minutes later. Candy and Meisha were inside huddled around Chanel at her chair.

"Y'all heard about Chase?" Meisha asked.

"Some kid tried to rob him just now," Chanel said.

Vanessa was amazed at how fast the news had traveled. Chanel said she was getting into her Escalade, when she saw the botched robbery. She said Chase had just stepped out of a jewelry store, when a light-skinned teen pulled a gun on him. Chase grabbed the gun and tussled with the kid until a few shots rang out and the kid fell to the ground with the gun, still firing as Chase took off."

"We saw both of them," Leah said. "They turned the corner when we was walking down Two-Fifth. That kid was trying to kill Rich, for real."

"He even shot out the windows of a truck," Vanessa added.

"He must got a death wish," Candy said.

"'Cause everybody know Chase will kill a dude's mother to get to him," Meisha said. "And Rich ain't no altar boy. Wait 'til he find out. That lil boy is through."

Oh, no. Vanessa had not thought of Rich responding to the

situation. She was happy that he was no longer running the streets. But for the first time, it dawned on her that Rich had an inseparable bond with Chase. If anyone could pull him back in the game, it was Chase. She contemplated calling Rich to try and keep him calm because she was sure that word was probably circulating to him, if it had not already. But Rich was in Connecticut on business and would not be back in New York until the evening. So Vanessa figured that it would be best to see him face-to-face to speak to him about the drama with Chase. Then she began pondering whether she was overacting? Rich was a man, a responsible man who had proved that by leaving behind a world of drugs and death. He had proved to Vanessa plenty of times that he was a rational thinker. *I hope he thinks rational about this situation with Chase.*

* * *

Vanessa's iPhone rang later that night as the shop was about to close. Her heart jumped when she saw Rich's number on the screen.

"What's up, baby?"

"Where are you?" she questioned, nervously, pacing in front of her chair.

"I'm getting undressed, about to get in the Jacuzzi."

"Everything okay?"

"Yeah."

"How was your day?" Vanessa tried to feel out Rich. She was not going to bring up the situation with Chase if Rich didn't know about it.

"My day was cool. I just got back from Connecticut."

"You went straight home?"

"Yeah. That's why I called you. I knew you was supposed to be over at your crib working on your book after work, but I need to see you."

"Okay, I'll be right there."

RICH

Rich had just gotten out of the Jacuzzi. He was lying on a large inflatable mattress on the terrace, gazing at the stars. "Sky's the limit," he mumbled, thinking of how much he had overcome. He still could not fully grasp the reality of being out of the drug game and living a normal life. It was a good feeling to have the worries of beef and police out of his life, but the feeling was unusual.

Vanessa stepped onto the terrace and kissed Rich. He slipped his hand up her summer dress, inching for her pussy. "Be patient, I'm gonna take a quick shower." Vanessa said. "Stay right there."

"You know they say *time don't wait for no man*, women either."

"They also say *good things come to those who wait* and *patience is a virtue*." Vanessa smiled and stepped inside the penthouse.

Rich chuckled and lay back, gazing at the stars again. He thought about Vanessa for another ten minutes, then closed his eyes and took in the summer breeze flowing over his body. The only thing he was wearing was boxer shorts. A few minutes later, he opened his eyes, when he heard the sliding glass door to the terrace opening. *What the fuck?*

Vanessa was in a red teddy, walking toward him with Candy, who sported black negligee. As a smile overcame Rich and he opened his mouth to speak, Vanessa put her finger over her lips and uttered, "Shhh."

Unbelievable. Rich stared at their bodies—Vanessa was so petite and Candy was stacked in every place that counted. He found it hard to keep his eyes off her. Their meeting in the elevator flashed in his mind when the breeze brought him a whiff of the same perfume she had sported that day.

Vanessa and Candy stopped a couple feet away from Rich and began kissing. Rich couldn't believe how comfortable they seemed together. They slowly began undressing each other. Candy's melon-sized breasts popped out of her bra, landing in Vanessa's mouth.

Damn. Rich grabbed his rock-hard dick.

The women turned, facing Rich. Candy stood behind Vanessa. She sucked on her neck and rubbed between her legs, while Vanessa massaged her own breasts. Candy opened her eyes, looking directly at Rich as she nibbled on Vanessa's earlobe. She dropped to her knees gracefully, sliding her tongue between Vanessa's butt cheeks.

"Ahh," Vanessa moaned. Her eyes rolled in the back of her head.

Candy slid between her legs, peeking at Rich before kissing Vanessa's inner thighs and planting her mouth on her pussy.

Vanessa moaned louder, more passionately. She grabbed the back of Candy's head as Candy licked and sucked her into a climax.

Damn, they some straight freaks. I never knew Vanessa had it in her. Rich stood up, too hyper to continue lying on the mattress. He slowly paced next to the mattress Candy laid on and spread her legs. "Goddamn, girl." He was staring directly at the fat lips of her pussy when Vanessa dove face first between Candy's legs.

"Eat me. Yeah, eat my pussy," Candy called out. She licked her lips and closed her eyes.

Rich balled his fists and gritted his teeth. He was trying to be patient. As soon as Candy came, he planned to join them. He stood over Vanessa, gazing into Candy's eyes as she panted and moaned.

Candy leaned forward until she was standing. Vanessa then

lay down and Candy sat on her face. She slowly grinded, her lips quivering.

"Fuck this," Rich mumbled. He stepped out of his underwear.

Candy looked up at him and grabbed his dick with both hands.

Rich exhaled deeply, savoring the wet warmth of Candy's mouth engulfing the head of his dick. She worked it with her lips and tongue, then made her way down, swallowing as much of him as she could. He watched her eyes roll into the back of her head as she grinded hard on Vanessa's face. Candy used one hand to grab Rich's waist for balance, then suddenly her body quaked as she came. She still managed to keep sucking Rich's dick, savoring each slurp, bobbing her head with her eyes closed.

Vanessa eased from underneath Candy. She slid toward Rich, nearly swallowing one of his balls.

"Damn. Yeah, baby. Y'all work it." Rich reached down, pulling both of their heads to him as he came. Candy sucked him dry and swallowed all he had to offer.

Vanessa and Candy stood and sandwiched Rich. He palmed Candy's ass, kissing her, while Vanessa kissed on his back. They steered him to the mattress where he was forced onto his back. Candy faced Rich and straddled him.

"Damn, girl," he whispered. Candy's pussy was tighter and hotter than he anticipated. She was the closest he had been to a virgin in years.

Vanessa stepped over him from behind his head. Her pussy landed square on his face. She leaned forward. He could hear her and Candy kissing and moaning. Meanwhile, Candy's pussy locked on his dick and she rode him faster. She began slamming against him…hard.

"I'm cumming," Candy screamed.

Rich reached back and grabbed Vanessa's ass. He pulled her forward until his tongue was dancing between her butt cheeks.

"Stop," she cried. "Please. It feels so good."

Rich gripped her squirming body firmer. Reaching her climax, her juices leaked onto Rich's face.

They all got up and went inside the condo. They spent all night going at it in the bedroom, switching positions, sucking and sexing until they were asleep.

* * *

Rich awoke the following morning and sat on his canopy bed. His back was sore and he could feel scratches on it. He went to the bathroom, washed up and put on one of his Versace robes. Fresh on his mind were the memories of a night of steamy, passionate sex. His time with Vanessa and Candy had been all he expected and more.

Rich headed to the kitchen, following the scent of pancakes. *Look at this shit.* He smiled at the sight of Vanessa and Candy side-by-side in the kitchen, preparing breakfast. The only thing covering Vanessa was a tank top. Candy had on a t-shirt and panties. In Vanessa's hand was a skillet, while Candy stood squeezing fresh orange slices and strawberries into a juicer. Rich walked in between them, from behind, caressing both of their butts. He kissed Vanessa on the cheek, then pecked Candy.

"So, how was your night?" Vanessa smiled at him.

"Baby, you won't believe this." Rich sighed. "I got attacked by two wild animals." He grinned.

"You sure didn't put up a good fight," Vanessa said, laughing.

"Yeah, but he was swinging that baseball bat." Candy grabbed Rich's dick.

"That's a Louisville Slugger, girl," Vanessa said, looking at Candy's hand.

Rich enjoyed the moment, hoping it would not stop. When he

asked Vanessa for a one-night affair, he had no idea that it would come with an overnight stay equipped with breakfast and flirting. He was still amazed that Vanessa and Candy were so sexually compatible and comfortable together. More surprising was their joyful, friendly demeanor the morning after.

"We figured you worked up an appetite last night," Candy said. "Even though you did a lot of eating." She laughed.

"Speaking of our diet, I never would have expected you to be the type that likes drinking." Rich's eyes rolled from Candy's lips to his dick.

Vanessa and Candy laughed as they finished preparing breakfast. They sat beside each other at the large glass table, opposite Rich.

Rich looked at the soy bacon, tofu eggs and wheat pancakes on his plate. He picked up a piece of bacon. "Soy everything. This is my only problem with her, Candy."

"I could get used to it," Candy said, staring seductively at Vanessa who smiled.

"So you ladies thinking about having some more slumber parties in the future?" Rich chewed the piece of soy bacon.

"Can you handle it?" Vanessa asked.

"You know I like to sling pipe like a plumber," Rich said. "And I ain't never been a party pooper."

"We'll see," Candy said.

Rich was pleased but confused. Pleased that future threesomes were on the agenda, but confused about how open Vanessa and Candy were with each other. He hoped that he was not witnessing Candy taking the only woman in his life away from him.

CHAPTER NINE
CANDY

While Vanessa was in the shower, Rich was sitting on the couch, sipping the fresh smoothie Candy had made. Candy stepped in front of him, gazing into his eyes. She could not stop thinking about the feeling of his dick pumping into her, his firm hands flipping her body into countless positions. "Everything they say about you is true," she said.

"Everything like what?" He set his smoothie on the table.

Candy sat next to him. She reached beneath his robe and grabbed his dick. It expanded in her hand. "Everything about that. I been wanting to find out for myself since that day in the elevator."

Rich stared at her hand as she unleashed his dick from underneath his silk robe. "Now you know Vanessa gon' be out that shower any minute."

"I don't think she'll mind after last night. Besides, I just wanna see it close up." She leaned down, inches away from his erect penis. Candy had never seen a man so well hung. She kissed his dick, slid her tongue around the head, then closed his robe and stood up.

"After all that we been through last night, I would have never figured you was a dick teaser," Rich said.

Candy lifted her skirt and bent over, her ass just a foot away from his face. "You can have me anytime you want, any place you want, however you want." She turned and faced Rich. "With or without Vanessa."

* * *

Later that morning, Candy and Vanessa were at the shop before it opened. They were discussing their threesome. Candy had confessed that she had never been with a man that was as large and as experienced as Rich was. She leaned against her desk, near Vanessa. "And you. You just took what we do to the next level. It's like Rich brought something new out of you that I never saw before."

Vanessa grabbed Candy by her waist. "I couldn't have done it without you. You and him together." She closed her eyes. "It was unbelievable."

Candy had also felt the power of three. It was a first for her, just like Vanessa. Simply thinking of their experience made her wet. The threesome was the first time that Candy's body had been stimulated totally. No part of her body went untouched by the caress of a hand, lick of a tongue or stroke of Rich's dick. She had identified new feelings and erogenous zones that she would forever crave.

But Candy realized that she wanted all of Rich's attention. She needed his strokes to make up for all of the men who had entered and exited between her legs before she reached her peak. She desired the feeling of Rich inside her womb, his eyes staring into hers, as if she was the only woman who existed in the world, while her arms wrapped his body. She wanted Vanessa's passionate tale of her and Rich to become sensual stories of Candy and Rich. She did not want to steal Vanessa's man. She just wanted to borrow him.

"You know, he asked me 'how did I feel after last night?'" Vanessa said.

"What did you tell him?" Candy asked

"That it felt so good I didn't want it to end."

"Who in their right mind would want what we felt to end? I still can't believe I was with a man. And I loved it."

"So you're bisexual?"

"I don't know. It's been so long since I've been with a man. I thought that I could never feel like this again after Dez." Candy shrugged her shoulders. "Maybe I'm just going through a phase."

"You're no different than me," said Vanessa.

Candy had no intentions of putting men back on her "must-have" list. She was content with Rich, although she didn't know how long their new relations would last. Neither did she know how intense they would become. Would there be sex sessions monthly, biweekly, weekly? Their schedule would most likely be determined by their demand. Judging from what Candy knew of Vanessa and what she sensed about Rich, there would be a strong demand.

"I meant to ask you yesterday," Vanessa said. "What's up with Vera? I greeted her yesterday and she frowned her face up. She ignored me and damn near knocked me down when she stormed in here."

"She's a done deal. We're through."

"What happened?"

"She don't understand the concept of friends with benefits."

"You never talk to me about her."

"Nothing to talk about."

"How is she?" Vanessa asked, inquisitively.

Candy kissed Vanessa. "Nothing like you. That's the problem."

"What's so special about me?"

"You're open-minded, cool to hang with, you're very sensual, your lips are sweeter than chocolate, your pussy smells like roses, you make me cum harder than any woman has and I love you." Candy slid her tongue into Vanessa's mouth, kissing her lovingly as she wrapped Vanessa in her arms.

"I love you too."

Candy leaned back when the whispered words entered her ear. She stared directly into Vanessa's eyes.

"I love you," Vanessa repeated, without a blink. She said she had thought long and hard about Candy and she could not deny the feelings she felt for her. They were more than pleasure. Vanessa was beginning to have the same gut emotion when in Candy's presence that she had when she was around Rich. She felt wanted, needed and safe each time she was in the same room with Candy.

"I want you to understand that I don't expect you to leave Rich for me," said Candy.

"Okay."

"And I understand that what we have is between us."

Vanessa nodded.

Candy embraced her. The mood Vanessa's body generated within Candy was proof that they belonged together. The emotion Candy was experiencing was new and intense. It was something that she could not fully define or explain, but her heart, mind and body told her it was right. It did not matter that many people would consider their relationship taboo. It did not matter that Candy had to withhold truth from the woman she considered family. The only thing that mattered to Candy was that Vanessa continued to spark that inextinguishable flame within her that warmed her body each time they came together. What mattered was the love they each shared for one another.

VANESSA

The following month for Vanessa brought her closer to Rich than she imagined time would. She had moved into his penthouse. She had also been busy with her book, but she managed to make time for Rich. They spent time together throughout New York City when they were not at home. It was Vanessa's first time living with a man, and she learned that she enjoyed cooking, cleaning and comforting a man on a daily basis. She also appreciated that Rich often had the Jacuzzi or a warm bath ready for her after work, along with a meal she had cooked and Rich had reheated. Sex between them had become more passionate since they were spending more time together.

Candy had also been spending more time with Vanessa. They often had sexual episodes in Candy's office. Since Vanessa had moved in with Rich, but left her furniture and most of her belongings behind, she and Candy had also been using Vanessa's apartment for personal time together. The apartment had become Vanessa's second home. There, she and Candy cuddled and listened to neo soul and watched DVDs of *The Wire* when they weren't sexing each other.

Candy had begun spending weekends over at the penthouse with Vanessa and Rich. The trio had sex all hours of the day and night. They played strip poker and often Vanessa and Candy performed like strippers, dancing with each other and giving Rich lap dances. Vanessa had not discussed it with Rich nor Candy, but there seemed to be an understanding that Rich and Candy were not to have sex unless Vanessa was involved. Though weekends were the scheduled days for Candy to spend nights over, Candy often visited during weekdays, sometimes spending the night.

It was a Saturday night when Vanessa and Candy strolled through the front door of the penthouse.

"I'm gonna see if he's got the Jacuzzi ready," Vanessa said.

"Okay." Candy put down her Gucci bag and stepped into the bedroom.

As Vanessa neared the balcony, she heard Rich arguing. She posted up behind a grandfather clock where she could see the balcony. Rich was pacing back and forth in front of Chase.

"I tried to call you the day this little bastard Pana got at me," Chase said. "Your number changed. When the fuck that happen?"

"When I stopped hustling. That phone was for you and me on the drug tip. Even though we never talked reckless on it, it was for us to keep tabs on shit. You know that. Why you didn't use my legit line? My business line?" Rich asked.

"I lost that shit, man. Fuck, I ain't Free or one of the motherfuckers you be talking stocks and bonds with. It's me, man. Chase."

"And you shouldn't have disappeared for a month like you jumped bail or ducking the Feds. All type of shit was going through my mind. I don't know if you sleeping in a casket or lying in a hospital bed. I put the word out on the streets and half of Harlem was looking for you. Everybody acting like they blind or hard of hearing."

"Vanessa—"

Vanessa turned to Candy, silencing her with her index finger covering her lips. She pointed to the terrace, as Candy stepped over.

"It boils down to this," Chase said. "I went OT to lay low and let this shit die down so I can rock these motherfuckers to sleep. I told you who sent this little bastard to murder me. You know you the only one I trust. I got this shit planned, and it gotta go down tonight. I'm killing both of them motherfuckers. But I need you to hold me down." Chase pulled an automatic handgun from his waist.

Oh my God. No. Please don't take it, baby. Vanessa's heart was beating faster than Marion Jones, as she stared at the gun. She wanted to run on the balcony, snatch the gun and throw it off the twenty-one stories.

"I ain't that far removed from the game that I don't got a gun, so you can put that away."

Chase smiled and tucked his gun in his waistline. "Okay."

"But I left the game to get out of this shit," Rich said, shaking his head. "I ain't living for me no more."

Chase's eyebrows inverted and his lips twisted with anger. "It don't be for me, you don't be living at all. You'll be fucking dead. Another name on a mural on a fuckin' handball court in a park in Harlem."

"You right, Chase. I'm a hold you down, but you gonna put your own work in. And this is it for me," Rich said, shaking his head. "I told you game was over and to get out. I hope this shit is a wake-up call to get you up out of this street sleep you in."

Vanessa led Candy into their bedroom. Her tear-soaked eyes were wider than silver dollars. "What are we gonna do? We gotta stop him."

"Just calm down," said Candy.

"But we gotta do something." Vanessa had never been so scared. She felt helpless. Her world had become a fantasy when Rich swept her off her feet. Now the solid foundation they had created was crumbling before her eyes. She was faced with the reality that her life could change for the worse in a second based on the decision of the man she loved.

RICH

Rich stepped off the terrace with Chase.

"I'll be downstairs in the car," Chase said, walking out the front door.

Rich watched him close the door. He loved Chase. Chase had been the brother Rich never had. He knew Chase would do anything for him. He had already proven it. But Rich was coming to grips with the reality that he and Chase had grown apart. Yet Rich felt obligated to help him. His mind was made up. There was no choice.

Rich stepped into the bedroom, spotting Vanessa and Candy. "When y' all get here?" he asked.

Vanessa bolted into his arms and hugged him tightly. I love you so much. Please don't go with Chase. Don't leave this house. Please," she begged.

Candy stepped over. "Rich, you can't go. It's not worth it. I don't wanna see you end up like Dez." She wrapped her arms around him and Vanessa, forming a group hug.

Why the hell they had to be here? Rich rubbed their backs, comforting them. "I'm gon' be all right."

When Vanessa and Candy lifted their heads from Rich's shoulders, their eyes were puffy and red. Rich felt like someone had snatched his heart from his chest and stomped it. He had never seen either of them shed a tear. They had only brought joy to his life that came by way of smiles and seductive stares. They were too beautiful to cry, too delicate to face the hardship he was putting them through.

Rich sat down between them on the bed. He wiped away the tears from each of their faces. He kissed each of them on the cheek, then put his arms around their shoulders. "I promise y' all, tonight I'm coming back through that front door."

Vanessa took his face into her palms. Her eyes began tearing again. "Every time I look into your eyes I see me," she said. "I love you more than I love life itself. It was you who took me through Harlem and showed me how you escaped all of that madness. Don't go back and become a statistic." She hugged Rich for a minute and then slowly let him go.

"Listen to me, Rich," said Candy, as he faced her. "I been knowing you for over a decade, when you was knee-deep in the game and you felt you had no choice. You do now. Vanessa loves you and I care about you a lot." She kissed him on the lips. "You knew Dez. Her eyes began watering and Rich wiped them. "When Dez got killed, I didn't want to live no more. And Vanessa loves you way more than I loved Dez. The point is, what the hell are we supposed to do if you're dead or in Sing Sing?"

Rich got on his knees and faced Vanessa and Candy. "I didn't survive and thrive on these streets from age nine to thirty-five because I had a horseshoe up my ass and a rabbit's foot in my pocket. I know my way around. And I'm not even into bracelets, so you know I don't get along with handcuffs. Plus, we got a lot more living to do and that ain't gonna work if I'm hanging out with Biggie and Pac. I never let neither one of y'all down and I ain't about to start now. Trust me."

They stood and hugged. Then he stepped into his closet. Seconds later he came out with a handgun. He tucked it on his waistline and pulled his white mock neck over it. Rich squatted and tightened the shoelaces on his Wallabies. When he looked up, Vanessa and Candy were sitting on the bed, hugging each other and rocking back and forth. The sight of them crying was eating at Rich. He turned and walked out the room. He tried to rid the image of them from his mind. He knew that he would need to be focused for the mission he was going on with Chase. Distractions on the street could easily lead to death.

* * *

It was midnight and Rich was wheeling the black Ford Taurus with Chase in the passenger seat. Vanessa and Candy were still fresh on his mind. He had been on many missions like the one he found himself on, and never had a woman occupied space in his mind while he was focused on drama. Now he had two women clouding his thoughts. This new phenomenon indicated two things. First, although Rich once had virtually no feelings for women, he now had feelings for two. Second, while he used to be so deep in the game that nothing superseded it, he was now so far removed from the game that it was no longer his top priority.

"Park right there," Chase said, pointing to the corner in front of a Fish & Chips restaurant that was closed. Then he pointed to another building in the center of the block. "That's the building."

"That tenement?" Rich asked.

"Yeah."

Rich surveyed the six-story apartment building and the rest of the block where they were parked. It was deserted, an unusual occurrence for most Harlem blocks on a summer night. But there were many cars parked on the strip of concrete and tar that was lined with another tenement, brownstones and a large yard connected to the restaurant at the corner on which they were parked.

"These motherfuckers gotta get it," Chase said.

"So, what's poppin'? How it's going down?"

Chase said, "We lay until we see Biz pushin' that white Tahoe. It's gonna park in front of the tenement to pick up that little bastard Pana. By the time they get to this corner, I'ma be out there waitin'."

"Good, 'cause I'm just gonna be here laying to hold you down. That's it!" Rich said, emphatically.

"Right." Chase nodded. "But I need you to cut them off, so they can't drive away. Once they stop, that's when I'm airing the whole truck out."

The plan seemed simple to Rich. "Cool." He pulled out his .45-caliber Glock. He partially cocked it back, checking to make

sure there was a bullet in the chamber.

"Fourteen shots. I know you keep 'em full," Chase said. "Still know how to handle that hammer?"

"You never forget how to protect yourself."

"Shit, you was on offense a whole lot more than defense," said Chase.

Rich was silent, taking in the truth in Chase's statement. Most of the people Rich and Chase had shot or killed were not people who tried to kill them.

"Remember when I came home and you gave me that Smith and Wesson?" Chase asked.

"That nine. Dry sliver, twelve shots."

"I still got that shit," Chase said.

"Get the fuck outta here."

"I'm dead ass. You gave that to me along with a hundred one-hundred-dollar bills. I kept the gun and the C-note that was on top of the stack. Those is souvenirs. They in my basement. The gun is still in the box with both clips."

Rich remembered giving Chase the gun and money as coming home gifts. Fresh after serving five years, Chase had stepped back into the game with a fully loaded gun in his waistband and a pocket full of drug money. As they sat now, waiting to commit the same act that had sent Chase to prison, Rich felt guilty for welcoming Chase back into a life of lawlessness. The life that Rich had left behind, only to be pulled back into it by the man who he reintroduced to the game. Rich stared at the gun in his hand, then Chase, whose eyes were focused ahead of them. *This is karma, for real.*

"It's on, homey," Chase said.

Rich looked up, spotting Biz's white Tahoe.

Chase removed two masks from a bag, handing one to Rich. Then he took out an Uzi from the bag and set it on his lap. He pulled the mask over his head and face. Only his eyes, nose and mouth were visible. He stepped out of the car and ducked into the doorway of an apartment building next to the restaurant.

Rich slipped on his mask, as he started the Taurus. His sweaty palms soaked the glove that clutched the steering wheel. His other hand clutched the Glock. Rich shook his head, as Pana walked out of the tenement and stepped inside the Tahoe. *Fucking kid is sixteen. I'm more than twice his age.*

The Tahoe rolled slowly. Rich tapped his fingers on the wheel, while gripping the Glock, hoping Chase completed the job so his role would remain minimal.

Rich hit the gas, then stopped in the center of the street corner. The Tahoe skidded to a halt a second before the rapid fire of Chase's Uzi provided a soundtrack reminiscent of an old war film. He stepped into the street, riddling the SUV with 9-millimeter bullets. Paint peeled off the white doors and glass shattered from the windows.

"Come on, come on, come on." Rich slowly rocked back and forth, tapping the Glock against his leg. The adrenalin rush that came with crime was back. Then his mind flashed on Vanessa and Candy—the image of them curled up in fear as he walked out the door. He remembered Candy's comment about Dez being killed.

Chase stepped toward the driver's side, firing non-stop into every tinted window of the SUV.

"Oh shit!" Rich jumped out the Taurus when he saw Pana exit the Tahoe on the opposite side of Chase.

Pana fired, hitting Rich. "Motherfucker!" he barked.

Chase dashed around the back of the Tahoe and cut Pana down with six quick shots. "Come on!" Rich screamed to Chase, while looking around the block for witnesses and police.

Chase dumped a few more shots into the Tahoe and ran

over to the car, making it seconds before Rich did. Rich sped off.

A few blocks later, Chase said, "You should let me drive."

Rich looked at his bloody arm. "I told you it's just a graze. It's nothin'."

They rode through Harlem until they made it a couple blocks away from Rich's penthouse. Rich pulled over on the deserted block. He inspected his wound. The graze had torn just enough skin off his bicep to drench a portion of his shirt with blood. Rich tore a piece of the mock neck and wrapped his arm with it. Meanwhile Chase went to the trunk and grabbed an old sweatshirt and gave it to Rich to wear. Rich drove home and stepped out of the car.

"Yo, Rich," Chase said as he leaned his head out the window. He nodded. "Good lookin' out."

Rich nodded back and walked off. He was greeted by the doorman, who welcomed him into his building. Slowly stepping across the waxed marble floor of his immaculate building, he felt awkward. The gun on his waist and the wound on his arm did not fit the image of the building. *This ain't even my style no more.*

CHAPTER TEN
CANDY

Candy and Vanessa had waited up past midnight for Rich, hoping he returned home safely. Their night had been a cycle of crying, laughter and silence. They cried out of fear of the worse happening. They laughed when they joked about the fun experiences they shared with Rich. They were silent when their fears were overpowered by the presence of their circumstances.

The possibility of losing Rich showed Candy how important he had become to her. Her life had begun revolving solely around Vanessa. At work, Vanessa was present. After work, Vanessa and Rich were present. They were her sexual, mental and social support network. Without Rich, Candy's life would be incomplete.

Candy stepped into the living room, where Vanessa was seated Indian style on the couch. Sitting next to Vanessa, Candy gave her a cup of green tea, sweetened with stevia.

"Thank you," Vanessa said in a low tone.

Candy leaned back on the couch and watched the woman she

loved slowly sip from the cup. They both sat silent for minutes. Vanessa set the cup on the coffee table, then stretched out and rested her head on Candy's lap.

Candy began gently rubbing Vanessa's head. Seeing pain in Vanessa's face was almost as hard for Candy to think of as pondering the potential problems Rich faced.

"You believe in life after death?" Vanessa asked.

"Don't talk like that. Please."

"Just speaking my mind."

"Intelligent people like you have a lot more on their minds than that. How about living to the fullest in this life? Now, I believe in that. Let's talk about life."

"It sucks."

"Nothing wrong with a little sucking."

Vanessa laughed. "I want you to promise me something."

"What?" Candy asked.

"That you'll never hurt me like this, like Rich is doing."

"You've got my word." Candy kissed Vanessa's forehead.

The silent period returned, lingering like pollen in spring air. It was soon shattered by the sound of a key in the front door. Before the key could fully turn, Candy and Vanessa had raced to the door and snatched it open.

Rich smiled, as his women ushered him inside to the couch. "The door," he said. "Oh shit." Candy ran and closed the door, locked it, then returned to the couch. Rich peeled out of the sweatshirt Chase had given him.

"Oh my God." Vanessa stared at the bloody remainder of Rich's white mock neck that wrapped his arm.

"It's nothing," Rich said, nonchalantly. He removed the makeshift bandage.

"What happened?" Vanessa probed.

"Stop thinking about the past, baby. Let's focus on the future," Rich said.

Candy sat down beside Rich. She was silent, hoping that the few bits and pieces that came from Rich's mouth were enough for her to piece together the puzzle that Vanessa was trying to solve. Candy had dealt with enough hustlers to understand that the details of what happened in the streets stayed in the streets. But she knew details would not do much to change Rich obviously being shot in the process of retaliating with Chase.

Specifics were not important. What was important was Rich had emerged alive and he did not seem worried about the police coming for him.

"You okay?" Vanessa asked Rich.

"I only got grazed."

"We gotta get you to a hospital," said Vanessa.

"Not if you love me," Rich responded.

"What?" Vanessa was baffled.

Candy looked at Vanessa and said, "Police will come asking questions at the hospital if you have a gunshot wound."

Vanessa went to the bathroom and returned with a first-aid kit. She began cleaning Rich's wound. "Rich, I can't do this again. You don't know what the hell it felt like sitting here all damn night, not knowing if I would get a call from the morgue or the precinct."

"While you was sitting here thinking about me getting killed, I almost got killed," Rich said, visibly upset. "Now I'm home trying to move on, so the last thing I need is you killing me softly with this bullshit."

"Bullshit!" Vanessa screamed. She dropped the first-aid kit. "My love for you is bullshit? Okay." She stomped off onto the terrace.

Candy followed behind Vanessa, stopping next to her. "You know he loves you."

She explained that Rich had just been through something traumatic and he needed the sensitivity of a woman to readjust to the state he was in before he left home and entered a war zone. Candy knew that Vanessa had a sheltered background and had never been involved with a hustler. Candy explained to her the dynamics of the streets that had almost claimed Rich's life. "Ain't no love in these streets, Vanessa. When a man is caught up in all that bullshit, he wants to come home and get everything those streets ain't giving out."

Vanessa folded her arms. "What about us? Huh, Candy? What about what we went through tonight?"

"It's not about us right now."

Vanessa shook her head. "Well, you go tend to him."

"And you're just gonna stay out here, forever, huh?"

"I just need some space," Vanessa said, turning to look over Central Park.

"Okay." Candy walked back into the penthouse and finished patching up Rich, while explaining to him what Vanessa was going through. "You want something to eat?"

"I'm good."

Candy went to the bedroom with Rich and helped him undress.

"Vanessa just don't get it," Rich said, as Candy removed his shoes.

"She'll be okay." Candy looked up into Rich's eyes. "She just needs some time." Candy continued undressing Rich until he was seated on the bed in his boxer shorts. He pulled them off, staring at Candy.

Damn, it's like his dick is growing bigger by the day. Candy stared at Rich's long dick standing tall, through the slot of his underwear. It was finally the first opportunity to have it all to herself. She had been dreaming about this moment before, but she had never acted on her fantasies. There was no explicit rule that she not have sex with Rich alone, but there seemed to be a nonverbal agreement between all three parties. But tonight was different.

Vanessa needed some personal space, while Candy and Rich were in a space of their own.

Candy began undressing. "You've been through enough tonight." She pressed her palm against his firm, bare chest. "Lay down, so I can take care of you," she whispered in her most sexy voice.

"Whatever you say."

Candy crawled on top of Rich and slowly kissed him as his hands roamed over her back and stopped on her butt. She sucked on his neck, slowly working her lips and tongue south until his erection was hers to savor.

"Damn, girl. You serious."

Candy loved when Rich talked to her during sex. It confirmed to her that she was capable of pleasing him. She massaged his balls, while slurping away on his dick.

Rich leaned forward. "Let me hit it from the back."

Candy got on her knees and hands. She felt Rich's powerful hands grip her waist, as he entered her. She moaned. She felt like there was no more room left in her body as he began pulling her back into his strokes. They were in an air conditioned room, but her body was overheating.

"Damn, your shit is tight." Rich worked up a slow rhythm.

Candy gritted her teeth, bouncing her butt backwards to meet Rich's thrusts. He was giving her the satisfaction that no man had before. Just the thought of finally having him to herself made her wet and her nipples hard. She needed him to give her all he had. "Fuck me harder!"

Rich picked up his pace. He began slapping her butt, as he rammed into her harder.

"Yes!" Candy roared like an animal. Rich's smacks heightened the sensation that she felt throughout her body. She felt his hands pull her back and wrap around her breasts. She put her hands on top of his. They were both on their knees, her back to his chest, his mouth pressed to her neck. Her body almost lifting from the mattress as Rich stroked harder and faster.

"Yeah," Rich whispered.

"I feel it all in me." Candy's mouth was wide open, her breath heavy. "Ahh," she screamed like her life depended on it. "Ahh, I'm cumming."

"Me too. Come on."

Yes, yes." Candy's breath slowed, as she and Rich climaxed together. She could still feel his tongue on her neck. She opened her eyes as Vanessa opened the bedroom door. She watched Vanessa frown and walk away.

VANESSA

Vanessa awoke on the couch the following morning. Before she realized that she was in the living room and before she wiped the cold from her eyes, the image of Candy and Rich having sex flashed in her mind. She felt betrayed, double crossed by both of them. In Vanessa's mind, Rich belonged to her. When Candy was around, Rich was hers to love, make love to, laugh with, converse with. And when Rich was not around, Candy belonged to her. The girls nights out, the office freak shows, cuddling under the covers at Vanessa's apartment. It was Vanessa who had the upper hand—the best of both worlds. At least that was the rationale she had on her mind since she spotted Candy and Rich the night before.

Vanessa did not intend for her infatuation to turn into love and her love into a feeling of possession of human life. But she was realizing that her problems were her own. They dated back to the day she chose to experience sex with another woman. Candy's first lick on Vanessa's throbbing clit sparked a pattern of Vanessa withholding the truth of her sexuality from Rich. She now regretted that decision. Back then, she and Rich were in an open relationship. There was only lust and intrigue holding them together. That was the ideal time for her to be truthful. For even after they fell in love, Rich appreciated and accepted her sexuality. But it was that truthfulness that helped nurture, within Vanessa's mind, her deception that she had two separate relationships in which she reigned.

But as she lie on the couch with visions of Candy and Rich flesh-to-flesh on a bed that all three of them had been sharing, reality was apparent. Vanessa and Rich were not a couple and Vanessa and Candy were not lovers. Vanessa, Candy and Rich were a trio that was equally bound by powerful feelings. But Vanessa was still emotionally wounded. She knew the truth, but she couldn't handle it.

Vanessa rose and walked into the bathroom. She brushed her teeth and took a shower. As the hot water cascaded over her soft skin, she heard the bathroom door open. Seconds later, Candy slid the glass shower door open. "What the hell are you doing?" Vanessa barked.

Candy stood naked, with a surprised look on her face. "Come on, now. I'm getting in the shower."

"Not this shower."

"What?" Candy responded.

"Use the other shower. You and Rich." Vanessa closed the shower door. She listened to Candy rant for a few seconds, before she slammed the bathroom door and left. It hurt Vanessa to stop Candy from showering with her. They had showered together nearly every time Candy slept over. Having Candy caress her body with a soapy sponge was one of the most comforting feelings Vanessa had experienced.

After Vanessa showered, she got dressed and prepared some oatmeal, multi-grain toast, soy sausages and a slice of

grapefruit. She bit into her toast, while thinking about Candy and Rich. Just as she was almost done eating, Rich walked into the dining room.

"What's for breakfast?" he asked.

"Whatever you decide to make," Vanessa said, as she slipped the last bite of her soy sausage into her mouth. She stepped into the kitchen and put her plate in the dishwasher. Rich followed behind her. "Still got your panties in a knot, huh?"

Vanessa looked at him with venom in her eyes. "My panties are the last thing you have to worry about."

She stepped out of the kitchen and stormed out the front door.

* * *

Later that day, Vanessa was in the crowded shop working on one of her client's twists. She had been working beside Candy for hours, only speaking to her when absolutely necessary. Vanessa managed to squeeze in some indirect comments about loyalty and trust during the conversations among the women in the shop.

Vanessa had been peeping Candy's reactions to her standoffish demeanor. Vanessa also noticed Candy bow her head in silence once in response to one of the loyalty and trust comments.

Vanessa struggled to maintain her harsh stance, while inside she was hurting as much as Candy. She had never wanted to do anything to Candy other than please her. Hurting her feelings had never been a thought. But that changed the moment Vanessa's feeling were hurt by the sight of Candy and Rich having sex.

"You okay?" Leah asked Candy. "You seem like you been dealing with something all day. You wanna talk about it?"

Vanessa observed silently, as Leah placed her hand on Candy's shoulder.

Candy flashed a cheesy smile. "I'm good Leah. Just thinking."

"You sure?" Leah asked.

Candy nodded, then peeked at Vanessa.

"Hey, Vanessa," Chanel said.

Vanessa turned around to her, spotting Chanel clamping her cell phone onto her hip. "What's up, Chanel?"

"I just heard that young fool Pana who almost killed Chase got murdered last night. Six shots. Biz and his girl got it too. They was all in Biz Tahoe."

"Who was Biz's girl?" Meisha asked.

"Some silly heifer that was riding around with a young fool with a death wish. Damn if I know her," Chanel said.

Vanessa was trying to digest what Chanel said. *Why kill a woman?* She glanced at Candy, who seemed unfazed. Vanessa assumed it had to be Chase who pulled the trigger on the woman. She wanted it to be Chase, or anyone other than the man she loved and shared a bed with. It didn't matter that she watched Rich take a gun from Chase. The war stories that Rich reminisced to her about did not matter. She had heard a lot of things about Rich, but she had rarely witnessed him get angry, so she could not picture him shooting an innocent woman.

"They say who did it?" Candy asked Chanel.

Vanessa looked at Candy. *She must be fishing to see if anyone witnessed Rich do it.* Chanel snickered. "Go figure. Most people love they life more than they do kickin' it to police."

"I ain't seen Chase since Pana got at him," Meisha added.

"Who knows who did it." Candy said.

"But you ain't gotta be a rocket scientist to narrow down the possibilities to the usually suspects," Chanel said.

"We don't need to be speculating," Vanessa said.

"That's right," Candy added. "A lot of people in the Feds for conspiracy based on hearsay. And all that he-say-she-say is not even supposed to be allowed in court."

Chanel looked at Candy. "You right, girl. Let's change the subject."

Vanessa's heart was racing. Candy's talk of conspiracy charges and Federal prison kept replaying in her mind. She knew if Chanel was making assumptions, other people were too. Harlem was small, news traveled fast and bottom feeders were always trying to pull down the big fish on top. That was one of the things Rich had taught Vanessa about the streets. Her hope now was that Rich had not become a victim of the streets he knew all too well. Vanessa's anger with Rich was being replaced by her fear for him. She could be mad at him later, after she was certain he was not destined for a life behind bars. Now, she needed to help him.

RICH

Rich stood on the edge of his balcony, looking over Harlem, as if he were still one of the hustler who reigned supreme over the neighborhood. He was reflecting on the fact that he had flirted with death and his freedom less than twenty-four hours earlier. He was questioning his ability to remove himself from the street life he knew far better than his new life. Chase had showed him how easy it was to be pulled back into the game. But Rich felt his debt was now paid to Chase. There would be no more guilt trips...hopefully.

Rich had not spoken to Chase since the shootout. Under normal circumstances, they would have met up the day after the action to discuss their performance and their next move. But Rich knew these were not normal circumstances. There would be no rehashing the drama or developing new plans. Rich wanted the madness behind him and the future open. His lack of contact with Chase told him that Chase was ready to give him some space, or part ways with him permanently. Strangely, Rich wasn't sure how he felt about that.

He went inside of his living room and flicked on the wide screen TV to CNN, so he could check the financial markets. "NASDAQ is down," he mumbled to himself, watching the ticker float across the bottom of the screen.

Seconds later, Vanessa and Candy stormed through the door. "They said Pana, Biz and his girl got murdered last night, Rich," Candy confessed.

"Chanel was running her damn mouth in the shop," Vanessa said, before recounting the scene, emphasizing how she and Candy stopped Chanel from practically mentioning Rich and Chase as the killers.

Without disclosing any details, Rich assured the women that they had nothing to worry about. "Baby, me and jail don't mix. I can't get no money if I'm sitting in Sing Sing." He grabbed the remote and changed the channel to the local news.

"Did you kill that woman, Rich?" Vanessa asked, looking square into his eyes.

"No," he said, without flinching. "I don't even hit women." Rich didn't like that Chase had killed Biz's girlfriend, but he understood that collateral damage was a part of street wars. "I didn't kill nobody," Rich said.

"Nobody?" Vanessa needed a confirmation.

"Baby, I'd ignore you before I lie to you."

"Look!" Candy pointed at the TV screen. "Turn it up."

Rich turned up the volume. A reporter stood at the crime scene he and Chase had created:

Police say that at approximately one-forty this morning, a triple homicide occurred on One-hundred and Forty-Fifth Street and

Lickin' License

Madison Avenue in Harlem. There are no eye witnesses. Neighbors say they heard multiple gunshots. Police arrived on the scene where the driver of an SUV, thirty-eight-year-old Bismarck Jefferson of Harlem, was found dead from multiple gunshot wounds to the face and head. Twenty-six-year-old Debra Foster of Queens was found shot to death in the passenger seat. The third victim, sixteen-year-old Fernando Jimenez of Harlem, was also found outside of the SUV, dead from multiple gunshot wounds. A gun was recovered from the scene, which police believe belonged to Jimenez. Police have no motives or suspects.

Rich turned down the volume as the reporter vanished from the screen. He noticed Vanessa staring at him in shock. He knew she had never come this close to street drama, so he anticipated her reaction. There was not only surprise covering her face, but also there was a look of disgust. It served as a reminder to Rich how blessed he was to have her in his life. The fact that she was not desensitized to death was something he valued in her. She was a reminder that the life he had left behind was not normal, not to be tolerated.

Vanessa took Rich's hands into hers. "Please tell me you won't get involved with anything like this again."

"You got my word," Rich said. He pulled her close and hugged her, then turned to Candy. "You kind of quiet over there."

"Just observing."

Rich sat on the coffee table, facing both women seated side-by-side on the couch. He took a hand from each of them. He looked at Vanessa. "Baby, without you, I wouldn't know what love is. You taught me how to love and what it feels like to be loved, literally. And I gave you a picture of the pain in my life that nobody walking the face of this earth will ever get a peek at. Turning my back on you is something I couldn't do if I wanted to."

"I love you." Vanessa leaned forward and kissed Rich, then leaned back on the couch.

Rich turned to Candy. "When I asked Vanessa to bring another woman into our bedroom, I told her it would only be a one-time affair that would benefit us both. But I had no idea how important you would become to us in and outside of the bedroom. I would be lying if I told you that I loved you, but I got a feeling in my heart that's damn near as strong."

"You know I feel for you too, Rich," Candy said.

Rich took all of their hands and stacked them together with his. "We got something real special going on here and we can't let our emotions get in the way of that. The three of us pleasing each other is no different than two of us pleasing each other. If I'm not around and y'all get hot and bothered, what they say? One man don't stop the show."

"I see you got jokes," Candy laughed.

"I'm serious as cancer," Rich said. "If you're spending the weekend and Vanessa's not in the mood, you still need the same affection as me."

"I got a confession to make," Vanessa interjected. She looked at Candy, then to Rich. She began telling the truth of how she and Candy had been having an affair and how they fell in love.

Rich smiled. He thought about how comfortable they had been together since their first threesome. Suddenly it all made sense. He wasn't upset with them, just a little upset with himself that he had not detected their affair himself. "I knew you was a freak, Vanessa. That's why I asked you to have the threesome." He laughed.

"Yeah," Vanessa said.

"You didn't know," Candy added, then began mentioning how she felt about Vanessa and how her feelings for Rich were growing.

Rich sat on the couch between the women, sliding his arms over their shoulders, as they huddled beneath him. They each talked and joked about their unique relationship. Rich understood that he had something many men only dreamed of having. But he wondered how long would it last.

CHAPTER ELEVEN
CANDY

andy had been up since 3:00 a.m. and she had torn her bedroom apart during her search. She had invaded every crevice of the large room, but there was no sign of the video of her and Vanessa. It was obvious that Vera had stolen it. She had been in the bedroom the day before she stormed past Vanessa into Candy's office and announced that she wanted out of the relationship she and Candy had developed. Candy now assumed that Vera had probably spent a night watching the video, mustering the gall and anger it took to confront her and announce their relationship was over.

Fuck! Candy flopped down on her bed, wondering if Vera was planning on revealing the tape to someone, if she had not unleashed it already. They were living in an era of celebrity sex tapes and average Janes and Joes trading graphic photos and videos with camera phones. The last thing Candy needed was the video of her and Vanessa to go viral on line. She could withstand the drama, but she doubted that Vanessa could. Vanessa would be crushed and Rich would be vexed. Candy was at risk of losing the two people she cared about most.

Frustrated, Candy pulled out her cell phone and dialed Vera's number. She got her voicemail, so she hung up. She thought about going to Vera's apartment, but she changed her mind. She decided to try contacting her a few more times before tracking her down. Candy knew if she confronted Vera in person, their interaction could become explosive. Risking an altercation that could prevent her from getting the video was not an option for Candy. She would have to humble herself to get what she wanted.

* * *

Candy dug through her office drawers. Since the tape wasn't in her bedroom, maybe, just maybe it was in her office. "Damn, I knew that shit wasn't here," she mumbled, shaking her head and leaning back in her chair. She tried to clear her mind. She had twenty minutes left before it was time to open the shop.

Candy closed her eyes and dozed off. She was awakened by Vanessa tugging on her arm. "Come on, Candy," Vanessa said. "This is not the businesswoman I know."

"I only closed my eyes a minute ago."

"You look like you were out all night clubbing."

All night searching for this damn video. Only if you knew. She looked at her watch. "Anybody out front yet?"

"Everybody's there and clients are already coming in."

Candy stood up and turned toward her bathroom. "I'll be out there in a minute."

"Yeah," Vanessa said, then left the office.

Candy stepped in her bathroom and rinsed her face. She gargled some mouthwash and then walked out and made her way to the front of the shop. Meisha and Leah were working on their clients' hair. Chanel was in her seat, reading an *XXL* magazine.

"Check this shit out," Chanel passed around the *XXL,* pointing out an old picture of Lil Wayne and Baby kissing. "Now y'all tell me that ain't no gay shit. No offense, Candy."

"None taken. I ain't no gay rights activist," Candy said. "But I don't think Lil Wayne and Baby are gay."

"Didn't Baby try to justify that shit, talkin'' ,bout Wayne his son and he love him?" Meisha asked.

"He can try all he want," Chanel said.

"That's not his real son," Leah added. "He ain't got no business kissing him."

Chanel said, "I don't care if he busted the nut that made Lil Wayne. Two grown men lips ain't supposed to be touching under no circumstances."

"You see that's the same year Wayne's wife filed for divorce," Meisha added.

"Go figure," Chanel said.

The conversation made Candy question her sexuality. She had never understood how two men could kiss or have sex. The thought of two hard bodies rubbing together did not add up to her. But she never saw her attraction to women in the same light as gay men. She couldn't fully explain it, but the feminine and sensual nature of a woman made lesbianism seem normal to her. Yet as she watched and listened to the conversation in the shop, she pondered if there truly was a difference. Despite her thinking, she still had a strong urge to be with a woman. The fact that she kept glancing at Vanessa was adding to her desire.

"Vanessa, what you think about Lil Wayne and Baby kissing?" Meisha asked.

"People are allowed to do as they please."

Chanel looked at Vanessa like she was crazy. "Vanessa, I know you ain't justifying no doo-doo chasing?"

"I'm saying I don't care what somebody else does with their body. Another person's sexuality has no bearing on me.

There are a lot more important things to talk about than who's fucking who. Like what are we gonna do to stop global warming or when the hell are they gonna let our troops come home from this war over oil? Better yet, what are we doing about our youth right here in Harlem who feel they have no alternative to make money other than selling drugs? As for Lil Wayne and Baby, we don't even know them and I'm sure they're not talking about us."

Candy was proud of Vanessa. She always had a different perspective than the norm. And it was always laced with enough logic to get her point heard without creating an argument. There was so much Candy had learned from Vanessa, simply by listening to how she viewed life.

"Excuuuse me, Vanessa." Chanel shook her head. "I don't know why I asked your environmentalist ass anything anyway. What you think, Meisha?"

"I won't be surprised if they pop up on a sex tape gettin' it on," said Meisha.

Candy peeked at Vanessa. Her mind was back on their video and Vera stealing it. She pulled out her cell phone and dialed Vera. Voicemail again. She contemplated leaving a message, but she didn't. She needed to hear Vera's voice to gauge how to handle her. She needed to see Vera face-to-face.

* * *

It was ten o'clock that night. Candy was growing impatient. Her shiny red BMW was parked in front of one of the many buildings of Red Hook Housing Projects. It was her third time there and her first time without Vera. On the past two occasions, Candy had simply double-parked and dropped Vera off in front of her building, then peeled off before Vera's high heels hit the sidewalk. Candy had heard enough war stories about the dangers of the projects to know it was a place she wanted nothing to do with.

"Where the fuck is she at?" Candy mumbled to herself. She had called Vera a block before she parked, getting her voicemail again. She had walked up to Vera's building and rang the intercom, but got no response. Assuming Vera was out, Candy hoped she would be home any second.

Candy stared at the group of teens forming in front of Vera's building. *Fuck it.* She got out of her BMW. The click-clack of her Sergio Rossi pumps echoed as she walked the concrete path leading toward Vera's building. Her statuesque figure was hugged by a Prada dress that she had struggled to squeeze into. She could hear the whispers about her, as she got close to the teens in front of Vera's building. She found it amusing, because the baby face boys dressed in jeans and fitted hats looked to be half of her age.

"Let me holler at you, shorty," said a five-foot Latino teen that sported specs and peach fuzz.

"Shorty?" Candy smiled, staring down at the boy.

"Yeah, Mamita. What's good?" He stepped up to her. "Holler at ya boy."

That's just what he is, a boy. "I'm looking for somebody." Candy said.

"I know, Mamita. I'm right here, you heard?"

"You're cute, but you're too young and I like women."

"I like women, too. That's what's up."

"I'm looking for Vera."

"You talkin" ,bout short, dark-skinned Vera? Big ass and tits?" He pointed to the building they were in front of." She live in 3-B."

"Thank you." Candy realized she had rung 3-D earlier. She walked past the other four teens, noticing their eyes track her as she made it to the building lobby. She looked at the silver intercom and pressed 3-B.

"Who is it?" Vera's voiced echoed from the small speaker of the intercom.

"Candy."

"Foul-ass Candy from Harlem?"

"I need to speak to you, Vera."

"No you don't."

"About the video."

"Too late. I got plans for that."

"What?" Candy frowned.

"Goodnight." The intercom clicked off.

Candy screamed Vera's name into the intercom twice. Her slanted eyes were almost shut and her fists were balled tightly. She stormed out of the building.

"Mamita, you all right?" the Latino teen asked as he strolled beside her. "What's poppin'?"

"You live in this building?" Candy asked, still stepping forward with her fists balled.

"Nah. Over there." The youth pointed to a distant building in the projects.

"So, you hustling in front here?"

"Nah, Mamita. And you asking too many questions. What, you writing a book or something?"

Candy stopped and smiled. She liked the youngster's style. "I see you got jokes."

"I don't sell drugs."

"What's your name?"

"Domingo."

"I'm Candy."

"Candy?" The teen smiled and licked his lips. "You know your boy got a sweet tooth."

Candy grinned, giving him a thorough once-over for the first time. He had on at least $1,500 worth of clothes. Pulling down his right earlobe was a huge diamond—a baguette that was more carats than most of the women who entered Candy's Shop could afford. Candy also noticed the imprint of a gun on Domingo's waistline beneath his Gucci shirt. "You may not be selling drugs in front of this building, but I know your little ass is hustling somewhere."

"I get it in any way I can, Mamita. Just not here, you heard?"

"Any way?"

"Just about," Domingo said.

She looked back at the lobby of Vera"s building, then at Domingo. "Let me get your cell number. I think I got a job for you."

VANESSA

Vanessa sat Indian style in bed, typing away on her laptop. She had been in Rich's bedroom working on her novel for eight hours straight. It was her day off and Rich was out of town at a business convention. Candy was in the shower.

Vanessa was proud of herself for completing the first draft of her novel. She was now rewriting it to tighten up, before letting Rich and Candy critique it. She knew they could both help her story with the authenticity of the streets she was writing about. The book, like her experience with Rich and Candy, had started off as street erotica. But as Vanessa began to experience love, her feelings unconsciously affected her writing. Her book was now an urban erotic romance. She was aiming to create a new genre that was a mix of styles of authors Zane, Wahida Clark and Eric Jerome Dickey.

Candy stepped into the bedroom in a robe with a peach-colored towel wrapping her hair. She opened her Louis Vuitton travel bag, which was on the bed. As she began undressing, Vanessa peeked at her, then continued typing.

"You need to give that book a break," said Candy, as she slipped on a tank top. You hear me?"

"I'm drained," Vanessa said.

"You've been writing all day." Candy crawled in bed, moving behind Vanessa until Vanessa's back sunk into her embrace. Candy leaned against the headboard. "Stretch out. You and this half-lotus yoga shit."

Vanessa laughed. She extended her legs and continued typing. Candy's hands began massaging her shoulders and neck. "That feels so good," Vanessa said.

"That's what I'm here for, to make your life easier."

"Sometimes I feel like we're supposed to be sisters."

"We are," Candy said. "Sisters, lovers, friends and anything else that can mean something that's real and shared between women."

"You're right." Vanessa shut her laptop and set it on the nightstand. She closed her eyes and began to savor the soothing feeling of Candy's delicate hands. The pampering put her at peace. It was always like that around Candy, almost too good to be true.

"Why don't you let me do your whole body?"

"You brought your oils?"

Candy pointed to her overnight bag. "Right in the Louie bag." She removed two bottles of oil, then left to heat them up. When she returned, Vanessa was laying nude, faced down on the bed. Candy slapped her butt.

"Stop playing." Vanessa giggled.

"You know you like that shit." Candy sat on top of Vanessa and dripped some of the scented oil down her spine. She began working her upper back, rubbing the oil into her tension spots.

"You're a pro at this, for real. It feels so good."

"I just know what your body needs," Candy responded.

"Let me ask you something serious."

"Go 'head."

"You ever wonder how long we're gonna last? I mean us and Rich? They say fifty percent of marriages end in divorce."

"I wouldn't call this a marriage, but I do wonder sometimes."

"And?"

"I can't predict. I know that I'll do anything I have to in order to make our relationship work. And I won't let anybody come between us."

Vanessa was silent.

"What about you?" Candy asked.

"Sometimes I wonder could I handle losing just one of you. It's crazy, because I don't know if I could even be happy with just one of you in my life. I need you *and* Rich."

"We're a team." Candy smiled.

* * *

Vanessa pulled up in front of Mimi's home. She had not been there in what felt like years. Vanessa had been overwhelmed with working on her book and maintaining her relationship with Candy and Rich. But she had kept in contact with Mimi by phone and e-mail. On occasion, the two had met for lunch. Since Vanessa had some free time, she decided to pay Mimi a surprise visit.

Vanessa stepped out of her Altima and walked up the short staircase on the quiet SOHO block. She rang the doorbell, then looked in Mimi's first floor window. She was shocked to see a tall, dark-skinned man with a bare chest open the window.

"Who you lookin' for?" he asked.

"Mimi. Tell her it's Vanessa."

"One minute."

Vanessa's eyes were still aimed at the window as the mysterious man ducked inside.

"What's up?" Mimi asked, seconds later when she opened

the front door.

"I didn't know you had company," said Vanessa. "I just stopped by to see what you were up to."

As you can see, I'm busy tryin' to get busy." Mimi licked her lips.

"Who is he?"

"He works with me. Been all over me for weeks."

Vanessa's eyebrows rose. "Weeks?"

"I been meaning to tell you, but it's like when we kick it, the convo is always about Rich and Candy."

"Don't sweat it." Vanessa smiled. "We'll talk later. Get back to your company."

Vanessa strolled back over to her Altima and drove away with Mimi on her mind. She felt guilty for pushing her best friend away. They had communicated about every guy they had met since college. Now, Vanessa didn't even know the name of the man who was comfortable enough to answer Mimi's doorbell. She wondered if she would have learned about the mystery man had she not dropped by Mimi's apartment? The relationship Vanessa and Mimi shared had developed through open dialogue. Mimi was an outgoing person who said what came to her mind, and Vanessa always had an open ear. Vanessa was reserved, but comfortable revealing things to Mimi that had been hidden in the depths of her mind. The two women had contrasting personalities that complimented each other. But that cohesion was the result of open communication. Without that, Vanessa knew that she and Mimi had nothing.

Over the years Vanessa's relationship with Mimi had become her life. Her trust in Mimi was so strong that Mimi was the only person who Vanessa revealed the dynamics of her relationship to. Mimi had been the outlet that Vanessa had to express a joy she felt no one else would understand. But after speaking with Mimi minutes earlier, Vanessa realized that she had been spending too much time discussing her relationship. Mimi was tired of hearing her. Although Vanessa didn't get to spend much time with Mimi, the trip to her home taught Vanessa a valuable lesson. She had fallen in love with two companions and she was slowly losing her best friend.

RICH

Rich was driving a blue Audi R8 through Midtown, Manhattan. He had good news for Vanessa He convinced Ted to publish her book early, provided it met the expectations of the company's senior editor. So the book could be on shelves in a few months.

Rich turned on Lennox Avenue and headed Uptown. He parked in front of the shop and stepped inside. He kissed Vanessa then greeted Leah and Candy. The shop was about to close and they were the only people left inside besides Vanessa. He said, "I got an announcement. My baby about to be in it to win it in a hot minute." He explained the news about his conversation with Ted.

"You the man," Vanessa said, then kissed Rich.

"Ladies," he turned to Candy and Leah, "I'm takin' my baby out to celebrate and it wouldn't be right if y'all not in the building."

"Sorry," Leah said. "My husband is taking me to see his parents." She kissed Vanessa on the cheek. "Congratulations."

Rich was happy to see Leah leave. He rarely got the chance to spend time with Vanessa and Candy in public.

There was always an element of apprehension among the trio—a fear that if they were seen together too much, speculation could lead to rumors. Vanessa had expressed that it was the only thing she disliked about their relationship, because she was a free spirit who really did not care what people thought. But she knew that gossip could cause problems for business and disrupt the vibe among the women in the shop. She was also nervous that her relationship being made public could have some negative effect on her book. She knew of countless gay and lesbian authors who were defined by their sexuality instead of their writing skills. Vanessa was certain that her unusual relationship would be far more controversial.

Rich led them out of the shop and into the Audi. "You spending the night?" he asked Candy.

"Yeah."

Rich nodded.

Minutes later they were pulling up to an exclusive eatery in Upper Manhattan. It was a vegan restaurant that was Vanessa's favorite.

Once inside, Vanessa chatted with the maitre d'', who she had known for years. He seated the group at Vanessa's favorite table.

"Thank you," Vanessa said, as Rich pulled out her chair and helped her sit down. He did the same for Candy.

"Such a gentleman," Candy said with a smile. "Who would've known you were once a thug on the streets?"

"First law of survival is self-preservation," said Rich. "You been around and you know how it go down."

"It's sad," Vanessa interjected. "Some of the things people have to deal with on the streets, especially our youth."

"It's a struggle to survive and a struggle to thrive on every level," Rich said. "From the `hood to the Hamptons from the projects to the mansions. Life is a struggle, just different levels and manifestations."

A waiter arrived and handed them each menus. Everyone

at the table ordered, then continued talking until their food was served.

Rich glanced at a woman holding a newborn at the table nearest him. He looked at Candy and Vanessa, thinking about his future with them. They had recently discussed the possibility of having children. Rich wanted a son. Candy and Vanessa wanted daughters.

"See you thinking over there," Candy said. "What's on your mind, baby?"

"Us," Rich responded.

"Oh yeah?" Candy said.

Rich looked at Candy, then Vanessa. "Remember that conversation we had on the terrace the other day?"

"About kids?" Vanessa asked.

Rich nodded.

"What about it?" Candy asked.

Rich explained that he had been giving their conversation some serious thought because the night with Chase had been weighing heavy on his mind. Rich felt if he would have died that night, there would be no one to carry on his legacy. He had been questioning how he would be remembered. Many people in Harlem still saw him as a drug dealer and womanizer. Since it was hard to escape his past, Rich knew it would be easier to produce a reflection of him born into a privileged life he had nearly died to earn.

"I ain't gettin' no younger," Candy said.

Rich looked at Vanessa.

"I'm not ready yet," she said.

"You're about to be a famous author." Rich smiled. "Plus, you need at least another year to finish school."

"Are we ready to let the world know about our relationship?" Vanessa began citing a list of negative things that could come of Candy having a child and their relationship becoming public knowledge.

"I got a solution," Candy said. "We wait until next year. By then, Vanessa will be out of school. I'll have my hair care business up and running, so I can fall back from the shop. "I'll hire two girls to replace me and Vanessa."

"I don't know," Vanessa said. "Let's just wait a minute and see how we feel about this in the future."

Rich was silent. He knew Vanessa had made some valid points about the drama that could come of their three-way relationship being revealed. But he also knew he wanted a son as soon as possible.

***

Back at his penthouse an hour later, Rich's head was propped up on a plush pillow on his bed. He was breathing hard and his toes curled. His eyes opened. He watched Candy as her tongue circled the head of his dick while Vanessa juggled each of his nuts in and out of her mouth. Rich tried to reach out and palm her head, but he couldn't. The overwhelming sensation that filled him was too much to bear. His arms were paralyzed and he hardly had enough strength and energy to curl his toes. Candy began sucking every drop of juice from him. Rich moaned and his body trembled. He could feel the cum flow from his nuts as Vanessa sucked them.

Candy crawled beside Rich and slithered her tongue inside his mouth. He turned to her as their bodies touched, their hands roaming freely. He felt Vanessa's warmth as she wrapped her arms around him and put hickeys on his neck. Her leg slid over his and she slipped her tongue inside his ear.

Candy turned around, reaching back and grabbing Rich's dick, gently rubbing it until it was erect again. "Put it in me," she whispered.

Rich eased his rock hard muscle underneath her yellow butt cheeks and inserted it inside her burning wet flesh.

"Ahhh," Candy whimpered.

Rich wrapped his arm around her as he sucked and licked her neck, slowly shifting in and out of her insides. He could feel Vanessa's tongue all over her neck and back.

Vanessa crawled over and made her way to Candy. She kissed her, sucked on her lips and trailed down to her large breasts, causing Candy to moan uncontrollably.

Rich pumped harder and harder and Candy screamed with each stroke.

Vanessa eased between Candy's legs. She managed to get a few stabs of her tongue on Candy's clit as her body shifted back and forth into ecstasy.

Rich came shortly after. His rapid strokes slowed to a halt.

Vanessa made her way back behind Rich. He turned to her and kissed her, engulfing her in his arms. Candy turned and hugged him from behind, slipping her leg between his. The trio lie entangled in the nude until they fell asleep.

CHAPTER TWELVE
CANDY

andy was seated inside of a McDonald's in Downtown, Brooklyn. She was impatiently awaiting Domingo's arrival after speaking to him hours earlier. She had met with Domingo once after their introduction in Red Hook Projects. She had paid him $1,000 to monitor Vera's movements in and about of her apartment. Candy planned to pay him an additional $1,000 after he helped her with the final stage of her plan for Vera.

Candy's fingers tapped away on the table, as she snacked on some fries. She gazed out the nearby window, waiting for Domingo to make his appearance on Fulton Street. She glanced at her watch. It was 9:40 p.m. When she looked up, Domingo was stepping out of the passenger seat of a burgundy Acura truck. "About time," she mumbled, shaking her head.

Domingo turned his fitted Red Sox hat backwards as the Acura pulled off. He stepped off the curb and looked around at the huge intersection of Fulton Street and Flatbush Extension.

He lived just five minutes away in Red Hook, but he seemed like a tourist in Brooklyn for the first time. He put his hands in his pants pockets and paced into the McDonald's and flopped down at Candy's table. "Hey sweetness." He grinned.

"Candy. My name is Candy."

"Still sweet."

"Your little ass is too much."

Domingo touched her hand. "You ready to get married, Mamita?"

Candy smiled. "What could your young ass do with a woman like me?"

"First thing I'll do is revoke your lickin" license. Then I'll take ya ass for a ride and see what's up with all that junk in ya truck, ya heard?"

"Whatever." Candy laughed, shaking her head. "So what you got for me?"

Domingo knew when she picked up her mail, went food shopping, to and from school plus some other routine trips to destinations Domingo was not sure of.

Candy said, "You're sure about all this?"

"Never doubt the kid, Mamita. Ya boy handle his biz."

Candy took out her BlackBerry. "Run all that by me again." She began typing in days, places and times of Vera's movements. "I'm a be in touch with you," she said, after five minutes of typing. She stood her thick thighs at eye level with Domingo.

"Mamita?"

"What?"

"That's all I get?"

"I'ma be in touch. When the job is done, you'll get the rest of your money."

Domingo sighed. "Not that."

"What?" Candy's eyes squinted.

"I ain't good for a kiss?"

Candy smiled. Then she bent down and pecked Domingo on the lips. She jerked her head back, just as he opened his mouth and his tongue crept out."

"Damn, Mamita." Domingo shook his head. "I ain't know you was no dick teaser."

Candy grinned.

* * *

"Rich is my man and you need to get off his dick!" Vanessa barked at Chanel. Candy stepped from the back of the shop when she heard Vanessa's roar.

Chanel headed for Vanessa. "Ain't nobody on no fucking Rich dick!"

"I know because you inside his dick looking out the hole. I need to go home and give him some pussy so he can nut you out," Vanessa screamed.

Chanel pointed her finger at Vanessa. "Heifer, who the fuck you think you talking to?"

"Hold up, hold up," Leah said as she and Candy jumped in between the two angry women.

Chanel was huffing, her head shaking slowly. "Candy, you don't know. I will hurt that heifer."

No you won't. You'll get your ass beat. "Listen," Candy said. "This shit gotta stop, right now!" She pulled Chanel to the back of the shop.

"You don't even know what happened," Chanel argued.

"I know what Vanessa said about you wanting to fuck Rich is true," said Candy. "I told you before to be easy."

"That's how it's going down, huh?" Chanel asked.

"Business over bullshit. I told you," Candy said, emphatically. "Just leave her alone."

Chanel was silent for a few seconds, staring into Candy's eyes. "Whatever." She walked off.

Candy began breathing slowly, calming herself. She wanted to do nothing more at that moment than hurt Chanel. Chanel was unaware, but Candy had drawn a line a while ago. Candy's top priority was the well-being of the three-person immediate family of which she was a part. The women at the shop had become extended family.

Candy walked back to the front of the shop. "You okay?" she asked Vanessa, who was sitting and talking to Leah.

"Chanel was outta control," Leah said.

"I tried to talk to her before about Rich like you said, Leah." Vanessa frowned. "She said I was paranoid."

"Exactly what happened?" Candy asked.

Leah explained that they were the last ones in the shop and were talking about men being unfaithful. Chanel made a few snide comments about men manipulating women who were not street smart. Vanessa ignored her, but then Chanel looked at her and said, "These heifers will go for anything 'cause they never had a real man."

"That's when I had to say something," Vanessa interjected.

"I never seen you so mad," Candy said.

"You seen that vein poppin' out her head?" Leah joked.

"I don't like her and I don't trust her," Vanessa said.

"Don't sweat it," said Candy. "I just spoke to her."

"Yeah, you got bigger things to focus on," Leah said, picking up a copy of Vanessa's recently published book *Ghetto Love.*

"You're right. My first book signing is coming up next week."

"Yeah, girl. Focus on that." Leah said.

Candy was focusing on Chanel. She was fed up with Chanel's games and she knew she would eventually have to be more forceful if she really wanted to stop the drama between Chanel and Vanessa from escalating.

VANESSA

Vanessa was inside a small bookstore in the Fort Green section of Brooklyn. She was seated behind a long table with copies of her books stacked on each side of her. She sipped on a cup of green tea after signing her fifth book for the night.

I'm finally where I need to be. She stared at a huge poster of her book cover. Ghetto Love had been promoted online and she had received good reviews in *Essence* magazine and *The Village Voice* newspaper. She had been in the book store for a few hours as people wandered over to her, seldomly purchasing books. The book had been out for two weeks and she did not know how much it had sold. Judging from the sales at the signing, it would be some time before she became a best-selling author. But she was still happy to finally have her first book in print.

A 30-something woman with mocha skin and a bright smile walked up and purchased a book. "Can you autograph it, please?" she asked.

Vanessa smiled. "Sure."

"It's for my partner, Denise."

Partner? As Vanessa signed the book, the word "partner" was stuck in her ear like wax. She had heard the term used by gay and lesbian people, but she never considered Candy her partner.

"Thank you," the woman said. "She's gonna love it."

"I'm sure she will. Thank you." Vanessa noticed the woman's curvaceous figure as she walked away. Then she took in the sway of her hips. *She's definitely sexy.*

Vanessa didn't usually see women how she saw Candy. But if she knew a woman was gay, her lustful tendencies kicked in. It was some type of psychological glitch in her mind. It made sense because sex was mental for Vanessa. It was the mental intrigue of sex with a woman that had attracted her to Candy.

Another customer stepped up to the table. He was about Vanessa's s age and dressed in a preppy outfit with loafers and a cardigan. "How are you?" he asked.

"So far, so good."

"I read the book review in *The Village Voice.*" He nodded. "Sounded interesting, so here I am."

"What was it in particular that interested you?"

"There was something about trust, and how when trust is broken it can't be restored."

"Only if there is genuine love. That's one of the major themes in my book."

"Exactly. That's what it was. One of your characters grapples with being betrayed by his first love."

"You'll see. It's a very touching story."

The man paid for his book. "Thanks." He walked away, then doubled back. "What inspired you to write this book?"

"Life and love."

"Interesting.

As the man strolled off, Vera walked up from behind Vanessa. Vanessa immediately thought of the nasty look Vera had given her in the doorway of Candy's office. It was the last time Vanessa had seen Vera.

"Vanessa," Vera said. "I'll take one." She paid for the book and Vanessa remained silent. "I'd appreciate it if you signed it 'To Vera.' And for the record, I'm not your enemy. I actually came down here to warn you about Candy."

"Oh yeah?"

"Come on, Vanessa. I'm far from stupid and my vision is twenty-twenty."

"What's that supposed to mean?"

Vera looked around, then pulled her phone from her handbag. She flashed the screen at Vanessa.

Fuck! Vanessa's eyes expanded at the sight of a video of Candy eating her out. She knew immediately that it was their first tryst.

"There's a lot you need to know about who you're dealing with," Vera said. "It's much deeper than her making videos." Vera pulled a card from her pocket and handed it to Vanessa. "When you're ready to talk, you can find me here."

Vanessa was in shock. Visions of the video flooded her mind. She didn't even see Vera walk off. Everything about her relationship with Candy was spinning through her head so fast that she felt dizzy. Betrayal, mistrust, hurt were just a few of the emotions that were too many to number or name completely. It made no sense to Vanessa. Why would a person who loved and protected her undermine her? Vanessa realized the video was old—before her infatuation with Candy elevated to love. Still, that meant their love was rooted in a lie. There was no telling what else may be in play. How many other videos existed and who had them? But Vanessa knew who could tell her.

* * *

After the book signing, Vanessa drove straight to Red Hook. She walked into Vera's apartment. It was a small, nicely furnished home, scented by candles.

"I'm glad you came." Vera grabbed Vanessa's hand and pulled her inside. She locked the door and led Vanessa over to a sectional couch in front of a 50-inch flat screen television. "I take it you wasn't too comfortable seeing that video."

"I didn't know it existed. Did she give that to you?"

"Watch it first, then we'll talk." Vera turned on the television. In seconds, a wide screen display of Vanessa and Candy was playing. Vera stepped out of the room.

Vanessa was in awe. Her face was clearly visible on the

video. Then Candy kissed her. She remembered the unusually good feeling of her first kiss from a woman. It was like Vanessa was experiencing her first time with a woman all over again. Candy went lower, stimulating Vanessa's breasts, navel, pussy and ass. Vanessa shifted her legs on Vera's couch, becoming aroused. She never knew what her own ecstasy-fueled face looked like. She had never seen a tape of herself doing anything. Now she was watching herself cum on camera.

The tape paused.

Vanessa looked up, spotting Vera's luscious naked body waltzing toward her with a remote in her hand. Vanessa leaned back. She didn't know what to say or do as Vera sat beside her and set down the remote. Vera pulled Vanessa's hand on her soft bare breasts. Vanessa jumped up and stepped away. She was fighting the lust running through her overheating body. "This is not gonna happen."

"You sure?" asked Vera.

"Yeah."

Vera sucked her teeth. "Candy got you open like a research monkey." Vera stood and approached Vanessa, backing her into a corner. "She forced her tongue into Vanessa's mouth."

She tastes so good. Vanessa shook her face free, breathing heavy.

Vera said, "If you don't want that video on YouTube, I suggest you be a good girl. Let me please you."

Vanessa felt her world crumbling. All she had done with Rich and Candy to keep their relationship quiet could be compromised by one video of her and Candy.

Vera began unbuttoning Vanessa's blouse. "I wanted you ever since I first saw you on that video."

Fuck, Vanessa thought. She wanted to cry. But that changed when she felt Vera sucking her nipples and slipping

her hand between her legs. Vanessa instinctively pulled down her pants. "Ahh," she purred, as her insides were fingered.

Vera came up, easing her tongue back into Vanessa's mouth. They kissed passionately like old lovers. Vanessa felt Vera push her downward. Soon Vanessa's tongue was inside Vera. Her body was sweaty. The taste soaked into Vanessa's tongue each time she licked Vera's clit. She could feel one of Vera's thick calves wrapped around her neck, followed by Vera's hand cupping her head. Vera's grip was forceful, yet delicate, a comfort Vanessa enjoyed. Fingers roamed through her 'fro.

"I'm cumming," Vera yelled, as her body shook into submission.

As Vera loosened her grip on Vanessa, the reality of Vanessa's bittersweet predicament set in. She felt used. Used by Candy. Used by Vera. She felt dirty and cheap. And she still felt guilty for cheating on Rich. She realized that if she had been faithful to him in the first place, she wouldn't be in her current situation.

Vera licked her lips. "I see why Candy fuckin' you"

"Can I have that video now?"

"Not yet. You still owe me a few more sessions." Vera laughed.

"What? You trying to blackmail me?"

"I'm trying to show you a good time. Besides, I got copies of that video everywhere. If you really want one, I'll e-mail it to you," Vera snapped.

I'm fucked. Vanessa was trying to think of some strategy to solve her problem. But she felt helpless, stuck under Vera's control. Perhaps once Vera grew tired of her, she would free Vanessa from the shackles of the video.

"I suggest you keep this between us," Vera said.

"Is that the only video that you have of me and Candy?"

"Yup, but I can't speak for Candy. There's no telling how many times she got you on tape."

Vanessa wondered if there were other videos of her and Candy? Were there videos of their threesomes with Rich? She could hardly believe that Candy had actually recorded their most intimate moments. She decided the best way to find out about Candy's secretive actions was through Vera. "Why do you think she taped us?" Vanessa asked.

"She's a freak and she's slick. Take your pick."

"What else can you tell me about Candy that I don't know?"

RICH

Hours later, Rich was lying on the couch on his balcony. He was reading the business plan Candy had given him for her proposed hair care company. From the corner of his eye he noticed Vanessa walk onto the balcony. "What's up, baby?"

Vanessa bent down and kissed him, then laid down on the couch beside him. She rested her head on his chest.

"It's kind of late," Rich asked. "How'd the book signing turn out?"

"Not too good. I went by Mimi's afterwards. How 'bout you? What are you reading?"

"Just going over Candy's business plan." Rich tossed it on the end table.

"Exactly how long have you known Candy?" Vanessa asked.

"I think I was about fourteen when I met her, so we talking almost twenty-one years."

"Long time."

"Yeah. Candy was always a thinker, calculated. She had a lot of hustlers throwing money at her over the years."

"You love her?"

"I'm fallin'."

"Sometimes I question how much I can take from her or you."

"Example."

"You cheating on me. Candy betraying me somehow. How much could you take?"

"I would give y'all a second chance. You can get over once, but twice is a wrap. Rich was mouthing what he *felt* made sense. It was a good theory, but he didn't know how practical it was. Certain violations could not be tolerated even once. But that was in a normal relationship. Rich had something unique going with Candy and Vanessa—a blessing that was hard to come by. There was really no telling how much he would tolerate to keep two beautiful women who cared about him under his roof.

Rich and Vanessa talked for about an hour, discussing issues of trust and love. Rich was still finding his way through experience. Trust and love were new concepts he had never anticipated having to deal with before he met Vanessa.

"Rich," Vanessa said, gazing into his eyes. "You know I trust you like I trust myself, right?"

"I wanna hope so."

"Promise me that you won't ever break that trust."

"You got my word. But where is all this coming from?"

"My book signing. I had a conversation with a guy who bought the book."

"Oh yeah?"

"He was moved that my book deals with issues of trust and love and stuff."

"I got you." Rich held Vanessa tighter, realizing how fragile she was. He would never do anything that would crush her.

Vanessa and Candy were all he needed and all he wanted.

CHAPTER THIRTEEN
CANDY

A couple of weeks after Candy met with Domingo, she was watching him step out of a Lexus GS400 in the same place he had exited the Acura truck on the corner of Fulton Street and Flatbush Extension. Once again, he looked around like an awestruck tourist in Times Square. Then he walked inside the McDonald's.

"Hey, Mamita." He leaned down to kiss Candy.

She quickly flipped up her hand between their faces as his lips almost met hers. "I see you're horny *and* persistent."

"You really want something that's hard to get, you gotta go harder." He adjusted his gold-framed Gucci specs.

Candy snickered. "I meant to ask you something last time."

"You don't have to ask me. Of course, you can have my baby." Domingo smiled.

"For real. Why when you get out a car, you always look around like you lost or something?"

"Same reason I never leave home without a gun and a

condom."

Candy shrugged her shoulders. "What's that supposed to mean?"

"Dudes is grimey and you can't trust hos. This ain't Harlem, Mamita. They respect the hustle up there. In Brooklyn, every ten steps you take, you gotta look over your shoulder. There's always some grimey bastard tryin" to rob you, or some ho trying to set you up."

"Thanks for the warning."

"It's gonna cost you an extra kiss." Domingo grinned.

"I'm gonna do your horny little ass a favor and hook you up with one of the young girls that come in my shop."

Domingo's eyes squinted. "Shop?"

"I own a beauty salon."

"Say it ain't so, Mamita."

"On Lennox. Right in the middle of Harlem."

Domingo gasped, shaking his head. "You work in a room full of pussy all day and you just telling me about it? Instead of sharing, you want all the chocha for yourself."

Candy laughed. "I got you. Now let's handle this business." She looked at her watch."It's ten to eight. Vera should be gone from eight to nine, right?"

"Si, Mamita."

"You ready to do this?"

"What's that? A joke? Ya boy always ready."

Candy smiled. "That's what I want to hear."

"But I told you, we gotta be careful. Vera crazy-ass brothers be ridin" around the PJs in this old Taurus. I don't wanna have to gun nobody down 'cause you got us spotted."

"Just come on," Candy said, grabbing Domingo's hand and standing. They exited McDonald's and hopped into Candy's BMW. Domingo couldn't take his eye off the car since he first got a glance of it. "I see you like this M-Three," Candy said.

"The first time I saw you in it in front of my PJs, I was gonna jack you."

"Oh yeah?" Candy sucked her teeth. "What stopped you?"

"You stepped out in those high heels with them tig old bitties with that big old ass. I been in love ever since."

Candy shook her head, grinning. "You got a smart mouth."

"Better that than a stupid one, right?"

Candy laughed to herself. She enjoyed Domingo's charisma. She parked at the end of his block and he told her to stay put. He was going to make sure Vera was not home. If she wasn't, he would break in, then call Candy. She nodded as he spoke. The plan sounded logical.

"I'm a have a hot bath and some scented candles waiting for you with a little R. Kelly in the background, okay?" Domingo licked his lips and smiled.

"Get your horny ass out my car." Candy watched Domingo bop up the block and go inside Vera's building. Five minutes later, he called her and told her it was safe to come. Minutes later, she was lugging her Louis Vuitton knapsack into Vera's apartment as Domingo opened the door.

"Welcome to the Plaza Hotel." He waved his arm with a smile, like a proud doorman. Domingo closed the door when Candy stepped past him. "Don't touch shit," he barked.

Candy froze. "What?"

"I don't know if a pretty thing like you can last behind bars." He tossed her some rubber gloves. "Plus, you can't have my baby if you playing Spades in a cell on Rikers Island. You might like pussy, but them butches in them cellblocks is vicious."

"Thanks." Candy realized how her eagerness had almost jeopardized her freedom.

"What we looking for?"

"Anything that can play a video. Computer, disks, flash drive, phone, iPod, whatever," Candy said."

They began invading every crevice of the apartment. Candy started with the living room. Domingo searched the bedroom. Candy picked up a stack of DVDs and dumped them into her knapsack. They all had movie labels, but she wanted to make sure she didn"t leave behind the video because it was disguised.

Domingo stepped back into the living room and handed Candy a laptop and some flash drives. "Hold on." He raced back into the bedroom and returned with a hard drive and some CD ROMs. He stuffed them into the knapsack.

Candy went into the bedroom to make sure Domingo didn"t leave anything behind. She trekked through piles of strewn clothes and scattered papers. Domingo had hit the room like a tornado. She scanned the area for a few seconds. *What the hell?* She picked up a copy of Vanessa's book. "To Vera, From Vanessa Denay" was signed on the first page. Next to the book was one of Venessa's beaded bracelets.

Candy was convinced that Vanessa was having an affair with Vera. *Why else would she autograph a book and leave her bracelets here? She only takes her bracelets off before we make love.* Candy rationalized that they probably had been involved since shortly after Vera saw the video then broke up with her. She recalled the time that Vanessa had asked about Vera's sexual performance. *She probably wanted both me and Vera from the day she saw us together.*

Candy finished searching the bedroom, then she ransacked the bathroom and kitchen. The thought of Vanessa and Vera having sex pushed Candy to focus more on destroying the apartment than finding videos.

Candy was huffing and puffing when she walked back into the living room with Domingo. She pulled out ten crisp $100 bills from her pocket and handed them to him.

"I like your style, Mamita." Domingo nodded. "We can do

business anytime."

Candy hurled the knapsack over her shoulder. Then she handed Domingo a card. "Come by my shop so I can hook you up with a PYT like I promised."

"She gotta look like you or this ain't gonna work, Mamita." Domingo grabbed his dick through his True Religion jeans. "I'm a tits and ass man."

Candy blushed. "I like your little horny ass."

VANESSA

Vanessa and Mimi were sitting on a bench in Central Park after eating lunch at Tavern on the Green. For nearly the entire lunch break, Vanessa had been explaining everything that happened between her and Vera. She mentioned that Vera said she broke up with Candy because of her infidelity and she was physically abusive. Vera swore that Candy had manipulated her into becoming a lesbian after she became Candy's client.
Vera claimed to have been young and naive.

Vanessa told Mimi that she was careful not to show any signs to Candy that she was aware of the video. She mentioned probing Rich indirectly about Candy's background, but not finding anything. But, she thought it was interesting that Rich said Candy had always been a "calculated" person. That word seemed to fit with Vera's depiction of Candy being a predator that used her shop to hunt new prey. It also explained how she made sure that she had a camera set up during the first time they had sex.

"You wanna know what I think?" Mimi asked.

"Of course."

"You're caught up. Out of your league."

"What? You don't understand."

"And you do?" Mimi chuckled. *"You* came to *me* with this."

"I know, but—"

Mimi cut her off in mid-sentence. "You're in a relationship with a guy who had half of Harlem on lock and a chick who turned you out on tape. Now you gettin' blackmailed into eating pussy by some other chick who fell victim."

Vanessa wanted to admit that she was in love, but Mimi wouldn't understand. She would need to have experienced the harmony that existed within Vanessa's household. She needed to know that Rich cried on her shoulder and chose Vanessa as the person to confess that he was repeatedly molested as a child. She needed to see the light that resonated from Candy's eyes when they gazed at each other before kissing. Vanessa knew that Mimi could not comprehend the language that vibrated from three hearts so in-tune that their beats were synchronized. It was all of these-things that kept Vanessa focused on making her relationship work, in spite of the video. But she needed to understand the circumstances that preceded the video.

"Why don't you just ask Candy about the video?"

"Then I run the risk of her confronting Vera and the video viewing public."

"How you know Vera didn't make the damn video?"

"Vera?"

"She could've been spying on Candy, for all you know."

"I never thought of that."

Mimi shook her head and huffed. "I'm a keep it a hundred, Nessa." She took a deep breath. "You need to really reevaluate where you at and where you planning on going. Because right now, you in some real soap opera shit that could fuck your whole life up."

* * *

Vanessa walked into the shop after speaking with Mimi. She was strongly considering the possibility that Vera had made the video. She planned to question her about it the next time they hooked up. It would be the third time and Vanessa was feeling guiltier each time she thought of being intimate with Vera.

Vanessa greeted Chanel, though it hurt her to humble herself for the sake of the shop. Chanel had not said anything out of line lately and Vanessa didn't want to say or do anything to spark ant friction.

As the time passed, the shop filled with clients. A rap video flashed on one of the televisions as the music of 106 & Park blared from the speakers. Vanessa was talking to Candy, when she turned to the front door.

"Domingo." Candy's eyes lit up.

Everyone in the shop seemed to watch the short teen as he made his presence known and turned his fitted Yankees cap backwards. He unzipped his butter-soft leather jacket.

"Mamita, what's good?" Domingo smiled.

Candy bent down and hugged him.

"You wanna feel me in your arms but no kiss, right?" Domingo shook his head. "That's some bullshit."

Candy laughed and introduced Domingo to everybody in the shop. Domingo pointed at Leah, then turned back to Candy. "Now this is the real, Mamita. You fugazy." Domingo turned back to Leah, finding her laughing. "What's good, Mamita? Como te llama?"

"Me llamo Leah."

Domingo nodded. He looked Leah over with a sneaky grin.

"She's married," Candy said. "Not to mention too old for you."

He turned to Vanessa. "How you doing, my soul sister?" Vanessa giggled.

Chanel said, "You don't wanna mess with her, shorty. Her man run Harlem."

Domingo shook his head. "He can have Harlem, but he better have a pass when he cross that bridge, ,cause I rep BK to the fullest, ya heard?"

"Where you from in Brooklyn?" Chanel probed.

"I'm from Red Hook, ya heard?" He walked over to Chanel, sizing her up. "I know I seen you in my 'hood too. I don't forget faces."

"I'm from the East."

"That's what's up. East New York in the building," Domingo said. "Since we got this BK thing poppin', we might as well see what else we got in common."

Chanel grinned. "Tell you what. If you makin' six figures in six years, then you can get down with the Chanel Legacy."

Domingo turned to Candy. "Give me some of what Chanel sniffin". Shit, six years and six figures later, she'll be waving at me when I"m walkin' the red carpet with Zoe Saldana."

Everyone in the shop laughed.

"He's cute," Chanel said.

"No, baby. Puppies are cute. Domingo is the flyest motherfucka in Red Hook."

Candy watched Domingo and Chanel go at it with a humorous war of words. She could see the women in the shop falling in love with Domingo. Even Chanel liked his style. Hours drifted by until it was almost closing time. Domingo was still hanging out. Chanel had introduced him to one her clients, a girl two years older than him.

Rich walked into the shop and greeted the women and kissed Vanessa.

"So that's ol" boy, huh?" Domingo asked Candy.

Rich turned toward him.

"Chanel told me you run Harlem," said Domingo.

"She say whatever come to her mind," Rich responded. "She don't know no better."

Domingo's eyes landed on Candy as he nodded. "Smart man.

I like him already."

"Rich, that's Domingo, my little homie from Red Hook," Candy said.

Red Hook. The name of the neighborhood had bypassed Vanessa's ears when Domingo first said it to Chanel earlier. But now she wondered if Domingo knew Vera. But it wouldn't have meant much to Vanessa anyway. She needed the scoop on Candy.

RICH

About an hour later, Rich was inside of his penthouse office. He ran his hand over his cornrows, sitting in the swivel chair behind his desk. He was facing the screen of his computer. Rich had been downloading some new Beanie Sigel tracks from iTunes, when he decided to browse You Tube. "Author Vanessa Denay Gets Freaky," he read the title of a video after clicking on a link His heart sunk into his chest. He slammed his hand on his desk and sighed. "Vanessa, Candy, come here!" he yelled.

"What's up, baby?" Vanessa asked, as Candy trailed her inside of Rich's office.

"Y'all come check this out." He pointed at the computer screen.

Vanessa and Candy stepped behind the desk. There was silence, both of their eyes glued to the screen.

Rich turned around, watching the women staring in awe. "We can't all talk together, but somebody lips gotta start moving. Matter of fact, it's plenty of room on this desk for both of y'all."

Candy and Vanessa sat on the desk and faced Rich. They turned to each other. Tears trickled from Vanessa's eyes.

"Why, Candy?" Vanessa cried. "Why did you do this? You videotaped the first time we had sex and you never told me.

Then you had the nerve to give it to Vera? Why?"

"She stole the video," Candy pled.

"I trusted you. Why?"

"You really wanna know the truth?" Candy replied.

"I'm not sure anymore if you're even capable of telling the truth."

"First, you tell me why you sleeping with Vera."

"Sleeping with Vera?" Vanessa's flood gates opened and tears flowed down her face.

"Yeah, I know you and Vera gettin' y'all freak on."

"Hold on, hold, hold on," Rich said. "We got a whole lot of talking going on, but nobody ain't saying nothing. Candy, why the fuck you tape Vanessa? And how this shit get on the Internet?"

"I wanted . . . her . . . soooo bad," Candy said, pausing between her words. She explained how the scheme developed. She admitted that Vera had discovered the video and stolen it. She also explained how she ransacked Vera's apartment in search of the video. She mentioned finding the video on Vera's hard drive, but that Vera must have had other copies. Candy was sure that tossing Vera's apartment caused her to post the video on YouTube. "So I was in her crib, trying to fix what I fucked up. That's how I know you were in there too. You left your beads and you signed one of your books and gave it to her."

Vanessa sniffled, trying to wipe away her tears, but the emotional flow continued. "She forced me. She said if I didn't have sex with her, she would put the video on the Internet. I only slept with her three times." She paused. "I'm sorry."

Rich noticed that Candy had begun sobbing too. He got up and embraced her and Vanessa in a group hug. The room fell silent, except for the sniffling.

Rich felt that their relationship would never be the same.

Trust had been broken and the fears they had about their personal lives becoming public would soon be a reality. As he hugged Vanessa and Candy, he knew the three of them would need to be stronger than they had ever been to withstand the drama set to unfold because of the video.

Vanessa stepped back.

You all right, baby?" Rich asked.

Vanessa pointed at Candy. "This is your fucking fault! You shouldn't have made that damn tape." She bolted from the room.

Rich turned to Candy. Her face was covered in tears.

"I didn't mean for this to happen," Candy mumbled.

"I know you didn't, but it did. Now we got a whole lot of bullshit to deal with."

CHAPTER FOURTEEN
CANDY

T hings had changed drastically for Candy since weeks earlier when the video was posted online. Vanessa had been living in her own apartment for a week. Guilt overwhelmed Candy each time she remembered Vanessa telling Rich, "I'm not setting foot in this penthouse if Candy is here!" Candy pled with Vanessa to come back, but she gave up after Rich insisted that Vanessa needed some time and space. Candy had been sleeping with Rich in his penthouse on some days, while Rich often spent other nights with Vanessa at her apartment. Candy thanked Rich for forgiving her and trying to bridge the gap she had created between her and Vanessa. Rich had been a go-between, relaying the thoughts of each woman to the other.

Vanessa was adamant that she loved Candy, but she was too hurt to function in a relationship with her. She felt that Candy had taken advantage of her.

Rich had reminded Vanessa that although Candy had violated her, it took place long before the two of them had fallen in love. Vanessa understood that, but she was still left with a wound that had not healed.

Candy was pleased that there had been no backlash from the video yet. She contacted YouTube file a formal a complaint and had the video removed from the website. But another site posted the video and refused to take it down at Candy's request. Interestingly, no one in the shop had hinted about hearing of the video or seeing it. The shop was business as usual, except for the tension that lingered between Candy and Vanessa. But it was undetectable to the other women in the shop. Yet Candy knew that it was only a matter of time before the gossip began. Her hope was that it didn't destroy the delicate thread that was holding together her relationship.

Candy was curled in the fetal position in her bed with Rich clutching her from behind. They had been discussing their relationship for over an hour.

"How would you feel if you was in Vanessa's shoes?" Rich asked.

"Fucked up."

"Exactly. She still loves you, though. I can see it in her eyes when I talk to her about you."

"Feels like she's ready to kill me when we're down at the shop."

"She's hurtin'."

"It's hard to fix what I fucked up."

"Tell me about it."

"But it really don't matter if it's hard. Let's just hope it can be fixed.

* * *

The following night, Candy sat in a BMW X6 with Rich behind the wheel. They were parked in front of Vanessa's apartment. Rich had convinced Candy to come with him to see her and allow him to mediate a resolution to their problem. Candy was nervous because it would be the first time she saw Vanessa outside the shop since she left the penthouse. Candy was uncertain if Vanessa would hold her tongue like she had been doing at work. But Candy was willing to accept the repercussions of her actions. She was prepared to do whatever was necessary to restore the life she had come to love.

Candy held Rich's hand. She took a deep breath and exhaled. "I'm ready."

They stepped out of the car and walked up to the building. Rich inserted his key into the door, and then led Candy through a narrow hallway. He stopped in front of Vanessa's door. "Hold on." Candy closed her eyes and gripped Rich's hand firmly.

"Everything's gonna be all right," Rich said, then inserted his key into the door and stepped inside.

"Oh my God!" Candy whispered as they entered the living room. She stared at Vanessa sitting Indian style on the couch with a box of Kleenex tissues in her lap. Her watery eyes were puffy and red. Candy rushed over and hugged her.

"Get the fuck off me!" Vanessa barked. "These tears are your fault."

"No, no, I love you."

Vanessa screamed again before struggling free. She backed away from Candy. Her eyes glared at Candy. "Rich, get her out of here, now!"

Candy began crying as Rich stepped over to Vanessa. "Baby, we can't keep going through this and you know it," Rich said. "I go home to her, she's crying. I come over here, you're crying. I'm just trying to wash away the tears."

Vanessa turned to Rich, then slowly to Candy.

Candy looked square into Vanessa's eyes for the first time that night. She could see the pain—a pain that she had never seen before. Candy wanted to speak. She wanted to say so much, but she didn't know how. She didn't know what to say. What words were

capable of erasing the pain? For over a minute, their eyes were steady. Candy mustered the heart to say what she thought was the most important thing. "I love you, Vanessa. I love you."

Vanessa fidgeted, sniffling while her eyes teared. She seemed to be stuck in a zone. She slowly stepped toward Candy, walked past her and opened the door.

More tears ran from Candy's face. She turned to Rich. "I tried," she mumbled, then walked out of Vanessa's apartment.

* * *

Candy had cried herself to sleep the night she left Vanessa's apartment. She had never known that Vanessa was capable of being so cold. But Candy understood the root of Vanessa's actions. She realized the severity of her situation, how deep the wound that she caused Vanessa was. She saw it in Vanessa's stillness, the extended period in which they gazed into each other's souls. A mere glance would have signaled that Candy was not worth her time. But Vanessa's drawn out stare meant she saw something within Candy worth holding onto. At least that was Candy's interpretation of their face-off.

It was almost time to open the shop, as Candy sat inside of her office. She was gazing at the wall that Vanessa's back was pinned against during their introduction to each other's bodies. It was the wall now serving as the videotaped backdrop to Candy's downfall.

Candy snapped out of her daze. She stood and walked toward the door of her office. As she opened it, she heard Chanel's voice.

"You motherfuckin' fuck tape freak," Chanel barked. In a blur she was stomping toward Vanessa. Candy charged out of her office, grabbing Chanel by the throat and ramming her head into a locker. "Don't you ever fuckin' disrespect her!"

Candy squeezed her throat tighter. "You'll end up in a casket and I'll be in a cell." She slammed the back of Chanel's head against the locker a second time then let her go.

Chanel grabbed her throat and gasped for air as Candy

stepped off. Leah and Meisha had just run to the scene. They stood silently as Chanel leaned against the locker. She was clearly embarrassed and scared. Her short thick frame possessed merely half the physical power of Candy's towering body.

Candy's heart jumped when she spotted Vanessa crying. She wiped her tears away and hugged her. She turned to Chanel and the other women, one of her arms still embracing Vanessa. "Y'all knew me for a long time. Y'all supported me through mad drama. Y'all know I'm open with my sexuality. We joke about it all the time in the shop. How me and Vanessa fell in love and how that video ended up on the Internet is a long story. It's a longer story when you add that we share the same bed with Rich."

"You jokin', right?" Meisha asked.

"She's not," Vanessa said. She looked at Candy, then back at their audience. "It's not a normal relationship, but it's a loving relationship. I just ask that it not be disrespected."

VANESSA

Vanessa was still coming to terms with the reality that she had just expressed the truth about her relationship to the women in the shop. Surprisingly, she felt liberated. There was a satisfying power that resulted from releasing knowledge of the thing that had brought her so much joy, but that she kept bottled up out of fear that it would cause her pain.

"Listen, girl," Meisha said. "Like I told Candy a million times, 'You can lick who you want, as long as it ain't me.'"

Vanessa laughed.

"And Candy, I need to get this straight, no pun intended," Meisha giggled. "You telling me you go both ways?"

"Like the FDR Drive," said Candy.

Meisha shook her head. "Vanessa transformed Rich from a hustlin' ho, and Rich done got Candy messing with men again. Y'all some bad motherfuckers."

"Only in Candy's Shop is this possible," Leah said with a smile.

Vanessa was pleased that things were turning out better than she thought. She was comfortable with the jokes. She had no problem with comedy because it was the nature of the shop. But when the thin line that separated jokes from disrespect was crossed, that"s when she had a problem.

As everyone went to the front of the shop, Vanessa noticed Chanel was still quiet until Leah walked over to her. The pair were having a conversation built on whispers and their eyes shifted to Vanessa and Candy.

Vanessa didn"t trust Chanel and she was beginning to wonder about Leah. Vanessa hoped that Candy physically chastising Chanel was enough to end the string of stunts Chanel had been pulling. It was a lesson that Vanessa also hoped would serve as a warning to the rest of the women in the shop that there were boundaries that should never be crossed.

Candy put her hand on Vanessa's shoulder. "We okay, now?"

"Of course not. But we'll talk later," said Vanessa. Although she finally felt free, there was still a slight uneasiness about her relationship being made public. It was not what would surface in the shop that troubled her any longer. It was the potential for gossip outside the shop and potential negative results that worried her. And she seriously wondered whether Leah and Meisha truly respected her or her relationship? Did they simply say what was necessary to please the woman who was responsible for their weekly salary? Vanessa had always sensed that Leah was genuine and Meisha was a straight talker. But then again her perceptions had been wrong before.

Vanessa watched Candy busily organizing tracks of weave hair by color. She had no doubt that Candy loved for her. It was evident in her action that left Chanel's world shattered. It was the type of instinctive response intended to protect loved ones. The rage on Candy's face and the force that slammed Chanel's head was as powerful as her death threat. Vanessa was beginning the process of forgiving Candy, but there was stubbornness within her and a pain that still existed.

"I"m sorry y"all," Chanel said to Meisha and Leah, "I gotta get the fuck away from Candy." She stormed out of the shop.

Everyone looked at each other. The fact that Chanel needed a temporary or permanent break after being manhandled by Candy was inevitable. But her delayed response to the incident could be a signal she had reached her boiling point and would soon explode.

* * *

Vanessa strolled down Broadway on her lunch break with Mimi. She had just finished telling Mimi about the shop scene with Chanel and the video being on the Internet.

"So what you gonna do?" Mimi asked.

"What do you mean?"

"With Candy."

Vanessa was silent.

"Guess that's a I don't know," Mimi stated flatly.

"I love her. I know you can't understand that. But I love her and I love Rich."

"Did you find out if she made any other tapes?"

Vanessa shook her head.

"Un fuckin' believable."

"That didn't cross my mind."

"Nothing seems to anymore," Mimi said, sarcastically.

"What are you saying, Mimi?" Vanessa stopped on the

crowded street.

"You buggin' the fuck out. That's what I'm saying."

Vanessa"s eyes widened in shock. "You never cursed at me before."

"You never was buggin' the fuck out before."

"Mimi, I don't have to tolerate this from you."

"You toleratin' a whole lot of shit from Candy. I been your friend for years and never did no foul shit like she been doing to you from day one." Mimi huffed. "You know what? I don't have to tolerate you beating me in the head with ya fuckin' problems no more."

An eerie feeling burned deep inside Vanessa's chest as she watched her best friend turn her head and walk away. She never fathomed the day Mimi would literally and figuratively turn her back on her.

Vanessa stood in the middle of Broadway, oblivious to the people passing and the honking of car horns. All she saw was the unbelievable image of her best friend's back.

* * *

Vanessa moped back into the shop in silence. She spoke to everyone except Candy. She needed a break from the drama that had become her life, the drama that started the day she walked into the shop. The unpredictable atmosphere was slowly breaking her down. She felt out of place.

Candy walked up to Vanessa. "Please, Candy. Not now." Vanessa walked by Candy. She made her way to the front of the shop and out the front door.

"Vanessa," Candy called, jogging behind her until they were side-by-side. "Where you going?"

Vanessa's eyes never veered from in front of her. "I need a break." She stopped at her car and slid behind the wheel.

"You buggin' out, Vanessa."

Vanessa started the ignition and pulled off, never looking

back at Candy.

* * *

A week had passed since Vanessa drove off Lennox Avenue in Harlem. She had kept driving her Altima until she was at Yellowstone National Park in Wyoming. The historic park was an oasis that her parents often took her to on vacations as a child. The tranquil place always brought her peace. The smell of the endless marsh of grass she would play in, the canyons, the fossil forest, the geysers—they were all things that evoked good memories for Vanessa. She looked to the stars at night, contemplating exactly where she fit in the world. During the day, she walked barefoot through the grass, taking in the sight of bears, elk, deer and other wildlife in the park. She slept at a nearby motel where she meditated and pondered life in silence. Seven days of stillness with herself and nature assured her exactly where she was in life and what direction she should travel in the future.

It was dark outside when she walked through the door of the penthouse. Candy dropped her plate of food on the floor and darted toward her. They hugged each other firmly for what seemed to be forever. Tears soaked both their faces.

"I was so scared that something had happened to you," Candy said, taking Vanessa's face into her hands. "I'm sorry. Please don't ever leave me again. I can't take it." Candy shook her head and hugged her tighter than she ever had.

"I'm sorry too," Vanessa said. "I love you."

RICH

Rich watched Candy and Vanessa from a distance. He was relieved but furious. He had endured sleepless nights and mornings that felt awkward waking without Vanessa's body against his. Rich and Candy had many heated arguments,

because Rich blamed Candy for Vanessa's disappearance. Both Rich and Candy had a clear picture of how painful life would be without Vanessa. It was an image they never wanted to see again.

Vanessa spotted Rich, as she and Candy walked slowly in his direction. She wiped the tears from her eyes and stretched out her arms, attempting to hug Rich. But he raised his hand, stopping her.

"Do yourself a favor and play that couch." He pointed to the leather love seat and paced in front of the coffee table.

"Rich, Vanessa—"

"Not now, baby," Rich cut Candy short. "You and me been doing plenty of talking all week. Even had arguments because she wanted to play Terry McMillan."

"Terry McMillan?" Vanessa blurted.

"Yeah," Rich said. "Ol'' girl that wrote *Disappearing Acts.* Why don't you take us on the journey of your disappearing act, Terry?"

"I just needed some space."

"Space? It's a whole lot of motherfuckin'' space downstairs in Central Park."

"This is not called for," Candy said.

"Speaking of calls, did you tell her that you called the police, Candy? That you cried all the way to the station and damn near fell apart when you filled out that missing persons report? Did you tell her that you couldn't eat the first two days? Or that you almost had a nervous breakdown, because she wanted to play hide-and-go-seek?" Rich shook his head. "Yeah, I hope you told her all of that."

"Reminds me of that night that somebody ran outta here with a gun and left me and Candy crying on the bed," Vanessa said, staring at Rich. "Why? Because he wanted to play *Scarface.* Then he came back in here shot, like it was nothing.

And had the nerve to get mad at me for caring about him."

Rich was silenced, his mouth wide open. He didn't want to think about his old war story through Vanessa's eyes. He knew he had done her wrong, caused her pain and ignored her concern for him. But he still felt that Vanessa had caused a lot more pain than he did.

"You fucked up, Rich. Just like Candy did with that video. Just like I did. But you know what I realized when I was gone?" Vanessa asked. "I'm still in love with you and Candy. I just needed some time alone to look inside of me. The deeper I looked, the more I saw you two. No Mimi, nobody from the shop, no online viewers of the sex tape. As far as I'm concerned, both of you are the only two people that exist besides me in this world."

Vanessa's words moved Rich. He knew they were true. He knew they were coming from the only woman who had an understanding and love for him based partly on truths that no one else in the world knew. They shared a bond that was unparalleled. He could not deny it. "You know I love you, right?" he said.

"Of course," Vanessa answered.

Rich stepped around the coffee table to her. "And I agree with everything that just rolled off your tongue. But you gotta understand that I was laying it on you kind of thick just now for a reason." Rich paused. "Baby, I done been shot, seen friends killed and a whole bunch of other things I don't even want to remember. But I could handle all that because I knew what I was dealing with. It was all a part of the game. But not knowing where you were, if you was safe, or if I was ever gonna see you again was killing me. It was unexpected."

Vanessa burst into tears. She got up and hugged Rich. Afterwards, Rich sat down between her and Candy. Vanessa began explaining what happened from the moment Mimi

walked away from her to the minute Vanessa walked through the door of the penthouse.

Rich looked back and forth at Candy and Vanessa. It felt good to see them smiling and talking again. They had overcome one of the biggest obstacles they could face. Rich's only hope was that all the drama was behind him. But in the back of his mind, he knew his life would always be filled with drama. It was a reality he could not deny.

CHAPTER FIFTEEN
CANDY

Candy, Rich and Vanessa had become popular within publishing circles and among fans of Vanessa"s book and the sex tape. A tweet from a famous rapper about the video sparked over a half-million views and an interview of Vanessa by Wendy Williams. Vanessa mentioned the main male character was similar to Rich and that they were in a three-way relationship with Candy. Vanessa also admitted that her relations had also influenced other elements in her book. With public interest in their relationship growing, Ted Stevens suggested that the trio write a tell-all book. The video they once feared would destroy them had become the ultimate promotional tool for Vanessa"s book.

Rich was seated by Vanessa's side at a table inside a Barnes & Noble in Atlanta. Promotional posters were displayed on easels and stacks of books were on the table. Candy, Vanessa and Rich were coming to the end of a question and answer session with the nearly 100 people seated and standing in front of them. The diverse group transcended race, gender and age brackets.

"My question is for Rich," said a twenty-something black man. "Does it get tiring holding down two women? On the mental side?"

"Not at all," Rich responded. "When you truly love someone, being with them and tending to their needs becomes second nature. Things become a strain for me when I don't want to do them. And it's nothing I wanna do more than keep these women happy." He kissed Vanessa on the cheek, then did the same to Candy.

"I don't understand how one man can have two women," said an older black woman.

Vanessa said, "That's because we live in a society where a so-called normal relationship consists of a man and woman. But there are countless societies throughout the world that are filled with relationships like ours. The only way we can begin to understand things that are different is to expose ourselves to things that are outside the norm."

That statement ended the Q&A session and people began to line up and buy books. Candy watched the stacks of books dwindle. Soon, more than 120 books were sold.

"You putting up numbers, girl," Candy said.

Vanessa smiled. "I owe everything to you and Rich."

An older white woman walked up and asked Vanessa, "How does it feel knowing that people are watching a video of you getting ate out?"

Candy was thrown off by the bold question, even though it was not intended for her. Vanessa was cool and collected. "It feels good," she replied nonchalantly. "It's a turn on."

Candy stepped out of the Barnes & Noble with Rich and Vanessa. They got inside of a Land Rover and Rich pulled off. They discussed Candy's new business, which was soon set to open. Nature's Beauty had been incorporated and the first Candice Cream was in production. Rich had invested a 30% stake in Candy's company. He had also introduced her to a distributor that agreed to make her first product available in forty states across the country.

Before Candy knew it, Rich was parking in front of the shop, which was packed inside. There had been more people hanging around the shop than usual since Rich and Candy had been appearing with Vanessa at book signings and receiving media coverage. Fans had often found their way to the shop. The very thing that Vanessa feared would be bad for Candy"s Shop had become her strongest asset to attract new customers to the shop.

"I'm a be waiting at the crib," Rich said.

Candy and Vanessa kissed Rich, then climbed out of the Land Rover and walked into the shop. They were warmly greeted, as they flopped down in their chairs that their clients usually sat in. Candy noticed Leah and Chanel talking. Leah had been the negotiator who arranged a sit-down with Candy and Chanel. Leah stressed that they had been friends for too long to part ways. Chanel agreed and came back to work after Candy apologized. Candy was really concerned with having Chanel"s help, because with Candice Cream and the book tour, the shop was short-staffed. Candy had allowed Leah to manage the shop when she was not there.

"So what's good? Y'all move them books on that tour or what?" Meisha asked.

"Did really good," said Vanessa.

"I'm drained," Candy interjected. "City after city, listening to people hit you with some of the wildest questions."

"Like what?" Leah asked.

"Have I ever had a train ran on me?"

"Whole lot of heifers in the 'hood was getting gang banged," Chanel declared.

"I ain't a whole lot of heifers."

"People don't know that," Chanel said. "They see you on a sex tape and you in a three-way relationship. What they supposed to think?"

Vanessa cut her eyes at Chanel.

"I really don't care," Candy said, emphatically. She stared at Chanel, as she braided a man's hair. Candy was trying to figure out the nature of Chanel's comment. Was it a genuine analysis or one of her infamous snide remarks? Chanel had managed to censor her tongue since the incident with Candy. But Candy was always wondering. She knew Chanel was still attracted to Rich and she was probably just as jealous of Candy now as she was of Vanessa.

"So how things been going here?" Candy asked Leah.

"A new order of India hair came in yesterday. The invoice is in your desk. We got some chemical orders in because stock is low. The booth rent was paid on time by everyone. It"s all deposited in the bank. So you can verify that on your iPhone. As long as I"m here everything is under control," Leah said.

Candy was impressed with how Leah had been managing the shop. Leah always conducted herself in a professional manner. Candy had not told anyone, but she was planning to offer Leah the opportunity to run the shop full time. Candy would soon need the help, because she would have to dedicate most of her time to running her new business.

VANESSA

Vanessa watched a smooth, young man a few years older than her step inside of the shop. He was sporting a freshly trimmed 'fro and a ton of jewelry.

"That's a fine brother, there," Meisha said to Chanel.

"Shit, what's fine is all that platinum and diamonds. Look like he got his weight up enough to get down with the Chanel Legacy."

The young man smiled when he spotted Vanessa and Candy seated feet apart. He walked past Leah and stopped in front of them. "Vanessa Denay and Candice Johnson." He flashed a sly grin. "They call me Cash and I'm from Philly. I'm double-parked outside," he said, waving his hand toward a blue Mercedes S-Class. "I'm just out here to handle some business, but I wanted to shout y'all out quick fast and let y'all know I was feeling the book almost as much as the sex tape." He reached inside the pocket of his Red Monkey jeans and handed Candy and Vanessa two business cards. "I own a few clubs in Philly. If y'all ever wanna play the stage, just holler."

When Candy and Vanessa looked up from reading the cards, Cash was already gone.

"Did he say 'club' and 'play the stage' as in strip club?" an older woman asked.

"Yeah. According to this card, he owns four strip clubs," Vanessa said.

"Child, I know you ain't gonna be up on no stage swinging around no damn pole," the woman said.

"Definitely not," Vanessa stated. Stripping was far from her style. But Cash's offer was one of many she and Candy had received since their video went viral. They had received e-mails from swingers clubs, pornography producers and strip club owners. No one seemed to understand that the video was simply a private affair that leaked into the limelight. And only a handful of people realized that Vanessa and Candy were in a loving relationship that encompassed more than steamy sex.

Leah said, "Cash. He got some damn nerve coming all the way from Philly to New York with a proposition."

"That man own four clubs and his name is Cash. He tryin' to get gwap like everybody else. Money to blow," Chanel said. "Money to blow."

"Yeah, yeah, Chanel," Leah said.

"You should understand, being that you going to school for business," Chanel added.

"I didn't notice you telling him you was interested," Candy said with a sly grin.

"I ain't the one with the fan base from a book and a sex tape." Chanel waved her hand from her head to toe. "And strippin' is not a part of the Chanel Legacy."

"Mine either," Vanessa said, visibly upset.

"It ain't much difference in somebody looking from their chair in front of a computer or somebody looking from a chair in a club. Still an audience," Chanel said.

"You don't get tired of making indirect statements?" Vanessa's voice rose.

"What you need to do is calm down," Chanel said.

"Or what, huh? I'm tired of your shit, Chanel!"

Chanel laughed. "Seem like you grew a heart since you found out Candy gon' protect you."

"Watch your mouth, Chanel," said Candy, pointing at her.

"I ain't say nothing that ain't true. You know you ain't gon' let that heifer fight her own battles."

"You know what? You really think you get busy," Candy said, standing up.

Vanessa grabbed her arm and looked at her. "I'm not scared of her. I can fight for myself," Vanessa said, knowing that Candy doubted that she could hold her own. Vanessa just needed to release the tension that Chanel had ignited within her.

"You better fuck her up," Candy whispered to Vanessa. She grabbed a few rubber bands from her station.

Chanel was busy taking off her earrings. "We can go right outside and get it poppin' as soon as the shop closes."

"Okay," Vanessa said. She sat impatiently for the next ten minutes until closing. The only voice in the shop came from the music playing.

"Come on," Chanel said, as she finished the hair of the last client in the shop.

"Come on," Candy told Vanessa.

Vanessa's heart was racing. Her palms grew sweaty. She balled her fist, preparing for the fight and stopping herself from trembling.

"Listen," Candy said, pulling Vanessa to the side, as they stepped outside. She pulled Vanessa's huge 'fro into an afro puff and strapped on a few rubber bands. Next, she covered Vanessa's face in Vaseline. "You grab them long-ass curls she got and pull her to the ground, then stomp her ass out."

Candy's strategy blew by Vanessa like an Olympic sprinter racing a handicapped senior citizen. Vanessa was too focused on Chanel, who was stepping out of the shop. She took off her Gucci heels and handed them to Meisha. Chanel had Vanessa by at least thirty pounds, but Vanessa was a couple of inches taller.

"You ready?" Candy asked, tucking Vanessa's shirt in her spandex.

Vanessa nodded. She was so focused on Chanel that she didn't feel the chilly air outside.

"I'ma bust ya ass," Chanel said, as the crowd of a dozen people was forming in front of the shop.

"Remember what I said," Candy mumbled.

Chanel put up her hands like a prized fighter, stepping toward Vanessa. "Come on, heifer. Come on."

Vanessa rushed Chanel and swung a haymaker. Chanel sidestepped the blow and punched Vanessa in the jaw. Vanessa stumbled and grabbed her face. "Damn," she blurted as the pain shot through her body.

"Yeah, you wanted to fuck with the Chanel Legacy!" Chanel barked, before charging in and delivering two more blows to Vanessa's face, dropping her instantly. "Get up, heifer!" Chanel screamed. "So I can knock your ass back down."

Vanessa was expecting the typical cat fight of wild swings and hair pulling. But Chanel had clearly picked up some formal boxing skills over the years. Vanessa followed suit, raising her fists like Chanel did.

"Yeah, heifer." Chanel charged her, swinging wildly, connecting a few punches and a hard slap on Vanessa's face and head.

Vanessa screamed, punching Chanel in the stomach. When Chanel bent over and held her stomach, Vanessa grabbed a handful of her hair with her left hand and pounded Chanel's face with her right.

Chanel charged forward, forcing her weight on Vanessa's petite frame, until she slammed against a parked Chevy Envoy. She wrestled Vanessa to the ground. They rolled around until Chanel was on top, choking Vanessa. Vanessa was fighting to breathe. She tugged at Chanel's hands. She punched Chanel on the side of her face and ripped her blouse open as her hand came down. She reached up again, snatching Chanel's bra.

"What the fuck!" Chanel stopped choking Vanessa and grabbed her arm. Vanessa's hand fell. She was holding Chanel's bra and her huge D-cup breasts swung widely.

While Chanel reached to cover herself, Vanessa punched her and she tumbled over. Vanessa stood and kicked her in the stomach twice, and Chanel balled up in the fetal position. Vanessa continued to stand over Chanel, breathing hard, relieved of all the frustration Chanel had caused her.

"Come on." Candy put her arm around Vanessa and walked inside the shop as the crowd watched Meisha help Chanel to her feet. Candy took Vanessa into her office and got a first-aid kit. "She scratched your neck all up," Candy said. "But you put the blows on her. I'm proud of you." Candy smiled.

Vanessa laid back on the couch. She stared into Candy's eyes as Candy dabbed a peroxide-soaked cotton ball on her wounds. Vanessa thought of how protective Candy had always been over her. How she had always been so gentle and affectionate to her needs. Neither Rich, nor any other man had ever been so attentive to her. As she stared into Candy's eyes, Vanessa realized that she would never desire another woman besides Candy.

After they were done, they headed to the front of the shop. But Candy doubled back to get the first-aid kit in case Chanel needed it. "She's not our enemy," Candy told Vanessa. "She wanted a fair one and she took a loss. She'll get over it." Vanessa, unsure if she was ready to speak to Chanel, entered the front of the shop.

"You okay?" Leah asked.

"Yeah," Vanessa said as she sat down.

Meisha was talking to Chanel in the corner furthest from Vanessa. Chanel was pacing back and forth, shaking her head and frowning. The look in her eyes told Vanessa there would be no peace between them any time soon.

"Fuck this shit!" Chanel yelled and charged at Vanessa. Vanessa ran at her and the two women collided, fists swinging.

Candy was stepping from the back of the shop, as Vanessa and Chanel pulled and swung each other around, knocking over hair care products. Chanel rammed Vanessa's head into a mirror, shattering it.

"Ahhh, hell nah." Candy ran over and pulled Chanel from Vanessa and slammed her on the floor. Vanessa and Candy both were stomping Chanel.

"Stop!" Meisha screamed, as blood began leaking from Chanel's nose and lips.

Vanessa suddenly realized that Chanel was severely hurt. She stopped and tried to pull Candy from her. "That's enough, Candy."

Meisha and Leah raced over and helped pull Candy off Chanel.

Chanel scrambled to her feet. She stumbled back down, dazed. She shook off the beat down and stood up, staggering for a few

seconds.

"Get the fuck outta here and don't never come back!" Candy barked.

Meisha grabbed Chanel's Prada bag and helped her leave. Candy looked at the mess in the shop. "I'll clean this up tomorrow."

"I'm sorry," Vanessa said. Aside from the physical damage done to the shop, Vanessa wondered how much financial damage her fighting that night had caused. She knew that turning the shop into a battleground was not good for the customers. Chanel would not be coming back, and there was no doubt that the night's fights would have a negative effect on Leah and Meisha. The future of the shop as a viable business was in jeopardy and Vanessa faulted herself for that.

RICH

Rich was lying in bed when Vanessa and Candy came home. They flopped down onto the mattress on each side of Rich, resting their heads on his bare chest and stomach.

"I had two fights with Chanel," Vanessa said.

"Me too," Candy added. "But just one."

Rich put his hands on each of their faces. He noticed the scratches on Vanessa's neck. "Y"all all right?"

They said, "Yeah," in unison and began telling Rich the details of the night's action. Rich knew that Chanel had been provoking Vanessa for a while. In his eyes, Chanel deserved what she got. But he was worried about how the fights would affect the shop.

"Come on, Candy. Let's take a shower." Vanessa kissed Rich, then pulled Candy off to the bathroom.

Rich closed his eyes and dozed off. When he awoke, he headed for the kitchen. Stepping inside, he saw Candy propped up on the counter and Vanessa licking between her legs. Both women were naked, their bathrobes strewn on the floor. Rich assumed that their lust had gotten the best of them after they showered.

"Ahh," Candy moaned. Her eyes were on Rich as she gripped the edge of the counter.

"Damn," Rich mumbled. He felt an erection coming on. His dick climbed through the slot of his boxer shorts. He grabbed his dick and gritted his teeth each time Candy licked her lips and closed her eyes. Facial expressions always turned him on. When his eyes shifted down to Vanessa's firm butt cheeks, he lost control. He stepped out of his boxers and slid into Vanessa from behind. He gripped her waist, pounding inside of the slippery slit between her legs.

She bounced her butt back, while slurping away between Candy's legs.

Rich looked into Candy's eyes, feeling the hot juices inside of Vanessa. The clapping of her butt cheeks and Candy's moans were driving him insane.

"Eat me," Candy whimpered. She moaned and groaned until she climaxed and her body went limp. Candy laid back on the counter, trying to regain her composure.

Rich pulled out of Vanessa, as he was about to cum. He quickly turned her around, lifted her against the refrigerator and slammed into her. He stroked faster with each pump. She screamed, clawing into his back. He gripped her ass tighter as he came. He slid her sweaty body down the refrigerator.

Rich stepped back until he felt Candy's body against his. Her tongue began roamed his neck. He stood still, helpless to her overwhelming affection. He watched Vanessa pull a bag of ice from the refrigerator. She ran a piece over her nipples, while fingering herself. *I love her little freaky ass.*

Vanessa screamed, as she slid a piece of ice inside of her

pussy and crossed her legs. She rubbed her legs back and forth, until the ice melted while she fondled her small breasts. She grabbed another piece of ice, put it in her mouth and dropped to her knees while chomping on the ice.

Rich watched her walk toward him. She grabbed his dick with both hands before, sucking the head. "Shiiit." Rich closed his eyes, inching back. The small pieces of crushed ice circled his dick along with Vanessa's warm tongue. She removed her hand and began working the shaft of his dick.

When the ice melted, she stood, smiling. Candy eased from behind Rich. She grabbed his dick and guided him on top of the rectangular dinner table in the dining room. She slowly climbed on top of him and eased her pussy into his mouth, while deep-throating him.

Rich palmed her large round ass, lapping his tongue between her legs. Soon, he felt Vanessa's hands on his. She leaned over him, parting Candy's butt cheeks and diving in between them face first.

Candy quaked, soaking Rich's face. She continued bobbing up and down, sucking Rich into a second climax.

Rich opened his eyes as Candy slid off him. Leaning up from the table, the reality of what had just taken place set in. Once more, Vanessa and Candy had taken their sexual encounters to another level. It was the first time that the kitchen and dining room became as useful as their bedroom. It was the spontaneous nature of their sexual episodes that helped make lovemaking with them special for Rich. He looked at Vanessa and Candy, wondering what they had in store for him next.

CHAPTER SIXTEEN
CANDY

andy rose from bed with Rich and Vanessa. Their episode that spanned from the kitchen to the dining room the night before was fresh on her mind. Then the madness at the shop hit her. She did not know what to expect when she opened the shop. Candy was sure the rumor mill had circulated the news, but she hoped it would have only minimal damage on her business.

After driving to the shop, Candy and Vanessa walked inside.

"Sorry," Vanessa said, looking around at the mess she created during her melee with Chanel. Bottles of conditioner and shampoo with specks of glass from a broken mirror littered the floor.

"Chanel needs to be apologizing."

"Won't be seeing anymore of her."

"You right about that." Candy put her Gucci bag away and began cleaning up. She was upset over losing Chanel. Candy had grown attached to her over the years as a friend and an employee. She was a person who brought life to the shop and kept it real with Candy on personal issues. But all that became irrelevant once she violated Vanessa. Chanel was the enemy.

Vanessa began helping Candy clean up. "It's sad that it had to come to this," she said.

"Shit happens."

"It did feel good to beat her ass on my own, though." Vanessa giggled. "I know you thought I was gonna lose."

"Chanel's a street chick. Been fighting all her life." Candy put her hand on Vanessa's shoulder. "I just can't see myself letting nothing happen to you."

"I know." Vanessa smiled. "It really makes me feel good to know you're so protective of me."

"You're like my little sister."

"Little sisters don't make their big sisters cum." Vanessa licked her lips and smiled.

Candy kissed her and continued sweeping up.

Shortly after they finished cleaning the shop, Leah stepped inside. She hugged both of them. "I was thinking about y'all all night."

"Yeah?" Vanessa said.

"Yeah." Leah nodded. "I was mad because y'all really fucked Chanel up. But the more I thought about it, I couldn't front. She deserved it."

"For a long time," Candy said.

"I think y'all destroyed the Chanel Legacy." Leah laughed. She began setting up her station. "So I guess it's replacement time."

"Yeah." Candy thought of how the last replacement had become one of the two most important people in her life. She glanced at Vanessa, remembering the day she walked into the shop.

Meisha stepped through the door. She stopped, just a few feet deep inside of the shop. Her eyes beamed at Candy. "That was some bullshit last night and you know it."

"When people keep pushing buttons, they'll eventually get a reaction," Candy said.

"That's what go down in the shop. Talk shit all day, brush it off ya shoulder at the end of the night," said Meisha. "When did we start jumping each other at the end of the night?"

"She practically called me and Vanessa hos. Then she asked to fight, got her ass beat and couldn't handle it."

"You was outta control, though. We supposed to be family up in here, but you damn near stomped Chanel to death."

"Family fight, then they get over it. They don't go crazy because they lose a fight. I was coming in here with a first-aid kit to make sure Chanel was okay 'cause that's what family do. But what do Chanel do? Go for round two and tear apart my business in the process."

"Business? That's what this is about?" Meisha was silent for a few seconds. She looked at Vanessa, then at Leah, before focusing back on Candy. "Well, I came to tell y'all that I'm gone." She shook her head. "I can't work here knowing that I can get stomped out at any minute. Ain't no love lost. I just don't pump like that." She turned and walked out.

"You know she was mad close to Chanel," Leah said.

"Yeah." Candy huffed. "Life goes on." At least she hoped it would. The record high of two employees lost in less than twenty-four hours began weighing on the businesswoman in Candy. The fact that they were old friends was affecting her personally. Although Candy knew Meisha was biased because of her closeness to Chanel, Candy was forced to question her own actions. *Did I go overboard when I was stomping out Chanel?*

Shortly after Meisha left, her first scheduled client walked into the shop. Candy tried to reschedule the woman, but the woman was not interested. She wanted her hair done only by Meisha. By the end of the day, each of the clients who had entered the shop looking for Chanel or Meisha left after learning the women were no longer working at the shop. Candy had gotten on the phone during her lunch break and tried to reel in the list of clients she had scheduled for Chanel and Meisha. Some were comfortable with working with the remaining hair stylists. But they could only be seen by Candy, Vanessa or Leah when their scheduled clients canceled. Most of Chanel and Meisha's clients were unwilling to wait on a list. Candy was left with the task of quickly finding new, qualified beauticians. It was the only way she would be able to keep her salon alive.

VANESSA

Vanessa still could not believe it. Two weeks after her fight with Chanel, Candy found out she was pregnant. It was now a week later and Vanessa stood in the bathroom of the penthouse with a positive pregnancy test.. The test was the third she had taken in the last half hour. Undoubtedly, she was pregnant. The more Vanessa thought of the countless times she and Candy sexed Rich at the same time, unprotected, it made sense that they were both pregnant.

But Vanessa was not ready for her own child. She wanted to bear Rich's seed, but the timing was off. She was a best-selling author with book tours and interviews scheduled. She needed time for her career. She had dropped some of her college classes and was anxiously waiting for Candy to hire a replacement for her at the shop. But Vanessa would have to find a way to balance her pregnancy and her career, because she wanted to have Rich's child and that superseded everything.

Vanessa walked into the living room. She smiled, staring at Rich on the couch with Candy. Her shirt was pulled up and Rich was rubbing her stomach. That had been part of his daily routine since he learned Candy was pregnant.

"You gotta stop this," Candy said, as Vanessa walked over. "Get him, Vanessa. I ain't even showing yet and he still carrying on."

Vanessa sat beside Rich and pulled up her shirt. "Feel mine, baby," she said, clutching the pregnancy test in her hand out of sight. "Feel it."

"You gotta let me fill that thing up, first."

"Look." She handed Rich the pregnancy test.

His eyes lit up and he passed it to Candy. "Vanessa, don't tell me that's Candy's test from last week."

"Oh my God." Candy covered her mouth with her hand.

"I just took that test," Vanessa said. The third one in thirty minutes."

Rich jumped up, smiling. "Stop frontin". You serious?" She nodded. He sat down and kissed her. "I can't believe this." Rich put his ear to her stomach and began rubbing it.

"Now you can keep him away from my stomach," Candy said with a smile.

Rich got up and started pacing. "We gon' have two kids that's the same age," Rich grinned.

Vanessa watched the happiness on Rich's face. His life was complete. He had skated past jail, skipped over death, ducked out of the game with riches, and claimed two beautiful women as his. Now he had two children coming forth to carry his legacy. Vanessa was happy to make that a reality for him.

She reflected on when she first met Rich and how she was intrigued by his mystique and image of power. She remembered how he stripped all of that away to reveal to her his true self. Vanessa loved everything that she learned about him. She knew he would make the perfect father. He had the benefit of street knowledge and corporate insight to help him as a parent. He could warn his children about the perils of the streets and show

them the importance of work ethic. He could teach them through experience.

"Y'all know we having a boy and a girl, right?" Rich said.

Candy countered, "Two girls, Rich."

"That's right," Vanessa said.

"This the thanks I get? I bless both of y'all with babies and y'all don't know how to act."Rich chuckled.

"Can't give y'all nothing."

"Two beautiful little girls that's gonna grow up and be women that will change the world," Vanessa said.

"Pretend that we know one is going to be a boy," Rich said. "What would you name him?"

"Richard," Candy said.

"Nah, baby." Rich shook his head. "I got that name from a hustler. My son is gonna break that cycle of selling drugs. Only drugs he gonna know about is Viagra."

"How 'bout Jamel?" Vanessa added. "That's your real name."

"Nah. That's still hustling backwards," Rich said. "If he gonna be three times better than his pops, his name gotta be next level."

"See, that's why we having two girls," Candy said. "Boys is too much damn trouble. Gotta go through hell just to name 'em. Imagine after they born."

"I got it." Rich smiled. "Future."

Candy squinted her eyes and turned up her nose. "Future?" she mumbled, as if the word hurt her coming out of her mouth.

Vanessa said, "Explain that, Rich."

"Our son is the future. It's a whole lot of throwback and old school shit going on, but our son gonna be the next level. That's where we at as a family. Baby, people say a woman can't raise no man. That's not us. They say that same sex couples can't raise a child. That's not us either. Our son is gonna have a father and two mothers. That's some futuristic shit right there."

Vanessa thought Rich had a point. They were bringing children into a world where the love their parents shared was not the norm. As far as Vanessa was concerned, the norm was the past. They were the future. Their children would be the finishing touches of a family that transcended regularity. "You're right, Rich. If we have a son, we should name him Future."

RICH

A month had gone by. During that time, Rich had learned that Candy would be having the son he wanted. The trio agreed that the baby's name would be Future. It was too soon for doctors to determine the sex of Vanessa's child.

Rich felt reborn with just the thought of having children. Each day brought him new visions of all the things he wanted to do for his children. He vowed that he would never allow them to be placed in danger. The memories of his mother renting him out to be sexually exploited always lingered in his mind. Rich would die before he allowed anyone to do anything remotely close to that to his child.

Rich was sitting in Candy"s Shop reading a *Forbes* magazine. The shop was about to close and he was waiting on Vanessa and Candy. He had planned to take them to see the movie *Brooklyn's Finest.* Just as he put the magazine down, he noticed Chase walking through the door. It was the first time he had seen Chase since the shootout. Desperation was plastered on his face. Chase did not greet anyone in the shop. He had the same creepy eyes and frown that he had when he stood on Rich's terrace the night he convinced Rich to risk everything that mattered to him.

"Let me holler at you, homey," Chase told Rich.

Rich stood and walked behind him.

"Rich," Vanessa called.

Rich turned to her, detecting the fear that oozed from her eyes.

"I'll be done in a minute," she said, while braiding a client's hair.

"I'll be waiting outside," Rich responded.

Candy walked over to Rich and whispered in his ear, "Please. Not again."

He thought of the night Candy and Vanessa had begged with him not to risk his life and freedom for Chase. He winked at Candy and kissed her. "Don't worry." He stepped outside, catching up with Chase.

"I need you to make a move for me," Chase, said.

"I ain't see you in months since I got shot and risked my freedom for you. And that's the first thing you got to say to me."

"I ain't trying to argue with you, Rich. Bottom line is the connect went sour and I need you to plug me in with somebody."

"I know your eyes and ears work, so you see it in my swag and you heard it out my mouth and in the streets. Me and the game ain't got nothing in common but old memories."

"Come on, homey. I ain't asking you to go cop no bricks. But you gotta make a call or something. Let somebody know I need ten of them thangs."

Rich shook his head. "Just get on the phone and talk myself into a conspiracy charge, huh?" Rich shook his head. He noticed Vanessa step out of the shop. She was gazing at him. "I"ma be with you in a minute. Get in the truck." He tossed her the key to a white Hummer parked feet away.

"When you start giving bitches the keys to the whip?" Chase asked.

"You gotta curve your tongue. That ain't no bitch. That's wifey," Rich said, as Candy stepped out of the shop and walked over to Vanessa.

"Wifey?" Chase's face wrinkled like a prune. Rich had never referred to a woman as wifey before. Chase looked at Vanessa and Candy. "That's what the fuck this all about? All this game over shit is about some pussy-eatin' bitches? Motherfuckin' hos got your nose open like a line of coke? I knew it."

Rich clenched his fist, holding back the urge to hurt Chase for disrespecting the two people who mattered most to him— the two women who were bearing his seeds. He turned to Vanessa, who stood beside Candy in shock. Leah and a couple of clients were nearby. Rich turned back to Chase. "I'm a let that bitches comment slide. Matter of fact, I'm gone." He turned to walk away.

"Fuck is you going?" Chase said. He yanked Rich's arm.

Instinctively, Rich swung. He connected square with Chase's jaw. Chase stumbled back and pulled out a gun, but Rich grabbed it. They tussled for control of the .357-caliber Glock.

"Rich!" Vanessa screamed.

As Rich twisted Chase's arm. A shot went off. The hot lead tore through a car window, sending specks of glass to the ground. Rich head butted Chase and the gun fell to the ground. Chase kneed Rich in the balls, then dropped him with a right hook to the jaw. He began stomping his Timberland boots into Rich"s chest.

A thunderous clap from a gun sounded and a bullet ripped through Chase's shoulder. He fell against a parked Toyota Camry. Rich looked up and saw Vanessa holding Chase's Glock. Smoke rose from the barrel.

"Bitch shot me," Chase blurted.

Rich scrambled to his feet and took the gun from Vanessa. He aimed it at Chase, ready to squeeze the trigger. Then he noticed the small crowd gathering around the scene. He took a step back and turned to Vanessa. "Come on." He pulled her toward the Hummer as Candy opened the passenger side door.

* * *

Rich drove straight to his penthouse, followed by Candy in her BMW. In minutes, Rich was packing a duffle bag. He didn't anticipate Chase snitching, but he was not certain what anyone else who witnessed the shooting would say. More important was what Chase would likely do to Rich, Vanessa and Candy. Chase was not only capable of killing, but he liked killing.

"Come on, y'all gotta get packed," Rich said, stepping into the living room.

Candy was hugging Vanessa, rocking back and forth. Vanessa needed to be comforted after having just shot Chase. She was shell-shocked, mumbling about her nearly killing another human being.

"You did what you was supposed to do," Candy said, caressing her back.

"Candy, go pack y'all shit. I wanna be outta here in five minutes," Rich said. After Candy left, Rich sat beside Vanessa and turned her face toward him. "Baby, you ain't do nothing that Chase wouldn't have done to me if he had the chance. You hear me? You saved my life."

Vanessa nodded and hugged Rich. "I love you."

"I never doubted you, but you just proved that in a whole different way tonight."

Candy retuned with her overnight bag. "I got everything," she said.

Rich stood and wiped the tears that began to fall from Candy's eyes.

"When I saw that gun, I just froze," Candy said. "I thought I was gonna lose you like I lost Dez." She looked into Rich's eyes, fighting back tears. "I don't wanna lose you, Rich. I love you."

"I love you too." The word "love" had slipped out. But it felt right rolling off his tongue. At that moment, Rich was certain he was in love with two women. He grabbed Candy's overnight bag and his duffle bag and set them on the couch. "We gotta get outta the city."

Candy nodded.

"Where we gonna go, Rich?" Vanessa asked.

"Up State. I got a hideout up there."

"I didn't know that," Candy said.

"Me either," Vanessa said.

"It's for emergencies. The less you know the better for all of us. If you don't know about it, police can't scare it out of you, thugs can't beat it out of you and it won't slip out of your mouth to your friends if you're drunk or high. But that's irrelevant. Right now we gotta go. Candy, you follow us in your car."

Rich stepped out of the door, holding both bags. As they took the elevator downstairs, Vanessa kept breaking down and crying. At the ground floor, Rich dropped the bags, and held Vanessa's hands. "Everything is gonna be straight. I promise you."

When the elevator opened, Candy grabbed the bags. "I'll a take these to my car and wait for y'all."

"Good." Rich turned to Vanessa. "Baby, you gotta listen and you gotta listen quick. You went through a serious situation tonight, but it ain't nothing you can't overcome. You ain't by yourself. You got two other people supporting you. Two people that love you to the fullest. Ain't nothing we can't do or get through together. Now, come on." He put his hand around her shoulder and they began walking.

"I'm scared, Rich," Vanessa mumbled. "I don't wanna lose you."

"I don't wanna lose me either, baby. Just like I don't wanna lose you or Candy. We a team, baby, and ain't nobody gonna come between us." Rich stopped and looked into her eyes. "You hear me?"

Vanessa whispered, "Yeah," and hugged Rich.

"Now come on, baby." Rich unhanded her. "We gotta go." They began walking through the hall toward the entrance of the building.

The doorman ran inside. "Call the police!" he screamed to the receptionist. "A woman was just kidnapped outside."

Rich's eyes expanded. He charged through the door as a black Taurus turned the corner. *Chase. We used that same fuckin' getaway car used to put in massive work. Now it's coming back to haunt me.*

"Mr. Thomas. It was Ms. Johnson," the pale doorman said to Rich. He pointed to Candy's BMW that was parked across the street. Her overnight bag and Rich's duffle bag lie on the street beside it. "She was getting inside, and out of nowhere, this car pulls up. Two guys jump out, snatch her and pull off."

Rich turned toward Vanessa. Her face was covered in tears,she dropped to her knees. Rich knew there was no avoiding what circumstances were dictating. He was being forced to revert to the life of killing and crime from which he had struggled so hard to free himself. He was facing the worse drama he had ever been in. But he was prepared to kill whoever he had to in order to save one of the two women he ever loved.

CHAPTER SEVENTEEN
CANDY

verything was dark. It had been that way for Candy since the masked villains forced her inside the Taurus and put a black pillowcase over her head. She screamed and tried to fight back, but her useless attempts to free herself came with a price. She was beat into submission, gagged with an oily rag, her hands tied. Her wrists felt like they were on fire. She assumed it was a gun that hammered her head, which was throbbing. And there had to be a gash because she felt the flow of warm liquid slowly trickling down from her forehead between her eyes and over her nose.

The ride was short and silent. Short indicated to Candy that she had not left Harlem. No talking was a sign that she was dealing with professionals. Not some James Bond-type professionals who could beat a man to death in ten blows and evade police with the help of high-tech gadgets. Candy's captors were the type of professionals who had snatched up so

many people in the 'hood and done so many robberies, that no matter how dramatic a mission was, they never uttered a word in the presence of witnesses. A familiar voice could convince a jury to convict. And professionals never were convicted of crimes. Candy had dealt with enough hustlers and street thugs to know real beef when she saw it. But for the first time in her life, she was experiencing it.

She was snatched from the car. The firm grip on each of her arms felt like gloved hands—another professional sign of calculated criminal experience. One of her Gucci pumps came off while she was being drug down a short flight of concrete stairs. *They must be taking me to a basement.*

The first thing Candy heard was the barking of a dog. There was a third set of footsteps behind her, presumably the driver of the Taurus. Tears began flowing from Candy's eyes when she felt a hand squeeze her butt.

They stopped. The irritating sound of chains seemed to come from every direction. Candy's body was slammed face-first onto a table. Her wrists and ankles were chained separately, then pulled apart until her body was stretched out.

"Get the fuck off me," Candy tried to yell through the oil-stained cloth that gagged her. She shifted and scrambled to free herself to no avail. The chains were locked somewhere on the table. She heard clicks. Candy kept kicking and turning until another set of chains slammed against her head and back. More blood. Her hair stopped it from leaking too far.

Her ankles were simultaneously gripped by the gloved hands. The chains jingled as they tightened, pulling her limbs further apart. Her body was outstretched on the table, a limb at each end. She felt as if something inside of her had torn, muscles, ligaments, arteries—it was as if anything within her that was capable of expanding was stretched beyond limit.

The pillow was partially removed from her face for a second.

She got a glimpse of the basement. It was covered in soot and debris. Tears leaked from her eyes as she felt her clothes being cut off. The snip of scissors was deafening. Candy was certain that a harsh reality awaited her once she was nude.

Heels. Candy could hear the click-clack of shoes. It must have been hard bottoms of another professional thug. The steps grew louder, closing in on her. The steps stopped and a hand wrapped in a latex glove trailed from her ankles upward. Her butt cheeks were parted and what felt like a thick tree branch was rammed inside her anus with full force. Candy tried to wiggle away, but the more she moved the more her body seemed to tear apart. More chains lashed her head and back. More blood exited her body.

Candy's tears increased when she heard the clicking of a plastic-encased razor being opened. The sound was familiar. She had carried a razor all her life. Everyone in the shop seemed to have one. Leah, Meisha, Chanel—everyone but harmless Vanessa. Candy's muffled screams did not go much further then the rag in her mouthas the razor dug into her butt cheek. Each one of them was slowly and carefully carved. It was the type of precision that went into surgical incisions and sculpting fine art.

The chains were removed from her limbs and she was turned over. When she tried to break free, chains slammed down on her face and stomach, over and over until piss and shit leaked from her. She was beat back into the toxic pool of blood, feces and urine that covered the table. Candy had been so focused on trying to avoid the severity of her situation and block out the pain, she forgot there was a child in her womb. That agonizing truth set in when Candy could not scream. She could not think. She did not know who she was or where she was. All she knew was she did not like what she was experiencing.

* * *

Candy had been bleeding all night. She awoke when the

Taurus hit a pothole. She was in a steamy trunk filled with the hot the stench of her waste that covered her body. Her entire body was sore and she was too fatigued to move. The Taurus came to a halt and the trunk was opened. Through the pillowcase covering her face, Candy could feel the sun and see some of its glimmer. Then she felt a pair of hands lift her. Her body cringed as she slammed against the hard, tar-paved street. The door of the Taurus slammed and its tires peeled off. There was a haze of burnt rubber that Candy could hardly smell through the waste ingrained on the pillowcase and her clothing.

"What the—"

Finally. A familiar voice. Tears rushed from Candy's eyes. The voice had snatched her back into the harsh reality of her life. The pillowcase was removed from her head. When the blinding sun wore off, Candy looked into Leah's eyes. Both women were in the center of one of the lanes on Lennox Avenue in front of the shop.

Leah took off her jacket and wrapped Candy's naked body. She removed the oily rag from Candy's mouth and screamed for help.

VANESSA

Vanessa was snatched from her sleep at 9:03 in the morning by the sound of gunshots. She crawled from bed and crept out of the bedroom in search of Rich, but she couldn't find him. She peeped through the curtain of another room, toward the sound of the gunfire. She exhaled when she saw Rich shooting at bottles in the woods behind the cabin they had arrived at the night before. She ran out the back door and called Rich. He kept shooting. She covered her ears, walking closer, noticing a small arsenal of guns and bullets spread out on a bed sheet on the grass.

Rich turned to her. In his hand was a .50-caliber Desert

Eagle. In his eyes were tears. Vanessa slowly approached and hugged him. She remembered that Rich had not gotten much sleep when they arrived at the cabin tucked discretely in the woods. Rich had blamed himself for Candy's kidnapping. Vanessa had tried telling him it was not his fault, but he insisted that had he not punched Chase, Candy would be with them.

Vanessa had also wallowed in self-pity since the incident. She shouldered the blame because she shot Chase. She felt that if she had not been so weak, Rich would not have been consoling her inside the penthouse lobby, leaving Candy to exit the building alone with the bags Rich was supposed to be carrying.

Staying cooped up in a cabin in Balmville, New York only enhanced Vanessa's frustration and guilt. The wealthy Orange County enclave was just an hour and twenty minutes from Harlem, but Vanessa felt like she was in another world. During the ride upstate, she took in the scenery—the country club, mansions, golf course, a seemingly endless sea of trees and perfectly trimmed lawns. The nearest house to Rich's cabin was a large two-story ranch backed by towering hills. The peaceful atmosphere of Balmville was the type of environment Vanessa would enjoy under normal circumstances—circumstances in which Candy was safe and present.

"What are we gonna do?" Vanessa asked as she parted from Rich's embrace.

"I got a plan. Don't worry. I made some calls late last night. People got they eyes open in Harlem. Don't worry. Candy gonna be back and motherfuckers gon' get it!" He looked down and pointed at his guns. "Pick that gold one up."

"Huh?"

"Pick it up," he demanded. "The little gold one."

"Why?"

"Because I don't want you having another nervous breakdown if you have to use a gun again. And the way shit

going down, you need to learn how to protect yourself."

Vanessa stared at the gun, then back at Rich. She took a deep breath and picked up the weapon. Rich laid his on the bed sheet. Vanessa's hand shook nervously. Her mind doubled back to when she shot Chase.

"That's a Three-Eighty Lama. Three-Eighty is the caliber of the bullet."

"Exactly what is a caliber?"

"The caliber is the diameter of the bullet based on an inch. So the bullet in that gun is three hundred eightieths of an inch. It's all fractions, baby. The gun I put down is a Fifty-Caliber. That means the bullet is a fiftieth of a inch, which is mathematically a half of a inch."

"Oh." Vanessa nodded, twisting the .380 in her hand.

Rich stood behind Vanessa, placing his hands over hers. He showed her how to aim through the sights of the gun, how to use the safety, load and cock the gun, then fire. Within half an hour, Vanessa had gone through over 100 bullets. Her aim needed improvement, but she had become comfortable holding and shooting the gun. She was surprised how empowered she felt with it in her hand.

She sat back, watching Rich shoot bottles. She kept thinking of how just days ago, everything in their lives was perfect. Now Candy was missing and a man who had left the streets behind was teaching Vanessa to shoot. She wondered if things would ever be how they were.

Rich's phone rang and he answered it. He stood speechless, dropping his BlackBerry to the ground.

Vanessa rushed to his side. "What happened?"

"Candy's in the hospital."

***

Vanessa had been quiet during the ride to St. Luke's Hospital in Manhattan. Neither she, nor Rich knew what Candy's status was, only that she had been beaten and dumped in front of the shop naked.

Vanessa and Rich neared Candy's room. Besides Leah being present, Vanessa was surprised to see Chanel, Meisha and Mimi outside of Candy"s room. Everyone was moping around with teary eyes. They gave Rich and Vanessa a group hug.

It was Leah who had called Rich to relay the bad news. She now revealed that a large "C" had been carved into each of Candy's buttcheeks.

Rich held Vanessa up, as her knees buckled in response to the heinous details of the crime to which Candy had been subjected. "It's my fault," Vanessa kept screaming until Rich managed to calm her.

When the doctor stepped out of Candy's room, everyone swarmed him. "She suffered severe trauma to most of her body." He told them that Candy had also been sodomized. One result of the blunt trauma was a miscarriage.

Vanessa's head dropped and everything became a blur. Faces turned to silhouettes and voice seemed slurred. She staggered to a chair as the doctor continued talking. Vanessa wanted blood. Chase had to pay for killing the child Vanessa looked forward to helping raise. Candy did not deserve the punishment she had received. She was suffering simply because of her association and love, Vanessa rationalized. Within a few days, Vanessa had been transformed from a joyous young woman with an open heart to a callous soul shattered by the unwanted destruction of her family.

RICH

Rich cried as he stared at Candy's swollen face and the IV running into her body. The bruises, dry blood and gashes in her head made her almost unrecognizable. There was little left of the woman with the face and figure of a model. She tried to smile, but it was obvious the pain was too much for her to completely remove the frown from her face. Rich kissed her forehead and held her hand. He noticed welts on her wrists. He wiped her watery eyes and whispered, "I love you." He called Vanessa over, sliding his hand on her shoulder.

"I'm so sorry," Vanessa said, hugging Candy.

Rich sat on a nearby chair, allowing the other women to speak to Candy. He had never felt so weak, helpless and guilty. The loss of his son kept haunting him. The fact that his child had not yet been born did not matter. There had been a million visions in Rich's mind of his son. Now, those visions would not materialize.

Chanel sat next to Rich. "I ain't even gonna front like I know what you going through, `cause I don't. And I know I ain't been on the best terms with you or your women. But I know nobody deserves this shit. And I know that you get busy, or whatever. But I'm gonna tell you to think before you make a move. You got two women who love you and you still got a baby on the way from one. You don't wanna give all of that up going after Chase."

Fuck that. Nothing would stop Rich from his murderous plan. Chase's selfish desire to stay in the game had disrupted everything that Rich was building outside of a life of crime. Chase had earned every bullet that Rich had reserved for him.

Rich stood and walked outside of the room. He paced for a while, thinking of how he would function on a daily basis, while being haunted by the image of Candy's scarred body. The sight one of the two women he loved in such a brutalized state would push Rich to murder anyone,

even if he did not want to. But Rich *wanted* to kill Chase, so the *need* for revenge was a logical reaction.

Rich had seen so much in the streets, but he had never predicted the man who had saved him in the streets would attempt to destroy him. The deceit and friends-turned-enemies were parts of the game that Rich felt he and Chase were above. Rich had outlived enemies and survived street wars with rival crews only to be blindsided by his star teammate.

Rich stepped back into Candy's room and squeezed through the crowd of solemn faces. He stood beside Vanessa at the front of the group. He had nothing to say. No word would do anything to remove the pain he, Candy or Vanessa were experiencing. No language could convey what he felt. So he watched, silently—accepting the punishment of seeing Candy removed the furthest from herself that he could imagine.

Time drifted by and visiting hours ended. Rich and Vanessa were the last to leave the hospital. They walked through the parking lot toward a Range Rover. The atmosphere set on Rich. He and Vanessa were no longer in Upstate, New York. They were in Manhattan—the Rotten Apple that had spoiled everything for Candy. Rich kept his eyes open. "You got that gun on you?" he asked Vanessa.

Vanessa held up a brown clutch.

"Where the hell you get a clutch from?" Rich asked.

"I bought it Upstate."

Rich grinned because it took Vanessa needing to carry a gun in order for her to own a purse. She had never used clutches or handbags. Rich's mind was so off-balance that he had not noticed the small black bag until Vanessa held it up.

Vanessa got in the Range Rover after Rich. "So we got two days left and we can take her home, right?"

"That's what the doctor said," Rich pulled off in the Range Rover.

"Well, she could be a lot worse."

"I'm sure you can think of something different to say to make me feel better."

"I don't know what to say, Rich. In a split second, life has totally changed for us."

"I been saying that to myself since all this shit happened."

"I can't believe Chanel and Meisha showed up, not to mention Mimi," said Vanessa.

"Yeah. Chanel gave me a speech about not risking everything trying to get revenge."

"We've already lost one baby. You need to focus on the one we have left."

Rich knew he was responsible for Vanessa's well-being as well as that of his future child. Losing another child was not an option for him. But letting Candy suffer in vain was not an option either.

***

A day had passed since Rich and Vanessa made it back to the cabin. They spent almost an entire day on the makeshift shooting range behind the cabin. In the middle of the night, Rich shifted in his sleep until he awoke. Vanessa was gone. Rich grabbed his .40-caliber Taurus from underneath his pillow and crept out of bed in his boxers. He tiptoed past two empty rooms, and then saw Vanessa sitting in the front of the fireplace crying. He walked over and set the gun down before hugging her in silence. They sat in each other's arms for almost an hour. The only communicating done was with their hearts, confirming that their love would hold them together. Vanessa had told Rich several times how she felt so safe in his strong arms, so Rich knew that she now needed to be held more than ever.

"I couldn't sleep," Vanessa said. "Couldn't get her off my mind. Then I dozed off and I had a nightmare. Chase had killed you."

Rich could feel her tears on his neck as Vanessa's sobbing increased. "I'm gonna be all right. It was just a dream."

"But it seemed so real."

Rich and Vanessa sat in silence a little longer until she was ready to go back to sleep. They lie on the huge rug in front of the fireplace, her head resting on Rich's bare chest until sunrise.

After showering and eating, Rich was back behind the cabin, shooting bottles. It had become a stress release. It was also practice that would be useful for when he crossed paths with Chase.

Rich turned to Vanessa as she walked over with her gun in hand. He watched her switch from safety to fire. She cocked the gun back and took aim at her target twenty yards away. She squeezed two shots that missed. The third reduced the 16-ounce Pepsi bottle to pieces of glass. Vanessa turned to Rich with a sneaky grin.

"I would never believe it if I ain't see it," he said.

"Do something enough, you get good at it."

"Accuracy is one thing. I'm talking about something else."

"Oh yeah?"

"Baby, you took to that gun like a duck take to water. Few days ago you almost passed out after you pulled that trigger. Now you flickin' the safety and cocking it back like you grew up on a Army base."

"Things were a lot different a few days ago."

"Baby, if it's one thing for sure and two things for certain, everything gon' be all right in a minute. Trust me," Rich said.

"But you can't erase memories. The pain of the past will always remain."

Rich thought of the memories of him being abused. Not only were they permanent, but they had affected how he viewed and related to women for years. He could not help but wonder how Candy's experience would change how she viewed and related to him.

CHAPTER EIGHTEEN
CANDY

andy had been recouping in Rich's cabin for weeks. The swelling of her face was practically gone, but she still had trouble sitting down. The thirty staples in her butt were a painful reminder of her assault, as was the pain she endured when defecating. But the experience that hurt the most was losing her child. She felt she had neglected her motherly duties, that she had failed as a mother before she even became a mother. Candy questioned whether she was qualified to raise a child because she could not protect her unborn.

Vanessa and Rich reminded her that she could become pregnant again. But Candy didn't want to become pregnant. She wanted to give birth to the child that had been growing inside her womb.

She was not alone in her grief. The effect that her ordeal had on Vanessa and Rich scared Candy. For weeks, she had watched the two of them firing guns daily, for hours. Vanessa walked around, protesting that she would never allow Candy or Rich to be harmed again. She told Candy that if she had not been scared of guns before, she would have fired enough bullets to kill Chase and he would not have been alive to harm anyone.

While Vanessa was on defense, Rich was on offense. Candy pled with him day in and day out not to seek revenge on Chase. She argued that Rich had everything to lose and nothing to gain, because the damage she experienced could not be undone.

"I lost my son, Candy. Chase gotta die. His mother needs to lose her son."

"What if we lose you in the process?" Candy asked.

"I"ve been planning Chase"s death for a while. Ain"t no failing."

Candy stared at Rich in silence. His claims did little to stop the fear Candy had for his safety.

Days later, Candy was lying on her stomach on the living room couch. Vanessa walked into the room after hours of shooting outside. She twirled her gold-plated gun with her index finger as if she was a cowboy in a western film. "Look at you!" Candy barked. "What if that goes off?"

"It's not loaded. See?" Vanessa cocked the gun back several times, then flashed the bottom of the butt, showing there was no clip inside. She pulled a clip from her pocket and quickly jammed it in and cocked the .380. "Now it's loaded." She flicked on the safety. "But it's on safety."

"This Rambo-Nino Brown shit gotta stop, Vanessa," Candy demanded.

Vanessa was silent for a moment. She looked like she wanted to cry and kill. "What happened to you is not gonna happen again. Nobody is gonna destroy what we have."

As Vanessa left the room, Candy gazed at Rich.

"Baby, not today. Please," he uttered.

"Come here."

Rich tucked his Desert Eagle into his waist and stepped over to Candy. He squatted beside the couch so he was face-to-face with her.

"I'm scared," Candy whispered.

Rich put his hand over her cheek, pressing her face against his. "You don't have to be."

"That's easier said than done."

Rich leaned back, gazing into her eyes. "You know I love you, right?"

"Of course."

"Do you know I'll die for you?"

Candy was silent, noticing Vanessa step back over.

Rich wrapped one of his arms around Vanessa's shoulders. "I'll give my life for either one of y'all. And this ain't some shit you hear in a R & B song, watch in a romance movie or see a pimp tell his hos. I'm dead-ass serious."

"Don't talk like that," Candy said, coming to tears.

"Baby, I done lived my life two times over," Rich said. "I traveled outside of the country more that once and been to damn near every state in America. I slept in Trump Tower, I own a penthouse, and I done drove any car you can name that cost upwards of fifty stacks. I done literally slept with a different freak everyday of the week. And on top of all of this, I know what it's like to love and to be loved. Not by one, but by two women at the same time. On some real shit, what more can a man ask for? I lived my life. So when I say I'll give my life for the women I love, I'm serious."

Candy could see the passion in Rich's eyes and hear it in his low tone. She knew the chances of him not risking his life to kill Chase were almost none.

"We all would like to see Chase dead, Rich. But if you lose your life in the process, that's something none of us would want to see. And it wouldn't be you giving your life to save us, because we're safe right here. We're miles always from Chase," Candy said.

"So we just sit here? Base our existence on not going where Chase is? Just forget about the one-point-two million dollar penthouse where we fell in love? Where we planned our future only to have Chase take it away from us?" Rich shook his head. "Not Rich. I been in the street damn near my whole life and nobody never took nothing from me. Then I leave the streets and help create the one thing I never had, the most precious thing in life, just to have Chase snatch it from us." Rich shook his head, gazing at Candy. "Baby, I can swallow a lot of things, but that ain't one. I couldn't live with myself and I wouldn't be no good to y'all if I let this shit slide. That's why Chase and everybody else that had something to do with this shit is a done deal." Rich stood and walked away.

VANESSA

Vanessa trailed behind Rich into the bedroom. She understood his position, but it troubled her. Not only because she feared for his well-being, but also because of the guilt she was feeling. The last thing she needed was for more guilt to kick in because of something happening to Rich—something rooted in the bullet she fired into Chase over a month ago. Since she could not stop Rich, there was only one alternative in her mind. "Rich," she called. "I'm coming with you to get Chase."

Rich turned to her. "Oh yeah?" he tossed his Desert Eagle on the bed.

"Yeah. You're not the only person who will die for the people

you love."

"You're much smarter than you're sounding right now."

"What's that supposed to mean?"

"First and foremost, losing another child ain't a good look. Besides that, you're a twenty-two-year-old woman working on a master's degree and your book is flying off the shelves like it got wings. And to seal the deal, everything you know about beef came from me talking to you on a tour through Harlem and you listening to them freaks bumping they gums down in the shop."

Vanessa sighed and folded her hands. "Well, you been training me to shoot and how to clean guns for over a month, like we're starting a militia."

"The word 'self-defense' mean anything to you?"

Vanessa sucked her teeth. "I've been shooting damn near every day."

"Baby, Pepsi don't shoot back. There"s a big difference between them bottles and hearing bullets whiz by your head. Or when you're shooting at somebody who don't run, because they got a gun too. Better yet, when you can't tell which way the bullets are coming from, but you know they got your name on 'em. These the type of details that mysteriously get left out of the war stories dudes brag about in the 'hood." Rich chuckled. "Everybody wanna be a gangster. Beef ain't just physical; it's a mental game. Some real psychological shit."

Vanessa was silent.

"Come here, baby," Rich said.

She took two steps. "I'm wallowing in my own guilt, devastated about Candy. I'm scared for you and frustrated about everything else."

"It's okay, baby. Real situations cause real emotions to flare."

"Tell me something I don't know," Vanessa said.

Rich sat on the bed with Vanessa. "You gotta have faith in me, baby. You and Candy. If I tell y'all this gon' get done right, you can believe I ain't just talking 'cause I got lips."

"I believe in you, Rich. I always have. That's why I fell in love with you."

"That's the type of talk I need to hear, baby."

Vanessa kissed Rich and smiled. She went back into the living room with Candy. She sat down, allowing Candy to rest her head on her lap. Vanessa told Candy what Rich had just explained to her.

"And you ate all that bullshit up, huh?" Candy shook her head.

"We both know his mind is made up."

"Yeah, you right."

"He's been through a lot in the streets," Vanessa said. "Maybe this is light work for him."

"I hope so."

Rich stepped in the living room and kicked back on the recliner, facing the women as they became silent. "You can't hide nothing from me." He grinned. "Go 'head and tell me what y'all was saying 'bout me."

"That we understand your stubborn ass," Candy said.

Rich nodded. "I'm glad to see you smile again."

Candy blushed.

"So what happens when this is all over?" Vanessa asked.

"We take a break for a minute. Then maybe it's time for us to spread out. Don't y'all think so?" Rich said that the shop was falling apart and Candy would need time to manage her new business. He also mentioned that Vanessa's career was soaring and each of them needed to promote the book. "It would be good to start focusing on a fresh place outside of New York."

"I don't know," Vanessa said.

"You don't know what? Whether to fly the coup, or where we should land?" Rich asked.

"How 'bout the A?" Candy added.

"Atlanta." Rich nodded. "I like that."

"They have the Bronner Brothers hair show down there. That's perfect for my hair care products."

"Maybe open a new Candy's Shop, too." Vanessa smiled.

The more they talked, the more Vanessa felt things would turn out right. It was the first time in a while that life seemed close to normal. Most of the time they had spent in the cabin had been filled with debates, guilt trips and pessimism. But now, as they sat together in unity, Vanessa felt like they were back in the penthouse.

Although she liked the idea of moving, Vanessa missed living in New York City already. Seeing Mimi and the women from the shop at the hospital made her realize that in spite of all the drama, they shared a concern for each other. It pained her not to call Mimi. But Rich had insisted that Vanessa and Candy not contact anyone from the city. Leah had been leaving messages on Candy's phone, informing her that she was running the shop while she was gone. Rich did not want to risk anyone finding out where they were located. He knew that in the midst of a conversation, Vanessa or Candy could unintentionally mention something about where they were. Vanessa argued that Rich had been to the city countless times since they left the hospital. But she knew Rich had not been out socializing in Harlem. He was discreetly riding through the neighborhood in an unfamiliar car, peeping through tinted windows for any sign of Chase.

"It's about that time," said Rich, as he headed to take a nap.

"Who would've ever thought we would end up here?" Candy said. "I never thought I would deal with another man."

"Falling in love with a man of the streets was definitely not on my agenda."

"That's life. Unpredictable," Candy said. "Even with all the bullshit we've been though, I wouldn't trade this relationship for anything."

"This is real love."

"Everybody is looking for it, but only a chosen few find it."

Candy smiled. "I watched women come in and out of the shop for years, always complaining about men trouble."

Vanessa thought of all the scorned women she had seen come in the shop in just months. They had told story after story about sour relationships and hopeless futures with men. Even Meisha and Chanel were crying out to be loved, though masking their craving by slandering men. Their vocal demeanors were smoke screens and Vanessa knew it. Leah was the only person in the shop who was in love and it showed through her levelheaded approach to life. Being in love could humble a person. For Vanessa, love was life. She could not exist without either one. She knew that, thanks to Rich and Candy.

RICH

Rich was sunk low in the seat of a Toyota Corolla. It was an old model he had kept parked outside his cabin for years. It was also the same vehicle he had used to creep in and out of New York City on the prowl for Chase. For two months, he had been unsuccessfully searching. He assumed Chase had vanished somewhere out of town like he had done after Pana had shot at him. It was a waiting game. But the game would be worth the wait.

Rich looked through the tinted windows of the Corolla, as he steered down Chase's block. He slowed down and pulled over at the sight of Chase's Mercedes. It was parked directly in front of Chase's brownstone. Rich was parked five cars down and across the street.

It was the first time he had seen the Mercedes during his hunt for Chase. This was the opportunity Rich had carefully waited for while he watched Candy suffer. It had been two months since she had been kidnapped and tortured. Although she had fully recovered physically, there were psychological scars Rich, Candy and Vanessa had that would never heal. The images of Candy lying helplessly in the hospital would be forever engrained in Rich's mind. For this, he was determined to give Chase a slow death. The usual penalty of a few bullets to the head was too kind for Chase.

Rich switched the safety off on his Desert Eagle. He pulled his hood over his head. He stalked down the street and stabbed one of the back tires on Chase's Mercedes, then doubled back to his Corolla. He pulled off and parked two cars down, across the street from the Mercedes. Rich watched the back tire deflate. It was almost midnight and no lights could be seen through Chase's windows. Rich knew it would be a long night.

With some luck, Chase might hit the street early like the mornings he had dropped by Rich's penthouse before 9:00 a.m., focused on having the edge on their competition. But no matter what time he left, Rich would be waiting. The stay was a small cost for the taste of revenge that was teasing his tongue.

* * *

The sun was up and Rich's eyes had not closed since he parked across the street from Chase's home. He had spent the night talking to Vanessa and Candy by speaker phone, before they dozed off around after 3:00 a.m. He listened to music on Hot 97 from the car radio until the morning. He had watched what seemed like all of Chase's neighbors head out of their homes. They held book bags, briefcases and other things that marked them as law abiding citizens starting a new day of normal lives. It was a normalcy Rich yearned. *Chase might be the only street dude on this block.*

Just after 10:00 a.m. Rich saw Chase finally surface on the deserted block.. Rich's heartbeat raced as he pulled out his Desert Eagle. Instinctively, he wanted to fill Chase's head with every hollow point slug in his gun. But he had a plan to follow. He rocked back and forth, impatiently watching Chase get inside the Benz and start it.

Rich"s cell rang and it was Candy. "She"s gone, Rich! She"s not here!"

"Calm down. What happened?"

"I just woke up and Vanessa is nowhere in sight. She didn"t leave a note or anything, like usual. She"s gone, Rich. I"m up in here by myself scared."

"Look under the bed." Rich said, watching Chase. He had barely pulled into the street, when he backed up the car and got out. "There"s a Timberland box under the bed with two ten millimeters in it," Rich continued. He was trying to comprehend what was going on with Candy and Vanessa, while he focused on Chase.

"Rich, I"m—"

"I gotta move." Rich cut Candy short and eased the car door open. He darted forward as Chase checked his tire.

As Rich closed in, Chase looked up, pulled his gun and fired in one swift motion seconds before Rich squeezed off two rounds. Both men scrambled for cover, Chase behind his Benz and Rich behind a tree.

"Fuck!" Rich said frustrated and angry. He peeped around the tree and a bullet whizzed by his face. He braced himself, then sprinted to a nearby Range Rover as a trail of bullets followed him, shattering every window of the truck. "It"s now or never," Rich mumbled his back pressed against the Range Rover. He crept around the back and began firing, stepping forward.

Chase ducked behind his Benz just as one of Rich"s bullets met his shoulder.

Rich watched Chase scramble on the ground for his gun, which he had dropped. As Chase grabbed the beretta and raised

it, Rich said, "Don"t even do it."

"That"s you, Rich?" Chase responded to the familiar voice. He frowned in anger, then rose his gun.

Rich fired, hitting chase in the arm sending him back to the ground with his gun beside him.

"Ahh," Chase blurted. "Fuck you, Rich!"

Rich kicked him in the face and snatched the .45-calibur Kimber Eclipse from the ground. He pulled out a pair of handcuffs and dropped them on Chase. "Put „em on."

"Fuck outta here." With what little strength the wounded thug had, Chase tossed the cuffs.

Rich picked them up, cuffed Chase and hauled him off towards his Corolla like a detective with a perp.

"This how it's goin' down?" Chase asked, trying to struggle free.

Rich slammed the bulky Desert Eagle into Chase's face. He pushed him forward and aimed the gun at the back of his head and forced him inside of the trunk. Just as he slammed the trunk shut, two of Chase's soldier stormed from his home, guns blazing. "Oh shit." Rich ducked behind the Corolla, as fully automatic fire tore through its tinted windows.

"Ya ass is dead, motherfucker," one of Chase's soldiers yelled.

Rich peeked around the back of the car and two bullets ripped through the taillights, nearly piercing Rich's head. Chards of the plastic light covers hit his face. *Fuck!* Rich eased to the front of the Corolla. He peaked up and fired six shots. Three hollow points hit the first soldier in the chest. His body slammed back, flipping over a fire hydrant. His finger was locked on the trigger of a Mac-11. The submachine gun continued firing, as the lifeless man lie in a rapidly growing pool of his own blood.

The other solider stepped forward, squeezing the triggers of two 9-millimeters. "Motherfucker!" he screamed like an insane lunatic.

As Rich ducked down, two bullets hit his chest. He was lifted off his feet like a bag of garbage hurled from the truck of a sanitation worker. Rich's back slammed to the sidewalk first, followed by his head. The sound of the bullets continued. Rich saw the second soldier's head emerge from behind the car. With a clear shot, Rich managed to aim and squeeze, but his gun jammed.

"Stupid motherfucker," Chase's soldier smiled, slowly stepping toward Rich. "You gon' bite the bullet for real." He stood directly over Rich, and reached down, trying to jam one of his 9-millimeters into Rich's mouth.

"Bong, bong, bong, bong!" Bullets flew, just as he stuck the gun in Rich's mouth.

Chase's soldier fell forward to the ground, beside Rich. Vanessa stood over the man with her smoking .380. She helped Rich to his feet, then turned and fired three more bullets into the head of the lifeless soldier. "Come on, baby," Vanessa said, as she pulled Rich toward the Corolla. "Give me the keys."

Rich was speechless as he handed her the keys. He got in the passenger seat and she sped off. "Where the hell you came from?" he said, pulling off his hoody and the bulletproof vest underneath it.

"A thank you would do," Vanessa said, as she tucked the .380 back in her clutch with one hand, while steering with the other.

Rich couldn't believe he was seeing Vanessa calmly drive away after having just murdered a person in cold blood like a professional hitman.

"I drove down here after we got off the phone. There's no way I was gonna let anything happen to you," Vanessa said.

I created a monster. But Chase definitely gotta get it. Rich's fingers anxiously tapped against his lap. He was hungry. The type of hunger in his blood was the same as the hunger that pushed wild animals to viciously hunt and devour their prey. Chase was destined for the pain and suffering he had caused Rich and the women he loved.

* * *

Vanessa pulled up behind the cabin and Rich hopped out of the Corolla. He stared at the red marks on the swollen skin caused by the plates in the bulletproof vest where he was shot. Vanessa gently ran her hand across Rich's wounds. "Don't worry, baby, I'm gonna take care of that for you. A nice bubble bath will make it all better." She planted a tender kiss on Rich's lips, then eased her tongue into his mouth. When their faces parted, she stared directly into his eyes. "I love you."

Candy came running outside. "What's wrong? I can see it in your face," she said, stepping closer to Rich. "What happened to you? What's wrong?"

"Nothing." Rich grinned. "This one of the best days of my life."

"It's hard to tell from looking at you."

"Trust me when I tell you."

Candy turned to Vanessa. "How you gonna leave me in the middle of the night and don't say shit?"

"I had to," Vanessa responded.

"You gotta do better than that."

"I had to hold down Rich."

Rich leaned against the trunk of the Corolla as Vanessa told Candy what happened. It amazed him to see how ruthless Vanessa had become. As he watched her, he thought of everything he had known about her. From the innocent woman he met who trembled when she nervously fired a single shot into Chase, to the woman he had trained until she became the warrior who saved his life by gunning down one of Chase's soldiers.

"Chase is gonna pay," Vanessa said, popping open the trunk of the Corolla.

Rich stared into the trunk. *I finally got this motherfucker.* He could not describe the feeling of revenge. It was a heartless thrill that came with knowing someone who had wronged him had to face him on his terms. "Revenge is like the sweetest joy next to getting pussy," Rich sang one of Tupac's lines.

Vanessa pulled out her .380 and stepped back.

Rich stared at her and Candy. Vanessa clutched her gun like a pro, her two large afro puffs and natural beauty evoked an awkward image of strength. Candy's long hair was wrapped in a French bun. Her hips swung, bulging from the tight pair of Moschino jeans she sported. Just a half-year earlier, Rich could not imagine being in a relationship with two beautiful women. Even as he ran through woman after woman, the thought of a three-way relationship never crossed his mind, just like love had never crossed his mind. Now he had it all and the man who had interfered with it was going to meet the wrath of Rich.

"What's up, baby? We gonna kill this bastard or what?" Vanessa asked.

Candy stepped forward, gazing at Chase until her eyes began tearing. She closed them tight, balling her fists. It was obvious to Rich that every thought Candy had about being kidnapped and abused was overwhelming her.

Rich pulled Chase from the trunk and Candy slapped him.

"You bitch," he responded.

Candy slapped him again and he smiled.

Rich noticed Vanessa crying also. The gold gun was shaking in her trembling hands. After Vanessa's recent performance, Rich was sure Vanessa's tears and trembling were rooted not in fear, but anger and other emotions that she could not control. She raised her gun to Chase's face.

"Not yet," Rich said. He grabbed a knapsack out of the trunk and made Chase walk, while he and the women trailed behind him.

"It ain't gotta go down like this," Chase said, trying to run. He fell after two painful steps.

"Shut the fuck up!" Vanessa yelled, as she held her arm around Candy's shoulders. She stomped Chase.

Rich picked Chase up. He pulled a rope from his knapsack and tied Chase to a tree. Looking into his eyes, for the first time it really set in Rich's mind that he planned to kill the man who had saved his life, the man who had stood side-by-side with Rich as they gunned down people, the man who Rich had made hundreds of thousands of dollars with, the man he had sexed women with and once vowed to go to the grave with. But as Rich turned to Vanessa and Candy, the more distant his past seemed, the more meaningless. What mattered was what Chase had done to Candy and the effects it had on the people she loved.

Just as Rich pulled out a scalpel, Chase's cell phone rang and Vanessa snatched it from his waist.

"Fuck you,, Rich," Chase barked

Rich cut through Chase's shirt and severed his flesh from his shoulder to his waist. Chase screamed in pain. Rich continued, digging deeper, ripping through his arms. He tore Chase's shirt off completely. "That should hold you, since you like cutting people."

"I ain't cut nobody, faggot!" Chase screamed.

"Rich." Vanessa held up Chase's cell phone. "Look at this."

There was a nude photo of Chanel on the screen and a text message: BCNU 2MORO LUV

Rich stared at the picture and read the message. "This fucking broad ain't shit!"

"And she had the nerve to be at the hospital with us, acting all lovey dovey," Vanessa said. "I knew she was poison."

"Chanel," Rich said.

"That's who cut her, stupid." Chase blurted.

Rich, filled with rage, slashed Chase's face like a slab of beef in a slaughterhouse, opening it to the white meat. "Stop fucking lying!"

Chase screamed in pain. He pointed at the cell phone. "Fuckin' dummy. She cut a 'C' on Candy for 'Chanel.' All them chicks in the shop was down. Y'all was too busy fuckin' and suckin' to see it."

And I thought that "C" was for Candy.

"It ain't my fault," Chase said, laughing.

Rich grabbed his face, slicing each eyelid off."

"Rich," Vanessa said, shaking her head as Rich faced her. "He's got all their numbers in this phone. Leah, Meisha, even Vera and Mimi."

"Vera?" Candy said, looking at the phone.

"Vera said you tossed her crib and stole a bunch of shit. She wanted some getback," Chase stated.

Candy paused, looking at Rich and Vanessa. "For him to know that, she had to tell him."

"I ain't cut her," Chase said. "I was just tryin' to get Rich away from y'all so Vera and her brother could kidnap Candy. That's why I came to the shop that night," Chase laughed.

"You think this a fuckin' joke?" Rich asked.

Chase grinned. "You always thought you was so fuckin' smart. Now look at your dumb ass, played by some beauty shop bitches," Chase laughed.

Rich sighed and slashed one of Chase's lips off. "That's for lying, motherfucker. I saw your car. That old ass Taurus we used to use."

Chase screamed in pain, then smiled. "The Taurus is Vera brothers' car dummy."

"Taurus?" Candy said, covering her mouth as Rich turned to her. "I forgot. Domingo said Vera's brother got an old Taurus. I didn't think of that when they snatched me up. Everything happened so quick. I just knew it was a dark-colored Taurus.

"Remember in the shop, Domingo said he saw Chanel in Red Hook?" Vanessa chimed in. Chase sighed. "Chanel was in Red Hook with Vera and her brothers plotting on Candy. This shit been in the making for so long, it"s ridiculous."

"When I heard shoes in the basement, it must've been Chanel," Candy said, slowly shaking her head. "Chanel always wears heels. I just thought it was a guy wearing hard bottoms. And the clicking of the razor—" Candy shivered as she recalled the traumatic event. "Chanel always carries a razor."

Rich remembered how in the hospital Chanel tried to convince him not to seek revenge on Chase. *She must've been trying to indirectly convince me it was Chase. But it was really her.*

"And Leah, she want the shop," Chase said.

Rich remembered that Leah had been helping Candy work on the business plan for her hair care products company and that she had always been mentioning that Candy should think of leaving the shop behind for the new business. Leah was the person who had given Candy the idea for starting a second business. And she had always been the one who volunteered to oversee the shop when Candy was out of f town. There was also the fact that Leah had always made it know that she felt Candy was taking advantage of younger women. Leah certainly had a motive for Candy's downfall.

"What about Meisha? Her number is in here too," said Vanessa.

"She just following Chanel," Chase mumbled with his one remaining lip covered in blood. "She said she quit the shop after y' all was wildin' out on Chanel. That was her way of fuckin' the business up, because she know Candy needed workers. She was hoping to fuck it up so much that you would just sell it to Leah and focus on your new business. All of these chicks was in on this shit. Y''all motherfuckers is blind," he grinned. "Three blind mice."

"Those conniving-ass broads!" Candy was furious. Her frustration with Chase was changing to rage for Chanel and her cohorts. There was an evil look in Candy's eyes that told Rich she was beyond the psychological pain of being attacked. She had been the peacemaker, while Vanessa thirsted for revenge. But Rich could see Candy was now hungry for the blood of everyone involved in her attack.

"Rich, I'm telling you. It was them hos in the shop," Chase said laughing.

"Fuck that! You still down with it. You came to the shop to get me away from Candy so they could kidnap her." Rich dug his scalpel into Chase's cheek and pulled it forward until it ripped through the skin of the small space that separated Chase's lip and the missing lip. Chase screamed, choking on his own blood.

Rich stripped him naked with the scalpel. He pulled out a bottle of alcohol and a large squeeze bottle of ammonia. He first doused Chase with the alcohol. As he screamed, begging for forgiveness, Rich poured the ammonia into his wounds.

"Motherfucker!" Chase screamed.

Rich pulled some lighter fluid from the bag and squirted it on all over Chase's face

"Fuck all of y''all dumb motherfuckas!"

Rich struck a match and tossed it on his face.

"Ahhhhhh," Chase screamed. His brown skin bubbled and the stench of burnt hair filled the air. Chase shook his face back and forth, but he could not escape the flames.

After a minute, Rich pulled the gun he had taken from Chase. He handed it to Candy. He wanted her to end his life with his own gun.

Candy slowly grabbed the semi-automatic and turned to Vanessa. They both stepped toward Chase until their guns were virtually touching the fire toasting his face.

Chase mumbled, as blood dripped from his flaming face.

The women slowly aimed their guns and squeezed them continuously until there were no more bullets. Chase's face and head were riddled beyond recognition. Candy and Vanessa turned to Rich, emotionless, smoke rising from the barrels of their guns.

Rich expected more tears, but there were none. There were no surprised looks or shaky hands. No fear in the eyes of Candy and Vanessa. They obviously enjoyed the thrill of the kill. Rich watched Candy staring at the gun as if it were something she had missed her entire life. Something she cherished. But Rich was certain that he wanted nothing else to do with guns. He wanted to pick up the life he started when he left the game behind. He wanted a normal life with the women who had tried their hardest to make sure he did not slip back into the game. But Rich did not know if they would ever be the same after experiencing the power that came with a revenge killing.

Vanessa had already proven she was no longer the free-loving bohemian who felt there was no reason a life should be taken. Now Candy had demonstrated that she was ready to manifest all the violence she had witnessed throughout her life on the streets of Harlem.

"Felt good, didn't it?" Vanessa flashed a sneaky grin at Candy.

Candy squeezed the empty gun and stared at it for a second, as if she were inspecting it with pleasure. "Yeah it feels good." She nodded and smiled. She kissed Vanessa and Rich. "Thank you." She paused, then turned and stared at Chase's dead body. "You got five friends coming to join you: Chanel, Meisha, Leah, Vera, and Mimi."

Vanessa looked at Chase. "Plus Vera's brothers."

THE END

Reading Group Discussion Questions
Lickin' License

1. Do you consider Rich a womanizer because of his relationship with two women at once?

2. Do you consider Candy and Vanessa desperate or naive for being in a three-way relationship with the same man?

3. Was it selfish of Mimi to turn her back on Vanessa?

4. After her reaction to discovering the sex tape, did Vera deserve the violent response she received from Candy?

5. Should Candy have detected early on that Leah was plotting on her business?

6. Did Chanel's jealousy justify her constant sarcastic remarks directed at Vanessa?

7. Did Candy deserve to be kidnapped and assaulted?

8. After leaving the streets, was it a smart move for Rich to risk his life and freedom for Chase?

9. Was Rich at fault for Vanessa's transformation into a killer?

10. Considering the bond that Candy had developed over the years with the women in her shop, was she wrong for siding with Vanessa over them?

About Intelligent Allah

Intelligent Allah's full name is Intelligent Tarref Allah, but he is affectionately known by family and friends as Intell. Born and raised on the chaotic streets of Brownsville and East New York, Brooklyn, Intelligent was a poet and aspiring rapper prior to becoming incarcerated in 1994.

Intelligent is a graduate of the Writer's Digest School's Writing Workshop. He also completed writing/grammar courses sponsored by Rising Hope Inc., Shawangunk Valley School, and Bard College through which he is currently pursuing his Associates in Arts. His writings have been published on the website, therubanbooksource.com, *The Five Percenter* newspaper and *American Vegan magazine*. *The New York Amsterdam News* has accepted his work as well.

Intelligent was contracted as an editor and copywriter for publishing companies such as Cinobe Publishing and Green & Company. He is the co-editor of Wahida Clark's bestselling novel *Thug Matrimony* (Kensington Corp.). He also served on the editorial board for prison newsletters, *The Lifer's Call and Ujima*.

Intelligent is certified by the Department of Labor as a counseling aide. He has completed numerous courses sponsored by Binghamton University, the Osborn Association, Exodus, AIDS-Related Community Services and the New York Department of Correctional Services. He is a member of Harvest Moon Poetry Collective, Rehabilitation through the Arts, the Nation of Gods and Earths, People for the Ethical Treatment of Animals, The American Vegan Society, Vegetarian Resource Group and other progressive groups.

WAHIDA CLARK PRESENTS
BEST SELLING TITLES

Trust No Man

Trust No Man II

Thirsty

Cheetah

Karma With A Vengeance

The Ultimate Sacrifice

The Game of Deception

Karma 2: For The Love of Money

Thirsty 2

Country Boys

Lickin' License

Feenin'

Bonded by Blood

Uncle Yah Yah: 21st Century Man of Wisdom

A Life For A Life

The Ultimate Sacrifice II

The Foreign Exchange

Under Pressure (YA)

The Boy Is Mines! (YA)

99 Problems (YA)

ON SALE NOW!

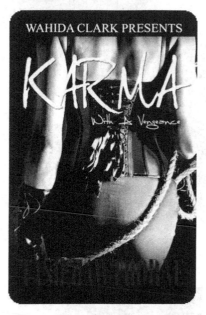

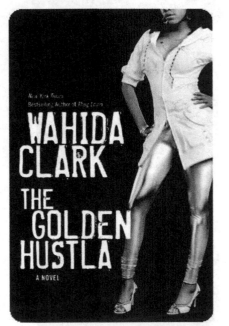

ON SALE NOW!

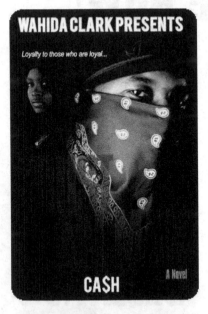

WAHIDA CLARK PRESENTS

Loyalty to those who are loyal...

CA$H

A Novel

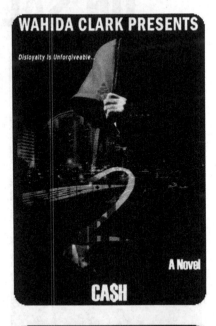

WAHIDA CLARK PRESENTS

Disloyalty Is Unforgiveable...

CA$H

A Novel

New York Times Bestselling Author of *Payback with Ya Life*

WAHIDA CLARK

THUG LOVIN'

WAHIDA CLARK PRESENTS

FEENIN

A NOVEL BY
SERENITI HALL

WWW.WCLARKPUBLISHING.COM

New York Times Bestselling Author of *Payback With Ya Life*

WAHIDA CLARK

COMING SOON!

WAHIDA CLARK PRESENTS

THE BOY IS MINE!

A WILSON HIGH CONFIDENTIAL

A YOUNG ADULT NOVEL BY
CHARMAINE WHITE

WAHIDA CLARK PRESENTS

A LIFE

MIKE JEFFERIES

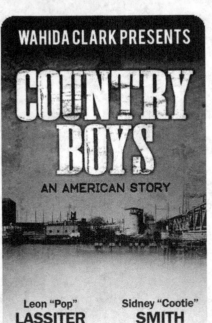

WAHIDA CLARK PRESENTS

COUNTRY BOYS

AN AMERICAN STORY

Leon "Pop"
LASSITER

Sidney "Cootie"
SMITH

WAHIDA CLARK PRESENTS

THE **ULTIMATE SACRIFICE II**
LOVE IS PAIN

A NOVEL BY
ANTHONY FIELDS

DISCARD

CPSIA info
Printed in th
LVOW04s1
439048LV00002B/243/P

9 780982 841426